BELLY UP

Also available from Eva Darrows:

The Awesome
Dead Little Mean Girl

BELLY
UP

EVA DARROWS

ink
yard
press

Recycling programs
for this product may
not exist in your area.

ISBN-13: 978-1-335-01235-7

Belly Up

InkyardPress.com

Printed in U.S.A.

For Greg. A sweet book for a sweet dude.

PART ONE:

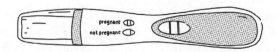

The snippa,
the speculum
and the womb goblin.

CHAPTER ONE

When my English teacher, Mrs. Thomson, went on that half-hour lecture-slash-tirade about "it was the best of times, it was the worst of times," she by no means had Michelle Levitz's end-of-year junior graduation party in mind, but I sure did. 'Cause that party, with its Boone's Farm Strawberry Hill wine that tasted like liquid Jolly Ranchers, its tent farm in the woods and high school kids from not one but *two* different high schools was one of the most memorable nights of my seventeen years of existence.

I played quarters for the first time.

I played spin the bottle for the first time.

I got pregnant for the first time.

…surprised you with that one, didn't I?

I didn't plan on it happening. In fact, it was the furthest thing from my mind that night as I stood in front of my open closet wearing a black bra and a pair of yoga pants, my toenails freshly painted, my face contorted in a full freak-out because I had (and have) no idea how to dress myself.

Basic life skill or not, clothes are hard. I'm not sure how you other humans manage it.

"What do I wear?" I motioned at the thirty-seven logoed T-shirts laid out on the bed behind me. My best friend, Devi, looked up from her magazine to rifle through them, her lip curled in distaste as she plucked three from the pile.

"Does it matter? They all look the same." She shook them at me. "Here's the hipster douchebag spring collection. Here's dumpster-diving chic. Oh, and my favorite, the secondhand store golden grab!"

Devi wore the pretty clothes—a floral blouse belted tight beneath her boobs, a crinkly teal skirt. Her long legs were tipped off by designer sandals that cost as much as my mom's ancient car. Her brown hair with the natural waves was tucked beneath a coordinating scarf with a flower barrette at the temple. She looked fresh from the festival scene, and perfect for a summer night out with her big Bambi eyes, hoop earrings and pink lip gloss.

I couldn't pull it off. I was short and roundish with a big ol' butt and thighs that could crush a walnut if I flexed hard enough. A deep-V collar like Devi wore? No go, not with my enormous boobs. I once lamented to my mother—who was blonde and blue-eyed and weighed a hundred and twenty-five pounds soaking wet—that I was shaped like a lawn gnome. Mom responded with, "You have curves for days, sweetheart. Curves for days."

It was true. I had curves for days. And days and days and days. I had *years* of curves and dressing them was a pain. Finding a pair of jeans that fit my tree-trunk thighs and bubble butt, yet still cinched in at the waist enough that I didn't look ridiculous? Needle-in-a-haystack-worthy. T-shirts had to be a full size too big or my chest stretched out the screen print until it cracked and looked like painted barf.

I would have killed for Devi's height and proportions. It was not my lot in life.

"Give me the Atari one," I said. She flung it at me and I caught it midair to tug it over my head. "And I'll have you know, *Devorah*, that the logo is the key to a successful T-shirt. It's the first thing new people see. Atari says, 'I'm fun and a little nerdy.' Guinness says, 'You probably like hockey or at least pretend you do.' My Little Pony says, 'I own at least one pair of glittery sneakers, which I do, and they're awesome, but if I wore them tonight, you'd kill me.'"

"You're seventeen, *Serendipity*," she said, because my mother was the type of person that saddled a kid with a huge-ass name. At least it shortened to Sara pretty easily. "Glitter was out in second grade." She pulled a Starbucks

T-shirt from the pile and held it up to her chest. "What does this one say?"

"That I prefer burnt coffee?"

We shared a grin as I gathered up the T-shirts and threw them back into my dresser drawer. The moment I walked away from the bureau, Devi tsked and nudged me with her foot. "No yoga pants. White girl needs to be less cliché. Jeans."

"…but they're comfortable," I whined. "I'm embracing my mother's culture right now."

"Yes, well, embrace whatever culture puts you in real pants. Those are pajamas."

I rifled through the stacks of pants in the second drawer. I'm half Swedish, half Spanish, and by Devi's decree, culturally confused. My mother raised me—she's full Swede. From her I inherited my porcelain complexion and an appreciation for ärtsoppa because *it's delicious.* My Spanish father isn't in the picture. He and my mother were married until I was two, but he fell off the map when they divorced and my grandmother's stories tell me I was better off without him. He was too *free with his hands*, she said, which made me grateful that all he left me was the last name Rodriguez, a mop of black curly hair and eyes so dark you can't see the pupils.

That's pretty much all I know about my Hispanic culture beyond the fact that Spanish-speaking people often aren't interested in me once they figure out I can't speak the language, and white people treat me like Speedy Gonzales with boobs because apparently Mexican and Spanish are the same thing.

I'm halfway in between, too much and yet not enough at the same time.

It's keen.

I swapped yoga pants for jeans, hopping to pull the damned things up over my hips. I made a beeline for two-dollar flip-flops, but a pointed Devorah groan and I went for some sandals with rhinestones on the bands instead.

"Lipstick," she said. "Or gloss, at the very least. Pretend you care, please."

"I care! Just less than you do!" I snatched a gloss from my vanity and even went so far as to mascara my lashes so Devi would leave me alone. "You're a fashion enforcer," I said, snagging my car keys and wallet from the table by the door. "If I don't follow the rules, you'll take out my kneecaps."

Devi unfurled from the bed, her six feet of gorgeousness making me look like I was standing in a hole by comparison. "I'm your best bitch. What best bitch lets her bestie go to a party looking like they just crawled out of bed?"

"An awesome one. Be more awesome, Devi."

Half an hour later, I stood at the end of a long driveway beholding a three-storied blue Colonial with a billion glass windows and a perfectly manicured lawn. Michelle Levitz's father was a swanky city lawyer with a huge swanky house and an equally-as-swanky Jaguar in the three-car garage. Michelle once said that her dad's name topped a partnership plaque on a skyscraper in the financial district of Boston. That meant he had bank, and he liked to travel to Bermuda with that bank. Thanks to his tropical wanderlust, Michelle had been left alone the last week of May to throw the biggest, most obnoxious party ever. Twenty tents were set up near the tree line beyond the shed. Another half dozen were being erected behind the pool. Nobody was in the pool on account of New England dumping snow on our heads two weeks before, but with enough alcohol, kids would be bobbing in the clear frigid blue within hours.

We'd learned some stuff in biology about teen brains being half formed and spongy. Freezing to death in a pool when it's subzero is a half formed, spongy brain kind of thing to do.

We walked to the house, my ancient Subaru sandwiched between two tiny economy cars, which were sandwiched between two SUVs. There was no hope of any car in that driveway escaping anytime soon, but that was okay. Devi's parents knew she was staying at my apartment overnight, and my mom was fine with us going out as long as I never ever drove drunk and we were home "at a reasonable hour." Her interpretation of "reasonable hour" and mine were probably different, but we'd hash out the details later, if and when I got into trouble.

As we crested the brick walkway leading to the front door, Devi reached into her over-the-shoulder bag to hand me a bottle of Boone's. Her twenty-one-year-old cousin, Jakob, had offered to buy booze for us if she'd agreed to fill up his gas tank, which she had, and so we were the not-so-proud owners of terrible wine. I'd had a drink or two at parties before, but never a bottle to myself. For that matter, I'd never been drunk before but there was a first time for everything, and really, it was Boone's. What could *possibly* go wrong?

Answer: a lot, but I wouldn't know that until a weird aversion to the smell of eggs. A hard lesson learned that night: if you're drinking, make sure you have a sober friend on hand at all times to keep your fat out of the fire. Or to keep your butt out of F-150 trucks at two o'clock in the morning with guys named Jack.

"Crap." Devi pointed to the side lawn at a cluster of kids setting up plastic cups in lines on the picnic table. "Aaron."

I frowned. "Hey, our first Skank One sighting. Is Skank Two with him?"

"Unfortunately."

Aaron Weller had been my on-again, off-again, but definitely-never-would-be-on-again boyfriend. We'd been together since eighth grade, had broken up a few times over stupid stuff, but we'd always reconnected. That all changed when Aaron left his cell phone on my coffee table over April vacation and I got an eyeful of Samantha Wuchowski's thonged butt in a text message. I wouldn't have cared that she was sending a dude pictures of her butt cleavage. What I cared about was that she'd sent *my* dude pictures of her butt cleavage and had messed around with him for three months behind my back.

Thus Skank One, Skank Two.

They could wallow in their skantitude together.

I surveyed the crowd until I found Samantha's blond head. We locked eyes and she quickly nestled herself into Aaron's side, like that would shield her from my contempt. She hated me as much as I hated her, mostly because after our breakup Aaron had sent me numerous messages on social media begging me to take him back, complete with videos of him ugly crying. It'd done nothing to sway me, but it sure pissed me off when I saw them together. She thought they were ready for their happily-ever-after. She only got it because I kept saying no.

She tilted her head up and whispered in Aaron's ear. He looped his arm around her waist and looked over his shoulder at me. Meeting his gaze was more difficult than meeting hers—I'd loved Aaron, probably still loved him a little. I'd given him most of my important firsts, had gone to formal dances with him, had visited with his family the previous summer at their lake house in Maine. We'd been the real deal, thought-we'd-be-together-forever type of couple, and though I was resolute in not wanting him back, seeing his face, his green eyes, his ash-colored hair and his chin with the butt dimple...

I still didn't want him back, but I did open the Boone's and take a long swig.

"Whoa, already?" Devi asked. "We're not even in the house."

"Don't judge me. You're not my real mom."

"Whatever, girl. It's your night."

And oh, what a night it was.

CHAPTER TWO

Being Devi's friend meant getting to witness the gravitational pull hot girls had on guys. Devi was the sun, the straight boys at the party were planets pulled into her orbit. Once they got a gander at her tight butt, swanlike neck and perky boobs, it was all over. I stood beside her, drinking my Boone's from a red Solo cup, and watched as dude after dude took a stab at scoring the prettiest girl there. Other girls were almost as pretty—they had good faces or nice bodies or glossy hair, but Devi had the whole package. Even my grandmother, whom Devi once affectionately called Genghis Khan with boobs, said she ought to model, but Devi had no interest.

"I want to be an astronaut," she said, and so she spent her time studying astronomy and physics.

We'd become friends in grade school, after Tanya Brides had threatened to beat me up if I didn't trade my pudding cup for her applesauce. Devi had defended me by telling the teacher, and for it, I'd given her half the pudding cup in thanks. Besties ever since. Behold the magical power of butterscotch.

After boy number twelve left Devi's side, dejected that she'd blown him off, she slumped against me, letting my much squatter self hold her upright.

"I should lie and tell them I'm a lesbian," she said. "They don't know what gray ace is anyway, probably."

Which was true. Devi dated, enjoyed romance and hand-holding and all of the sweetness associated with being with another person, but so far, and possibly forever, sex was not on the table. She thought about it sometimes, she'd told me before, but had no intention of acting on it. The interest wasn't there. Some boys would have probably understood that, but a lot of them were walking, talking boners, so Devi tended to date only among vetted, ace-safe spaces. Which meant a lot of online dating because New England wasn't a bastion of love and acceptance for the asexual community.

Or really a lot of people. It's pretty WASPy.

"No go on the lesbian-o," I said. I sipped my wine and blinked, trying to focus my eyes. The buzz felt pretty good, and it helped me not see whenever Aaron drifted by, but it was a little disconcerting, too. I was looking at the world through a hazy film that dulled colors and made the layers upon layers of noise hard to sift through. "They'd just ask to watch."

"True, and I love you, but you know, not feeling the sex thing, so." She grinned. "In another life, we'd make great porn together, though."

"Our theoretical porn is fantastic."

We tapped our cups together and drank.

A burst of laughter from the kitchen caught our mutual attention. Despite over a hundred kids milling around from at least four towns, it was Samantha cackling. Again. She'd been performative all night, her new-girlfriend game strong. Aaron joked, she bray-laughed. She clung to his arm. She nuzzled at his neck. She practically dry-humped him every time he sat down. Aaron seemed to enjoy the attention for the most part, but every once in a while, I caught him glancing my way while she climbed all over him.

Like he currently was. He held Samantha close but eyed me over her head while she nibbled on his ear.

"I can't tell if he's pretending to be over you or if he's asking you to save him," Devi said. "She's on him like white on rice."

"I don't care."

Except I did care a little, and we both knew it, so I poured myself another drink. And another after that. How we ended up playing spin the bottle, I don't know. I'm not clear on how I ended up making out with Jennifer Gill, specifically, though Devi told me her cheap-seats view proved that gender was absolutely not a hurdle for me when it came to kissing. I met Jack after the game ended. He was tall, almost six foot, with olive skin, black hair and eyes as blue as the Pac-Man Inky ghost on my Atari T-shirt. The boy was hot. Hotter-than-convenience-store-nacho-cheese hot. I liked how he had a ridge in his nose that skewed the angle a bit, like he'd broken it and never gotten it properly set. It added character to his face.

I was by the pool hanging out with Devi when he approached with another guy, whose name is unimportant (but only because I can't remember it, if we're being perfectly honest). The friend was hitting on Devi in the most awkward way possible, opening with a line about Cheetos, but Jack was all about me. Had I been more sober, I probably would have worried that he was doing the wingman, occupy-the-other-chick-so-my-friend-can-score-the-hottie thing, but after so many Aaron-and-Samantha sightings, and walking in on them swapping spit four separate times in four separate rooms, I wanted some attention of my own.

"Hey," I said, offering my best smile.

"Hey. I'm Jack. Cool shirt. My dad's got a 5200 set up in the basement."

"I'm Sara. Serendipity, but everyone calls me Sara." I grinned at him, he grinned back. He was drinking beer in a blue cup, which I only know because I remember how he smelled in the truck—Budweiser and Old Spice and breath mints. But at that point, he was just the tall guy with one hand wedged into his jeans pocket, the other holding his drink. Devi must have noticed me making eyes at him because she led her half of the duo away to talk to him near the tents. Jack and I watched them go before he nodded at the picnic table.

"Quarters? I haven't played that since...man. Last summer some time," Jack said.

"I've never played," I confessed, feeling shy that I hadn't yet experienced this particular rite of passage. Jack looped his arm around my back, his fingers brushing the bottom of my curly hair, to usher me over to the game. It wasn't complicated—you bounced quarters off the table to try to get them into the cups set up at the end—but after half a bottle of Boone's, I had the coordination of an inbred squirrel. I ended up missing every round. Fuzzy became full-on tipsy with an obnoxious case of the giggles.

Jack and I flirted the whole time we played, getting to know one another, casually touching. He was a year older than me and wanted to work on cars with his dad after he graduated. I told him about my plans to go to an Ivy League school and study English. He seemed interested in that, and my video-game hobby, and a few absolutely terrible jokes I made. I was interested in his lopsided smile and the low, quiet tone of his voice.

When Aaron walked by later, I brushed my hip against Jack's, hoping he'd take the hint. That glorious boy tangled his fingers with mine, pulling me into his side and leaning down to press a soft kiss to my temple. My eyes met Aaron's, he flinched, I smiled and he wandered off to find Skank Two. It was bitchy to be so satisfied, but I didn't care, mostly because Jack's hand had slid into the back pocket of my jeans.

"This okay?" he whispered into my ear.

"Oh, yeah."

I was suddenly grateful to Devi who'd insisted I not wear the yoga pants.

Another two rounds of quarters and we abandoned the game, still holding hands. Jack tossed our empty cups into a garbage bag hanging from the branch of some blossoming tree. We paused there, the ground carpeted pinky white with fallen blossoms beneath us. I leaned against the trunk, Jack leaned into me. We smiled at one another, his hands planted on my hips.

"I feel good," Jack said quietly.

I ruined it with, "Na-na-na-na-na-na-na," because of course I did.

He laughed and nuzzled at my throat. "James Brown. My dad listens to him at the garage."

"I wish that's what my grandmother liked. She's into the *other* seventies stuff. The Bee Gees. Donna Summer. ABBA, because of course she's a Swedish cliché. It's disco fever forever in the car with her."

"You poor, poor thing."

He expressed his sympathy with a nibble on my earlobe.

I slid my hands down his back, looping my thumbs into his belt. He grinded against me. I grinded back. It was obvious where things *could* go if I wanted them to. I debated with myself if I wanted to follow the slutty rabbit down the slutty hole. Jack was cute. He smelled good. He understood the pain that was ABBA.

He also wasn't Aaron.

It's not super flattering to admit, but that was the main reason I decided to do it, I think. My ex-boyfriend was thirty feet away with the girl he'd cheated on me with and they were all over each other. I'd loved Aaron once, still carried a torch, so to not have to grapple with that ugly truth, I'd entertain myself with a hot stranger. When Jack kissed me again, and walked me toward the driveway, I knew what I was in for: a hookup that'd put Aaron away awhile. A momentary distraction from a lot of old hurts.

I understood what it was—and what it wasn't—from the get-go, and I was okay with it.

Jack led me to The Truck—emphasized because it's the only truck I ever think of anymore when I hear the word—which was parked at the last spot on the right side, granting him unblocked access to the road. It was black and new and tall, and when he opened the passenger's side to invite me in, I had to take his hand and grab the door to haul myself into the cabin.

It had a new car smell. The dash was pristine, the seats were shiny leather. I was running my fingers over the radio plate when Jack circled around to the driver's side and climbed in. He turned the radio on and then lowered the volume, smiling at me from his side of the bench. His hand captured mine again, and I slid my butt over to sit next to him, my thick thigh up against his more slender one.

"Having a good time?" he asked.

"I am." I perched my chin on his shoulder with big eyes, my smile practically stitched to my face. I probably smelled like strawberries and potato chips, but he didn't seem to mind, not as he nudged my nose with his own. The kiss was soft and sweet at first, lips skimming and gliding and nestling together. His hand crept up to my cheek, then back into my hair, cupping my skull. I opened my mouth first, he took advantage, and the make-outs were epic. Perfect amount of tongue and lips, limited slobber. I climbed into his lap, straddling him. His free hand had drifted down to the small of my back, was running up along my spine between the top of my jeans and the band of my bra. It felt good; the fuzziness of my buzz and the gentleness of his touch. When his hands slid from back to front, gliding over the softness of my stomach and up, I was all in.

"We cool?" he asked. His fingers danced over the satin cups of my bra.

My answer was to pull off the Atari shirt. His answer was to drop his face into the cavernous valley between my boobs. His hair was thick and silky between my fingers. I liked how he looked. I liked how he smelled. I liked how he felt touching me, so when he kissed my neck, and then dropped my bra strap to nuzzle at my shoulder and squeezed my butt...

The humping was a natural progression. Drunk teenagers, a dark car, soft music, my ex about fifty feet away? It was all pretty inevitable. To Jack's credit, he asked me if I was sure I wanted it before he pulled down my pants. I groaned a *yes* and my hand plunged into his boxer shorts. Gratuitous bouncing, sweating and groaning were a matter of course.

...for three hours. Not straight through. That would have chafed. But we went, stopped, went and stopped again. I never asked about a condom. He never asked if I was on the pill.

Mistakes, as they say, were made.

CHAPTER THREE

I woke up in Jack's truck in my T-shirt and panties, my jeans and bra in a ball in the footwell. Jack was passed out cold beside me, his head tilted back, quiet snores rumbling from his throat. I slid from the truck's cabin and into the driveway to wrestle back into my clothes, hoping nobody came along and saw me. Unfortunately, jumping up and down to fit my pants over my butt made my stomach flop. I puked into the Levitzs' forsythia bush. Day-after wine burned like lava, and I swore then and there to never touch the stuff again. Two more hurls drove the point home, and I sagged against the side of the truck, my eyes trying to focus on the pale gray sky with the big ball of pain rising past the pine trees.

"Are you okay?" Jack asked sleepily from behind me.

"Yeah. I...gonna go find Devi. Think I need to pass out."

"I'm tired, too. It's not even six yet."

Jack poured himself from the truck and limped to my side. He leaned down to kiss me, but I offered a cheek instead. Not subjecting him to my hurl-mouth was the least I could do. He seemed to understand, and patted me on the butt instead.

"I should go before my parents kill me," he said. "Call me, okay? We'll go out. I had a great time."

"Sure," I responded, offering him a thanks-for-the-bone hug. He smelled like stale beer and sweat and I reeked like vomit and Boone's, but we got through it unscathed. I watched him drive away, my stomach all fluttery and not in the totally-going-to-puke-again way. Maybe Jack was my after-Aaron rebound. Maybe he'd be someone to hang out with over the summer when Devi went to visit her grandparents in Connecticut for what she called her yearly Jewish reprogramming.

Except I didn't have his number.

"Aww, crapcicles!"

He hadn't given me the digits and I'd been too worried about smelling like puke to realize it. Maybe that was his plan all along—an easy escape after a hookup—but he'd seemed like he liked me, so...

"Crap." I bumbled toward the house in search of Devi, hoping maybe she'd befriended Jack's wingman so I could ask him, but no, she was passed out on Michelle's couch alone, her arms wrapped around her mostly-empty bottle of Boone's like it was a teddy bear.

"Hey." I shook her foot, which was missing a sandal, though there was one on her other foot. That'd make walking hard. "Devi. Wake up."

"M'tired," she slurred.

Still drunk. Oh, good.

She grunted and rolled over on the couch so her back faced me. I sighed and wandered the premises in search of her missing shoe, finding it not near the pool but actually *in* the shallow end. I used the net to scoop it out, the leather straps warped and forever ruined. Good thing Devi owns sixty thousand shoes, though, so maybe her parents wouldn't care about the one ravaged pair, even if they were Gucci.

A quick spin of the property showed no sign of Jack's friend, though I did discover Aaron and Samantha curled around each other on a hammock. It wasn't what I wanted to see first thing in the morning, so I stalked back to the house, the realization that I'd just had my first one-night stand poking at my brain. I wasn't sure how I felt about it. Mom always told me to respect my body as it was the only one I was going to get. She didn't mean don't have sex, but to be safe and make sound choices I wouldn't regret later. Jack had been fun, but I probably should have been a bit smarter about our fluid swap. He could have had junk fungus or an infection or any number of diseases.

A baby never even occurred to me.

Maybe it was the booze. Maybe it was misplaced optimism.

Again, oopsie.

I pulled open the back door of Michelle's house and passed through the kitchen. Around me, kids groaned, heaved and crawled like extras in a zombie movie. Out back, tents started coming down. Out front, cars pulled from the driveway one after the other. The people who were blocked drove over the lawn to escape, the tracks left in their wake an awful way to thank Michelle for hosting. I roused Devi and loaded her into my old Subaru, tilting her head toward the window so if she had to throw up, she'd do it away from me and my upholstery. I drove us home and lugged her up the apartment stairs with my arms around her waist, supporting almost all of her weight while I wrestled with my house key. We stumbled inside like we were competing in a three-legged race, silent as we made our way to my bedroom. Mom's bedroom door was closed and her fan was on, so I knew she was still asleep. Grateful for the parental absence, I stripped Devi to her bra and panties and loaded her into my bed, leaving the trash barrel near her head in case of emergency spew.

I was tired and I wanted to sleep, but more than that, I was sore and sticky from all things truck. I hopped in the shower to hose off, scrubbing extra hard to eradicate Jack's nasty from my person. Did you know that sperm swim fast? Like, super fast? I didn't, and by the time I was topically de-sexed, it was far too late. Jack's little dudes were speeding past Cervix Town and rushing north for Uterusville.

It was only a matter of time.

★ ★ ★

"So, I have some news, and I know you're going to hate it, so I'm just going to rip off the Band-Aid. Do you want it now or do you want me to wait until after Devi goes home?" Mom asked at half past eleven from her position before the stove. She was all perky-looking in her tank top and size-nothing yoga pants, her blond hair piled on top of her head in a sloppy bun that made me think of a Real Housewife. I glanced back at my room. The door was still shut with Devi inside, so I was pretty sure my convo with Mom would be private unless Devi had developed bat sonar hearing overnight.

I looked up from my tea with sleep-soggy eyes. "Sure."

"We're moving in with your grandmother in August."

I'd been reaching for a coffee mug, but I froze mid-reach. I was the possum in the middle of the road, watching the headlights approach and waiting to be run over.

"Uhhhh…"

It was the best I had.

"Surprise?" Mom offered me a pained look over her shoulder. Seeing my trauma face, she stopped shoveling eggs onto a plate to pour me that cup of coffee. "She's getting older and could use the help. The house is huge. And it's only one town over. You have the car, so you can still see your friends. You'll have to switch schools, but this makes a lot of sense for us, Sara. Financially, family-wise. I told the landlord last night we won't be re-upping the lease."

I blinked at her incredulously. I loved my grandma— love her—but my mother also affectionately calls her the

Geriatric Battleax for a reason. She took no crap, and when it came to throwing shoes, her aim was Olympian. It was also her preferred method of correcting people; I needed extra hands to count how many times my butt had suffered one of Mormor's turbo-launched tennis shoes.

"She's going to drive you nuts. *Us* nuts," I insisted.

"Yep, you're right, but we'll figure it out. No rent means a lot of extra income, and someone I know is going to college in a couple years." Mom slid the plate in front of me. I hoped she attributed the gassy expression on my face to her news and not the hangover. She hadn't said much about the party or the previous night, probably because she was sitting on her ticking bomb of an announcement.

"You're serious," I said. "I'm going to Stonington next year?"

"I'm sorry. I know it's hard." She sat across from me and watched me not so much eat the eggs and toast as push them around and make interesting shapes with them. "I wanted to settle it before the end of the school year, so you could say your goodbyes and get contact info and stuff. Mormor's excited, thinks it'll be good for us."

"Mormor also thinks Tang is delicious. She's wrong a lot."

"Serendipity." Mom reached out to squeeze my hand. "I know it sucks, but Stonington has a great school. Better accredited than your current one. More AP classes, more languages to choose from than just Spanish and French. It's not all bad, I promise."

I wanted to argue that it was a heaping helping of bad, but I understood why she'd made the decision, even if I didn't like it. Mom struggled to support the household with her nine-to-five office job. She borrowed money from Mormor a lot to make sure she didn't bounce checks or make late payments. I *did* want to go to college, and I'd get some scholarships with my grades, but Mom made just enough money that I'd fall into the uncomfortable bracket of "not poor, but definitely not middle class, either," so financial aid was sketchy at best.

Moving was probably the best solution, I just hated admitting it. A new school with new teachers, a new curriculum and new students to navigate sounded exhausting.

"I get it," was all I could muster. I ignored the eggs and nibbled on the toast, wincing when it hit the acid vat that was my stomach. Mom kept stroking my forearm, and I let her curl her fingers around mine between bites.

"You'll have the summer, at least? And it's not far. You'll see Devi."

I glanced toward my bedroom door, hearing the vague rustling of human stirring within. Devi groaned and something thudded. I hoped it wasn't her body hitting the floor. "Yeah, I will. Once she's back from Connecticut."

Mom followed my gaze to the groaning on the other side of the apartment. "Should I make her some breakfast, do you think?"

"I don't know yet. Let me check..."

...if she's still drunk.

Mom rolled her eyes and got up to drop two more pieces of bread into the toaster. "Bread is probably a good start," she said, casting a sly look my way. "Lots of water, then aspirin. Probably some grease for lunch to suck up the nastiness. Steak and cheeses, maybe. Did you have a good time last night?"

I thought back to Aaron and Samantha and inevitably, Jack and his amazing bouncing truck. Not having his number bugged me. For the hours we'd been together, he'd been a ton of fun, but there wasn't much I could do about it. "All in all, yes? A few hiccups, but it wasn't bad. I met a guy but forgot to get his number."

"That sucks. Maybe someone else can get it for you."

"Yeah, maybe," I said.

Except no one did.

CHAPTER FOUR

"So that's the story. Surprise, everything is terrible forever," I said to Devi, rounding out my sad moving-in-with-Mormor tale. I wanted to talk about Jack, too, and fill Devi in on my rebound hookup, but Mom was floating around the apartment and I was pretty sure she didn't want to hear about her kid's sex life.

Devi blinked at me over her buttered toast, the only indication she'd drowned in a vat of strawberry wine the matching mascara smears beneath her eyes. She'd slept for six hours and miraculously emerged without a hangover, the witch. I kind of hated her for it. "It's only one town over, so that's good."

"Well, yeah." I shifted in my seat, cringing when my own stomach let out a shrieky wail. I was still battling the next-day demons. "But we won't get to go to classes together anymore."

"True, but we don't hang much beyond lunch, anyway."

"I know."

Devi sipped her water and shrugged. "I'll miss you, but you're a text away, and seriously, your grandmother's house is, like, ten minutes from mine, tops. We'll see each other all the time. I get why you're upset, but I don't think it'll be a big deal, and at least you'll get to avoid Mr. Brown's onion breath. I am not looking forward to AP Calc, dude."

My mother, who'd made herself absent upon Devi's appearance, yelled from the bathroom, "She's smart. Listen to her, Sara."

"Yeah, yeah, I will."

I frowned. It wasn't that I wanted to wallow in self-pity. It was just—

Okay, yes, I wanted to wallow, and no one was letting me. Devi made it worse-slash-better by saying, "Just think, no Skank One or Two. You'll be Aaron free, bay-bee."

That wasn't something I'd considered, and I perked up at the thought of not having to see him or his dingleberry of a girlfriend every time they walked down the hallway, twined together like snakes. And hey, new school meant new people. New people meant more options for dating. I'd had fun with Jack the night before. Kissing Jennifer before that had also been fun.

Maybe there'd be a thousand Jacks and Jennifers at Stonington. Maybe I could reinvent myself as an AP sex god-dess who just so happened to have the world's biggest butt.

"Maybe it won't be bad," I admitted. "It's a bigger school. More people. I've known everyone in this town since kindergarten and it's getting old. New blood is good."

"You'll be fine," Devi said. "I'm even a little jealous."

"I'm gonna miss you this summer," I blurted, watching her pick up her plate and bring it to the sink to rinse it. "How long are you at your grandparents' for?"

"The end of time, it feels like. The last week of July."

"We're moving in August, so we'll get a little hang-out time."

"...you're moving ten minutes away from me, in the op-posite direction of the ten minutes away from me that you are now. You're not going to Mordor, Sara." She smirked and stretched, and catching a waft of her own pit smell, winced. "I need a shower." I watched as she swooped down to grab her overnight bag from where I'd dumped it the night before. She was comfortable enough being in my apartment that she padded for the bathroom without needing help, stopping by the linen closet to grab herself a towel and facecloth. I heard the squeal of the door as she pushed it open. Right before she disappeared to rinse, she called my name.

"Yeah?"

"It's gonna be fine. Promise."

Four hours later, we were in the corner booth of a burger place at the mall recapping the events of the party, and oh, Devi was judging me.

"No condom, seriously?"

"I know, I know." I swirled my onion ring around in ranch dressing, plopped it into my mouth and then sucked a dollop of creamy goodness off my thumb. "I was thinking of getting a douche. I mean, I've never douched, but maybe that'll—"

"Vinegar, which is what douche is, does not cure or prevent STDs, you dink." She threw a french fry at me. It hit me between the eyes, bopped off my nose and dropped down into my pile of onion rings.

To be belligerent, I plucked it from the pile and ate it.

"I know that," I said, but I didn't really know, or I wouldn't have suggested it in the first place. But I really didn't want to go to a doctor. "I'm just trying to think of what to do the day after."

This wasn't how I'd expected our Jack conversation to go. I'd figured she'd give me the old attagirl for rebounding, for looking at Aaron and Samantha and, instead of shriveling because the thought of them turned my stomach, embracing my newfound sexual liberation with Handsome Guy Jack. Instead, she was scolding me.

Hardcore.

"Get tested." She jabbed me in the forehead with her nail, which hurt, and I winced away. "You don't know where he's been. Would you pick up food and eat it off the sidewalk? No? Well, this is worse."

"It's probably okay," I said, frowning. "I mean, chances are it's okay, right? He's young."

"Doesn't matter. You get tested. There's no such thing as a little gonorrhea."

No, there really wasn't. I knew she was right, knew that the 1 percent chance was worth having a doctor look at me, but my mind was spinning. How would I justify the appointment to my mom? She'd want to know why her healthy-looking daughter wanted to go to the doctor, and telling her that I'd gambled with my cooch didn't seem like it'd go over well. I was pretty sure that conversation would be worse than the one I was having with Devi.

"I know what you're doing," Devi said. "Stop it."

"Stop what?"

She rolled her eyes. "Go to a free clinic. They'll test you there."

"A clinic?"

"Yeah, like Planned Parenthood? They do a lot more than abortions. I'm pretty sure there's one twenty minutes away."

"Oh, right." And I knew that, too, but nothing was firing right in my head. The thrill of the hookup was over and the day-after regrets were hitting hard. Jack had been cool, but I still had no idea how to get in touch with him. Maybe I'd never see him again, which meant Devi was absolutely right. I'd effectively picked up food off the sidewalk and inserted it into my no-no parts.

"Craaaaaaap." I dropped my head back onto the top of the booth and stared at the too-bright overhead lights. "I just didn't want to think about Aaron. Like, all night, with him and Samantha—"

"I get it." Devi reached across the table to squeeze my hand. I didn't look at her, too intent on burning out my retinas with the offtrack lighting, so she slid along the curve of the corner booth until we were hip to hip. "I'm not trying to be insensitive, Sara. I totally get it. He hurt you and you wanted to feel better, and a hookup is cool! Just…as long as you're safe about it. I'm worried about you, is all. So promise me you'll go to the doctor? Or the clinic? I'll go with you if you want. It'll probably be less scary if you've got a friend with you."

"Yeah, sure," I said, my voice full of lead. "I promise."

"Okay, cool." She pressed a dry kiss to my shoulder and pulled over her fries and milkshake. "It's probably fine, like you said. I'm being precautious, but it's peace of mind, too. Speaking of which, when we get back to school on Monday? You should totally ask Michelle if she knows where Olly is from."

"Wait, who's Olly?"

"Oh, the friend I let flirt with me for an hour and a half so you could have your truck cabin romance. If you ever doubt my love for you, remember this conversation. He kept trying to impress me with his car. He has a new Mustang, apparently, that his surgeon dad gave him, except he didn't have it with him because he wasn't allowed to drive it at night, but if I wanted, I could come over to his house and—get this—*sit in the car to check it out*. We can't drive it, but we can sit in it."

That made me straighten up in my seat. "Seriously?"

"Oh, yeah. Seriously. That was his big pitch. To sit in an unmoving car." She grinned and offered me a french fry. I accepted it, biting her fingertip and earning a thwack upside the head for my efforts.

I deserved it.

"It's not his, you realize," I said, going back to my greasy lunch. "Like, it's totally his dad's car and he's trying to use it to get laid."

"Oh, I know. It's gross, but boys are gross."

As I tucked back into my lunch, my mind racing with thoughts of STDs and clinics and a couple hours of DNA swap, I could only hope boys weren't *that* gross.

CHAPTER FIVE

Monday came, no clinic. *Too much homework*, I told myself. Plus, I was stewing over Jack. Sadly, Michelle didn't know who he or Olly was, never mind where they were from. She looked at me blankly after I asked and then complained that her father had come home and grounded her for the rest of her natural life for the lawn getting torn up after the party.

It sucked to be Michelle.

Tuesday, I tried to psych myself up to go to the clinic, but no, that didn't happen, either. I justified it with the paper I had due for English class…next week. Devi read me the riot act again, and so I made a promise. Wednesday was the day. I'd drive myself to Planned Parenthood and get my testing done. I dreaded it still, but Devi's bit about peace of mind was spot on. I'd rather know that I had crotch fungawookie and get treated than to find out the hard way with itches or oozes or worse later on.

A plan. I had one.

But then Aaron came along and screwed it up because that's what he did best.

Logically, I understand that it's not his fault that I didn't make it to PP. He didn't hold me down and tell me I couldn't go. He didn't slash my tires or lock me in a closet. I already had a trash record of going because I was scared. No, what Aaron did was absolutely *ruin* my day, decimating me so much I shirked all responsibilities so I could lick my wounds over chocolate ice cream.

Wednesday afternoon, five minutes after last bell. I stood at my locker stuffing books into the pit of disorganized despair that was my book bag. We didn't carry many books anymore, a lot of our stuff was online or printed out in packets, but close to finals, three of my teachers had volunteered textbooks as study aids. Like a true nerd, I'd signed them out to take the chapter reviews to make sure I knew the material. I'd just wrestled my Algebra II book in between my file folders when Aaron appeared, sliding in beside me and leaning against the lockers.

He looked good. Collared shirt, white T-shirt underneath. New jeans and sneakers. He had a fresh haircut and he'd switched his cologne to something that wasn't the nose-killing Axe body spray he'd preferred when we were dating.

"Hey," he said in greeting. "Got a minute?"

"Nope." I slammed the locker in his face and brushed past him, my shoulder colliding with his as I stomped my way down the hall and toward the parking lot. I wished I wasn't wearing my old jeans with the faded knees. I wished that I hadn't gotten salad dressing on my *Evil Dead* T-shirt at lunch. I wished I'd brushed my hair or done anything with it beyond putting it up in a clip on my head. But that wasn't my reality. "Fake it till you make it" was in full effect. I might have felt like two pounds of garbage in a one-pound bag seeing him, smelling him, touching him, but I wasn't letting him know that.

He fell into step beside me.

"Are you okay, Sara? For real. I'm worried about you," he said.

"Don't be," I immediately snapped, though inwardly I was screaming. What had he heard? Who'd he heard it from? Was everyone talking about me? Maybe I wasn't ready for this liberated sexual-being thing after all. I was only seventeen...

"That guy. Like, you don't just go off with dudes. He didn't do anything to you, did he? Like, nothing in your drink or—"

"I said I didn't have a minute," I interrupted him. "My business stopped being your business when you boned Samantha, remember?"

I thought that was the end of it because he stopped mid-hall, brow furrowed, his hands slipping into his pockets. I was almost free, my hand was on the door handle, when he said, "I get it. I screwed up and ruined a great thing. That doesn't mean I stopped loving you, you know. If you went off with Rando Dude because you wanted a hookup, fine, but that's not the Sara I know."

I stopped in my tracks to eye him over my shoulder. He looked so earnest, like he'd just poured his heart out on the floor. His shoulders were tight, his lips tilted down into a frown. It's how he'd looked on all the sobby Snapchats, too, and for a fleeting second, I wavered. I remembered what it was like to love this guy, to be with him, to smile with him, to feel him stroking my hair after a bad day. I remembered why we were good together.

Then I remembered Samantha's thong-in-crack on his phone.

I am so, so glad to be getting away from this. From him.

Bring it on, Stonington.

"I said it's none of your business," I hissed, and before he could do anything else to hurt me, I ran to the Subaru. Bonus, I didn't cry till I left the parking lot.

I did cry all the way to Devi's house, having to pull over twice to blow my nose and wipe my eyes.

Screw you, Aaron.

Screw you and your girlfriend, too.

You know your best friend is a good one when she'll let you drop by her house unannounced, eat all her ice cream and snot up her favorite shirt because your ex-boyfriend decimated you with concern trolling.

"That's what it is," Devi said, handing me another tissue, probably in hopes I'd stop dripping all over her blouse. "Concern trolling. I don't think he really gives a crap about you being okay. He wants to let you know he knows about Jack and frame it as a good-guy-Aaron thing. It's a douche move."

"You're giving him an awful lot of credit for being clever," I said, digging into my ice cream, which was really her ice cream, but who was counting?

"Maybe, maybe not. If he's desperate enough to get you back, he might get clever out of necessity."

I didn't know what to say to that, so I shrugged and offered her a bite of ice cream. She waved me off and reached for her frozen chai instead.

"You sure? You're going to be eating kosher soon," I said.

"Actually, Ben and Jerry's *is* kosher. Most of it is, anyway, but thanks for the reminder, smart-ass. God, I'll miss bacon."

Devi's immediate family were pretty casual with their Judaism.

Bubbe, not so much.

"Sorry. When you come back from Connecticut, I'll have bacon double cheeseburgers at the ready."

"Gee, thanks, friend."

She winked at me. I winked back. I licked my spoon clean and flopped back into her mountain of pillows, my eyes sweeping her room. It was big, almost twenty by twenty, with dusky purple walls and off-white furniture. I didn't think people actually had things like matching bedroom sets, but Devi's bureau, vanity, desk and headboard were all the same style and color. There was a knotted rug on the floor and real lace curtains in the windows. The paintings on her wall weren't framed posters, but actual oil-painted reproductions.

In short, Devi's room > my hodgepodge room with matching nothing.

"Can I live here while you're gone?" I asked. "Just move in and be the honorary third Abrams kid?"

"Sure, my parents love you. But Ezra lives here, you realize, and he's back on SpongeBob reruns almost exclusively. Plus, he pees in the pool, so…"

Ezra was Devi's seven-year-old little brother. And he acted exactly how you'd expect a seven-year-old little brother to act, complete with the obsession with farts, Lego and bad TV shows.

"Yeah, okay, hard pass. I'd actually rather move. Speaking of which, I'm a lot more okay with it after Aaron's crap. I don't think I can deal with him anymore."

"Valid." Devi drained her chai and slid in beside me on her giant bed, her arms and yards upon yards of legs wrapping around me. She nuzzled at my hair and I settled into the hug. She was the one thing, possibly the only thing, I'd miss about my hometown, but like she'd pointed out, I was only ten minutes away in the opposite direction. I wouldn't see her during the school day, but we didn't have all our classes together, anyway.

I'd be losing a Devi lunch, but gaining an Aaron-free life.

"I'm gonna miss you, wifey," I said. "You're about all, though. I think I'm ready to get out of Dodge."

"I'll miss you, too, but you're right. Take out the trash. Aaron's part of that trash. You got this, girl."

CHAPTER SIX

Devi didn't bring the clinic up again after that and, honestly, I didn't kill myself to get there, either. I kept making excuses for reasons not to go, and eventually, I just told myself I was too busy and a symptom would have shown up already if I'd caught something so I must be fine. Instead, I focused on getting through school, acing my finals, getting phone numbers from classmates I wanted to stay in touch with—which was a lot fewer than I'd expected—and helping Mom pack. Devi left, but she texted me daily and sometimes at night we'd Skype, save for Friday night and into Saturday because she was observing Shabbos with her grandparents.

It was a whirlwind—often a lonely whirlwind—but the busyness helped with that. Aaron kept right on Aaroning at me, sending me check-in texts and Snaps that probably would have made his girlfriend's hair fall out, but I never responded.

"Block his nuuuuumber," Devi said to me on FaceTime. "Bloooock. Hiiiiim."

"I will," I promised.

But I never did. It was unhealthy, but those messages were a weird form of validation. He'd broken my heart. Knowing he struggled with it made my own suffering a little more palatable.

Bitchy, yes.

Regrets, no.

My world was sorting, boxes and trash bags. A third to keep, a third for the dumpster, a third for charity donations. With so much going on, I never really caught on that I'd come down with not an STD, but a fetus. I was more tired than usual, sure, but my days were long. My stomach was off. Not horribly so, but I chalked it up to the stress of the move. My boobs hurt, my nips aching so much sometimes I'd scream angrily at my bra and T-shirts for daring to graze them, but I'd gotten breast sensitivity with PMS before, so it didn't occur to me to worry about it. And the killer? I still got periods. Light ones, but periods all the same, which is why I didn't figure out something was really "wrong" until I was almost three months pregnant.

Eggs finally did me in.

I loved eggs, ate them all the time. It was a breakfast ritual between Mom and I where she'd get up in the morning, scramble up some eggs, I'd make toast and butter it, and we'd eat together. It continued into the summer, as I took point on packing duty with Mom working all the time. She'd wake me up and we'd chow down as per usual before we went in opposite directions to carry out our days.

Wednesday morning, early. I was tired. So was Mom. Neither one of us were talking as we sipped our coffees, doing how we normally did on a weekday. Mom broke out the eggs, dropped them into the pan and BOOM. The smell hit me. I'm not going to lie to you and tell you pregnant women get extra senses because of Preggo Magic, but they do react to stimuli differently, and in that moment, the smell of eggs became something horrific. It was farts and sadness. It was old garbage and sweaty armpits and every other atrocious stench all rolled into one. I fled the kitchen to toss my cookies into the toilet in the bathroom, wishing to God that all eggs, everywhere, ceased to exist.

Mom followed me, rubbed my back, asked if I was okay.

"No eggs," I warbled. Which, again, was weird because I'd eaten eggs fine up to that point, but that's something people should know about pregnancy—your tastes can and do change often and rapidly for no rhyme or reason beyond "hormones."

"What did you eat?"

I did a mental tally of all the stuff I'd crammed into my maw the night before. Half a tube of Pringles while I was talking to Devi. A bowl of ice cream. Enough Diet

Coke to float the Titanic. While it wasn't the healthiest fare in the world, it wasn't any different than anything I'd devour any other day of the week.

"Nothing special," I said, fighting off the gags.

"Do you want some toast?"

"No. I just—gonna go back to sleep, I think."

Mom was there with me, following, helping me into bed and tucking me in. She tutted and fussed over me, her hand on my forehead. She produced a thermometer. I had what she thought was a low-grade fever. She offered to stay home and nurse me but I told her I'd be fine, and I was fine a few hours later, if not slightly queasy. We both dismissed it as a bout of the flu. It wasn't until three days later when she hauled my sorry, pukey self to the doctor for said flu that The Question was asked.

"Could you be pregnant?" the nurse asked.

She seemed nice—Deb, her name tag said. She wore scrubs with cartoon kitties. A stethoscope looped around her neck. Her hair was salt-and-pepper gray and tied back in a ponytail. Her eyeliner was on point—perfect cat wings that could have cut a man who got too close.

"What?"

Mom was in the waiting room. I was sitting on the examination table with its crinkly paper cover, my feet dangling off the side and not touching the floor.

"Could you be pregnant?"

"No," I immediately said, because again, I hadn't missed a period at that point and I had no idea you could bleed and be pregnant. Deb nodded, jotted down some notes, took my temperature and blood pressure, and ducked out of the room. It wasn't until the door slammed behind her that I started freaking out about the Jack thing all over again. I never had managed to track him down. Calls to friends and having those friends call their friends yielded nothing—he was the amazing disappearing penis. I was disappointed, honestly, and it'd taken me a few weeks to overcome the self-doubt, confusion and paranoia about his potentially toxic pants parts, but eventually I'd accepted it as a thing that'd happened, live and learn. There were other Jacks in the sea.

It was, as Devi not-so-poetically put it, my sticky send-off to an old life in an old town.

But there I was, months later, sweating it again, literally days before I moved to Stonington.

Maybe Jack's back. Like a bad penny, Mormor would say.

I was chewing my fingernails down to stubs when Deb reappeared with the plastic sample cup and wipes. She motioned at the closed door of the doctor's office bathroom behind her. "Just leave that in the slot in the wall when you're done," she said. "Dr. Bhatia will be in shortly."

"Sure," I said. "Thanks—for the pee cup," I followed up with, because I'm a nervous talker and that's not *at all* awkward.

Deb eyed me like she might track a rabid lab animal. "You're welcome."

I decided, as I dragged my sorry, tired, pukey self across the clinic office hallway, that I'd tell the doctor about my hookup just in case it'd given me the dreaded funga-wookie. I'd had a pelvic exam once before. I'd hated that someone was all up in my guts and poking around with metal equipment cold enough to frost my ovaries, but if there was something wrong with me, I couldn't get better without honestly communicating what might have led to my being sick in the first place.

That doctor's office pee saw me wrestling the deepest thoughts I'd ever had in my seventeen years of life. And it all revolved around vaginal swabs and made-up names for STDs.

I washed my hands and headed back to the exam room, still feeling nauseated, more so when I got a waft of a cleaning chemical someone was using in the room next door to mine. I closed the door, breathing in and out through my mouth so I wouldn't paint the walls with the single piece of toast I'd managed to keep down. About ten minutes later, there was a soft rap on the door and a short heavyset woman with brown skin came in, her silky black hair tied back in a bun. White coat, blue-and-white-polka-dotted dress, sensible pumps. Dr. Bhatia smiled at me, her hand with pretty gold rings clasping onto a clipboard.

"Serendipity? What a pretty name."

"Sara," I said. "And thanks."

She nodded and put her clipboard aside, pulling a wheely stool out from under the counter. She folded her hands in her lap and adopted what was probably supposed to be a comforting smile, but the faint lines around her eyes made me think something was up. "Sara, before we start talking, you should know about some confidentiality clauses regarding your healthcare privacy as a minor. I am required, by law, to report any medical findings to your parent or guardian that I deem a threat to you or your personal safety. That said, my personal philosophy is to have a dialogue, to see what you think, and to make a plan with you that will ensure you are safe and as healthy as can be. We'll bring parents in only after we make that plan. You're seventeen, yes?"

"What? Yeah. Yes," I said, my stomach sinking to my knees. Why was she talking about threats to my safety? Had the pee test proven I had radioactive vag? Were my guts going to fall out?

"Okay, well, you're a young woman and I'm sure we can make a plan that'll work for you. Do you feel safe at home? With your mother?" The doctor reached for her clipboard, lifting it up so it hid the bottom half of her face. I concentrated on the dark vee of her manicured brows.

"I… Yeah. Home's fine. I get along great with my mom. Is something wrong with me? Like, am I dying? It was only the once. Well, three times in the truck, but—"

"We'll take some blood to rule out any complications after we talk. Sara, you're pregnant."

When this moment happens in movies, there's usually some dramatic reaction to it, like a scream or a whoop or something to indicate that the gravity of the situation— that you, a human, have another human parasiting it up in your midsection—is understood and-slash-or appreci-ated. I didn't flinch. I didn't make a sound. I just stared at her. It was the total reboot, the blue screen of death that lets you know the computer's operating system has shut down and needs a few minutes to hopefully patch itself back together again before it can function.

Preg. Nant.
Pregnant.
Baby.
Baby in me.
Jack's baby.

"Are you alright, Sara? Did you want your mother?"

I didn't answer.

Dr. Bhatia wheeled her stool in close so she was right beside me. She didn't touch me, which I appreciated—I'd have probably jumped out of my skin, but she was close and she was a presence and there was comfort in that. Being alone moments after finding out you are toting around an unplanned and not super welcome kid? Not a pleasant notion.

We sat like that for a few minutes, her waiting patiently for me to react. She expected me to cry; I know that because she brought over the box of tissues and put it against my leg on the exam table. I dropped my gaze to it, reading the word *Kleenex* on the side over and over again. I wasn't really thinking, more existing, but what was strange was that the existence itself was *changed*. There were other days I'd sat looking blankly at walls or ceilings, my mind on autopilot, drifting, but never before had I done that floating, thoughtless existing with the back-of-my-mind knowledge that I would be a mother.

It was different. I can't articulate how it was different, but it was. I was Sara. I was in the doctor's office. I'd just found out I was pregnant.

These were my truths.

CHAPTER SEVEN

"Okay. Okay, sure." Mom leaned against the clinic countertop, blinking fast, her hands curled over the lip of the Formica. She looked stunned, possibly as stunned as I'd looked a few minutes ago when I'd been told. A sheaf of blond hair had slumped down over her right eye, but she wasn't brushing it away. She was too busy staring at me like I'd spawned an extra head. "So we have some options. I… Wow. Okay."

Dr. Bhatia had offered to mediate our talk. I'd declined, and she assured me she'd be back after we had our family discussion—to just open the door and she'd know to come back. I needed blood work still, she reminded me, for *reasons* that included ruling out STDs that could potentially harm me and the baby, and they'd want to run some other screenings now knowing I was a walking, talking incubator but, *Don't worry about that right now.*

I could worry about that *after* I dropped the anvil on my mother's head.

She looked pretty good for having taken an anvil.

"I'm sorry," I said, looking down. "It was one night. Aaron was there, I was upset—"

"It's… Christ. I'm not going to tell you it's okay. This is life-changing stuff, Sara, but I will tell you we'll get through it. Your grandmother is going to be such an asshole about this."

What Mom wasn't saying was that she herself was only thirty-four. Mom had come home two weeks after high school graduation to tell Mormor she was pregnant with me. Mormor wasn't the type to pull punches; she'd see the parallel, like mother like daughter, and probably tell my mother it was *her* fault I'd done a boneheaded thing in an F-150 after a bottle of incredibly crappy wine.

…which I couldn't let happen. My mom had given me all the talks. I'd just been reckless, played sperm roulette and lost.

"I'll talk to her," I said. "Tell her it was my fault."

"It won't matter, but that's not… I mean, it's important, but it's not what's really important. What's important is what you want to do about it. You're seventeen, a great student. Is it Aaron's?"

"No!" I shouted, and she flinched like I'd whacked her. I immediately felt bad. "Sorry. God, no. It's Jack's—the guy."

I'd told her about "the guy." She'd listened to me bemoan the loss of "the guy" a few too many times over the last few months, so she knew exactly who I meant and why it was complicated. Jack was the phantom of my vagina. It was like *The Phantom of the Opera* only with less kidnapping.

"Aww, crapsicles." Mom finally brushed the hair out of her face and came to stand by my side. Her arm slid over my shoulders. "I could kill you, you know." But her words were softened by the soft kiss she pressed to my temple. She loved me, even if I was a colossal screwup.

I guess it helped that I was *her* colossal screwup.

"I don't know what I want to do," I said to her. I'd just digested the reality of the kid growing inside of me. My brain hadn't yet moved on to the next step, which was keeping it, abortion, adoption. My life was forever changed, yes, but I wasn't yet ready for the choose-your-own-adventure portion of post-conception reality.

"We don't need a decision right now, but we'll need one soonish, and honestly, I think we should talk this over with Mormor, too. We're moving into her house, she loves you, it's not like she hasn't walked this walk with yours truly before."

"Yeah, of course. Yeah. She's going to be a jerk about it, though."

"Well, of course she is, but she wouldn't be Mormor if she wasn't a jerk."

Mom gave me a pained, tight smile, the kind that suggested she had gas pains, and stepped away from my side. "We ready for the doctor?" she asked, her hand already extending for the metal door handle.

No.

"Sure," I said, feeling like I was going to be sick, and it had nothing to do with eggs, or the smell of cleaning chemicals, and everything to do with what I'd just learned and its myriad complications.

Mormor's house was one of those big New England farmhouses: two stories, gray with white shutters, a wraparound porch she'd decorated with flourishing window boxes, hanging plants spaced out between the second story supports, and too much wicker furniture. Mormor loved wicker. It was an essential part of her aesthetic.

Mom didn't call to announce us, because if she had, Mormor would have insisted Mom tell her why we were showing up on a Thursday when Mom should have been at work. She'd have been relentless, asked a thousand questions Mom would have had to sidestep or ignore, and then there would have been yelling. Mormor, as previously stated, was not a subtle creature, and when she latched on to something, she was about as delicate as a rabid wolverine.

So we decided to spring it on her.

We parked Mom's ancient black Jeep in the driveway, my finger toying with the edges of the Band-Aid from my blood draw. I don't know why the nurse chose a *Toy Story* bandage for a teenager, but it was at odds with the thoughts swirling about in my head, which were, essentially, that you really weren't a kid anymore when you got pregnant. You were an adult, or at least an adult in comparison to the little person you were supposed to spew into the world nine months later.

And what kind of an adult wore a *Toy Story* Band-Aid?
This one. Me.
My kid is screwed.

Mormor was in the garden. This wasn't surprising; the woman liked vegetables a whole lot more than she liked most people, and she spent any and all sunny days out digging in dirt. She wore a short-sleeved button-down shirt with loud orange flowers on it and a pair of khaki shorts. Her steel gray hair was tucked up under a wide-brimmed bonnet-type hat. Green gloves protected her hands from whatever noxious concoction she was slopping on her plants. I had my guesses, none of them were pleasant, but there she was, reaching into a bucket, producing a brown gritty mess and tucking it onto the roots of her vegetables.

She never lifted her head when we approached.

"Hi, Ma." Mom stepped up to the edge of a row of squash, her arms across her chest, sunglasses perched on the end of her nose. Her spine was so straight it could have been made of metal.

"There's a basket by the hose," Mormor said in greeting, her English laced with a hint of Swedish accent.

"I see it."

"Good. Pick the zucchini. Most people call before they show up, Astrid." Mormor lifted her face. She and Mom looked a whole lot alike with their pale eyes and pale hair and long noses. They also had the same this-is-a-load-of-crap face, which they were both wearing, with the curled lip and the crinkles in the nose. Mom broke first, though, because she always did, muttering under her breath as she grabbed the basket and stooped to snap zucchinis off the vine.

"It was important enough to just come over, Ma," my mom said, crouching down and reaching in beneath all the verdant green. She snarled as one of the leaves whacked her in the face. Mormor snorted and turned her laser-beam stare my way.

"What's wrong? Did someone die? Come here, let me look at you." Mormor stood up, brushing her knees free of garden dirt as she walked my way. She pulled off her rubber gloves and reached for my face, cupping my chin and turning it left and right, like she was examining a horse.

"I'm fine. No one died," I managed.

"Mmm. Swedish skin. You're freckling. Too bad you didn't get your father's coloring. He might have been an asshole, but he was a handsome asshole. Browned up like a chicken nugget." She took the hat off her own head and plopped it on mine.

"That's a little racist, Mormor. Comparing people to food?"

She ignored me, because that's just what she did, pulling me in tight for a spine-crushing hug. "Let's get you some lemonade. Your mother will join us when she's done."

"I... Okay," I said, being lovingly dragged toward the front porch. Mormor patted my shoulder and glanced back at my mother.

"Have you eaten yet, Astrid?"

From beneath a monster zucchini bush: "No, Ma."

"It's almost one-thirty. I'll take care of it. But you really should be on a regular eating schedule. It's bad for your pancreas."

"Okay, Ma."

Mom had the placating tone—the one she got when she was talking to bill collectors on the phone when they were demanding money she didn't have.

Hopefully, Mormor still lets us move in when she finds out I'm pregnant. Mom's struggling to go it alone.

Mormor led me into the house. She liked Americana decor, with furniture that looked old and distressed, lots of country landscapes and a dark red, navy and off-white color scheme. Her rugs were knotted, her drapes cotton and long. There was more wicker inside, but in the form of baskets, with plenty of houseplants tucked everywhere. We walked through the front room, which was the living room, with its big brick fireplace and overstuffed leather furniture. To the right of us were the stairs leading to the second story bedrooms, but it was the kitchen Mormor wanted, and it was the kitchen we went to, me a few steps behind her the whole way.

She motioned to a wooden stool at the island before washing her hands.

"What's going on?" she asked.

Or demanded, really. Because Mormor.

"I…uhh…wanna wait for Mom to come in, if that's cool."

"Why? Don't you think you can trust me?"

On the one hand, sure, I could trust Mormor! On the other hand, she'd just grabbed a tomato, put it on a cutting board and cleaved it in half with a single resounding thud of the knife.

…because, again, Mormor.

"I know I can." Mormor was gearing up to go at me again but, fortunately, Mom trudged inside with her zucchini crop, distracting her. The moment Mom left the zucchini on the counter, Mormor tutted and motioned at the sink with her machete.

"Rinse them. You know how I do things."

"Ma, I'm—fine. Okay, look, we have to talk to you."

"Are you not moving in after all? That'd be stupid, Astrid." Mormor went back to her tomato, slicing it into big slabs and laying them out on a paper plate. A touch of salt, a drizzle of balsamic vinegar—she slid it my way, reaching for a loaf of crispy bread she probably made herself and slicing off a hunk. It, too, went onto the plate.

I stared at it. It ought to have been a real treat for me, because Mormor's garden-fresh tomatoes were the best, except the idea of the squishy insides of the tomato with all those seeds made my stomach rebel.

I hunched over, squinting my eyes shut, willing the nausea to go away.

Stop trying to murder me, baby. That's rude.

"…what's wrong? Is she sick? If she's sick—I'm sixty-five. You shouldn't be exposing me to—"

"She's not sick, Ma. She's pregnant, okay? That's why we're here. Sara's pregnant." I kept my eyes closed, because then I wouldn't have to see the disappointment on my grandmother's face. Mom came to stand behind me, her hand going to the small of my back and rubbing in soothing circles. It helped me not hurl all over the kitchen island, but it didn't make me feel better. Mormor was silent save for the sound of her knife hitting the cutting board as she attacked another tomato.

Shunk.

Shunk.

Shunk.

"Well," Mormor said, speaking only after she'd finished cutting up her vegetables. I cracked an eye, daring to peek at my grandmother's face. No smile. No scowl. No anything. She was arranging more tomato slices on a paper plate when she said, without looking up, "It's good, then, that I have four bedrooms."

CHAPTER EIGHT

I asked to be excused from the conversation about my own baby. I know that's weird, but I was exhausted—emotionally and physically—and napping seemed like the best course of action, especially as a puke risk, which is like a flight risk, only more disgusting. Dr. Bhatia had prescribed medicine to help with that, but I hadn't gotten to the pharmacy yet on account of the Mormor visit.

Who, so far, was taking the whole thing pretty well. Thank God.

I climbed the stairs to the big beautiful spare room on the right. The bedspread was ivory. The wallpaper on the walls was ivory with little red-and-pink flowers with whorled greenery. The curtains in the windows were lace. It was pretty, at least two of my current room in size, and a lot fancier. I wasn't going to have a reason to be jealous of Devi's nice stuff anymore.

Right, Devi.

I have to call her.

This'll be fun.

I walked over to the bed and face planted into the pillows, arms to either side of my body, legs akimbo. Mormor walked in behind me to pull the shades. I had four windows total, three on one wall facing the neighbor's house next door, one on the adjacent wall pointed out at the backyard, overlooking Mormor's shed and frog pond. She made sure each of them was darkened before coming over to the foot of the bed to pull another crochet blanket up over my legs.

Mormor liked to crochet, particularly when she was watching *Jeopardy* and *Fox News* at night.

"Thank you," I mumbled.

"You're welcome. This is going to be your room. You can fix it up how you like."

"Okay." I lifted my head so I could look at her. There was no reproach on her face, only her tried and true austere expression of chin up, brows high on her weathered forehead, mouth pinched tight in a flat line.

"I'm sorry," I said. I didn't know what else to say. I wasn't even sure why I was apologizing, except maybe for putting everyone out, making everyone worry about me. I'm an honor student, top of my class—smart and al-

ways lauded for having it together. The mighty had finally fallen, and I'd done it *hard*.

Like, right onto my face before getting crushed by one
of those cartoon ACME anvils hard.

"Stop apologizing," she said. "You'll get through this.
Your mother did, and I did before her. It's not easy but
it's not insurmountable, either."

"You didn't have Mom until you were thirty, and you
were married."

Mormor sniffled, her hands, thin and riddled with
dark blue veins, clasped together over her flat stomach.
"I had an abortion, in Sweden in the seventies. I'd gone
to live with family awhile," she said. "There was a boy,
I loved him, but I was naive. Young women are often
naive. Trusting everything will be fine without realizing
you have to work for fine. We make our own fine." She
paused. "Frankly, I find it amazing our species continues.
We're all idiots."

"Yeah, I'm an idiot," I admitted, my fingers sweeping
over my throbbing temple. On top of the nausea, I was
getting a killer headache, which was probably tension,
but who knew with my freshly announced tenant. Weird
stuff was, and would be for a long while, happening in my
body. "Ugh. I feel so stupid. Like, I was so careful with
Aaron, but one night, and one bad choice—"

"That's all it takes. One choice. Bad is relative. If it's
any consolation, it's a mistake that's been made a million
times before and will be made a million times again. Such
is the way of youth and life. But you will get through it

because your mother and I will help you get through it. We're Larssen women. We persevere. It's what we do."

Except I'm a Rodriguez, my brain screamed. *What if we* don't *persevere?*

I didn't say it aloud. Mormor wouldn't brook a whiner, so instead I snuggled into the bed pillows and closed my eyes, hoping I could drift off and vacate reality for just a little while. Mormor took the hint, closing the bedroom door behind her and leaving me in the dark, alone. It should have been a time for rest, but my brain was on fire, the possibilities, the what-ifs, the what-do-I-dos endless. I felt like one of those babies who cried because they were overtired but refused to go to sleep. I wanted to, willed my body to, but it wasn't happening.

So I pulled out my cell phone and called Devi. I'd normally text her, but this was big enough news that it warranted the call. She was still in Connecticut, but was coming back after Shabbos that weekend.

"Killlll meeeeee," Devi rasped in greeting.

"Hi. Hey. Why?"

"I'm *melting*. Bubbe keeps the house at six zillion degrees and it's four thousand percent humidity. I'm going to have zits the size of meteors. Green tea sheet mask, thy name is God."

This was the part of the conversation where we'd normally spiral off into talking about skin care, both of us fully riding the Korean skin-care train, but not then. Then it was, "Devi, I'm in trouble."

"You okay? What's wrong? Who're we killing?"

"I just got back from the doctor and I'm pregnant. Please

don't—just don't… No 'I told you so' or anything, okay? I just found out and I'm really upset." And that was when the tears started. Not at the doctor's office. Not with my mom in the car when she told me we'd figure it out. Not with Mormor. With Devi, on the phone, by myself in the dark of a bedroom that didn't feel like mine but would be mine soon. Devi gasped and then went quiet, which only made me cry all the harder, because what if she didn't want to be my friend anymore? What if her parents decided I was "a bad kid" and didn't let Devi hang out with me because I'd corrupt her with my rampant slutitude?

If I get an abortion, they wouldn't have to know it'd even happened.

Except I wasn't sure I wanted one yet. I wasn't raised religious, I didn't have any dogma to contend with or staunch familial teachings. I'd always viewed it as a person's choice, to each their own. But the reality was, I was almost three months along. The fetus was maybe getting sorta human-like in there, and I wasn't sure I was comfortable with the idea of a medical eviction. I had nothing to say about anyone else making that choice! But for me, I just… It sat wrong. Mom would probably have something to say about it later, maybe she'd sway me one way or the other, but I was leaning toward a "don't do it."

Adoption? Possible, a good possibility, in fact, but again, I'd want feedback.

Devi's here, on the line, now. She's smart.

I trust her.

"I'm not sure what I want to do yet," I managed, warbling. I used my sleeve as a tissue because desperate times and desperate measures and boogers stopped for no woman. "About the baby."

"Holy crap. Okay, right, so. Right. Oh, my God." Devi cleared her throat. "So, yeah, I am totally down for talking about this with you. But…"

"Bubbe?"

"Ayep. She's got her soaps on. I'll… Give me a little bit, okay? And I will absolutely be down for a talk. I'll call you back?"

"Yeah, sure."

She apologized and ended the call. The idea that she couldn't even talk to me without risking grandmother ire did nothing for my nerves. I had another good cry, muffling it into Mormor's afghan, before tiptoeing down the hall to wash up in the bathroom. I splashed my face but the damage was done. I was not a pretty crier; my skin was tomato red, nose large and in charge. Half of my hair had escaped my rubber band, so black wormy frizz haloed my head like a Brillo pad. Crusts of snot soiled my nostrils. My eyes were swollen to the point I looked like a bug on a coke bender.

Yeah, this is the face of a woman who could be a mom.

I tried to swallow another sob and failed, which is what alerted my mom to the great crash of Serendipity Rodriguez going on upstairs. She called my name from the living room, and when I didn't answer, came running. I was sitting on the toilet holding my stomach and rocking back and forth when she found me. She slid into the bathroom and gathered me close. My little mom, that petite blonde thing who smelled like Chanel No. 5 and had for as long as I remembered, hauled me to my feet and led me back to the spare room. She half carried me there. I don't know how she managed such She-Hulk strength, but I wasn't asking questions as she dumped me into bed and pulled the covers up over me, sitting on the edge of the mattress beside me and stroking my hair.

I was crying so hard I didn't see Mormor come in, but I felt her when she sat on my other side and very efficiently tucked the blanket in under my butt, as gentle as the angriest drill sergeant.

"You will be okay," Mormor said.

"She's right, kiddo. You're going to be okay," Mom said. "We've got this."

I wanted to believe them. I *had* to believe them, or not only was it all over for me, it was all over for my kid, too.

CHAPTER NINE

I woke hours later, not of my own volition, but because Devi had climbed into bed with me and was spooning me, her arm thrown over my middle. I didn't care how she'd gotten there, I just knew she was there, and I rolled over and hugged her, burying my face in her neck.

"I probably smell rank. I haven't showered," she said in greeting.

Her arms wrapped around me and squeezed.

"You are the best wifey," I managed before catching a waft of...bacon? "You stopped for cheeseburgers on the way, didn't you?"

"Damned right, I did. Freedom, baby. But even with that bacon double cheeseburger with a double cheese-burger on the side, I did a two-and-a-half-hour drive in an hour and forty-five because I care. Also because I was trying to beat Connecticut traffic at rush hour. Thanks for ruining everything, New York."

"Is Bubbe going to kill you for leaving early?"

"Don't think so. I told her why I was going and she didn't try to stop me. I think she's glad to have her house back to herself. She said I kept getting a weird look on my face after a few hours without my phone on Shabbos. I'm pretty sure looking at me *actually* makes her angry." She smirked. "She loves me. She just wants to punch me a little."

"Well, yeah, but so does everyone."

"Exactly. I'm just that kind of girl."

The banter was easy, light. Familiar. Familiar was good, and the brick I'd been trying very hard not to shit soft-ened a little.

...wow. Gross analogy, but you catch my drift.

Devi kissed the top of my head and smiled. I think it was supposed to be reassuring, but she looked like she had gas. That was okay, though—finding out your bestie was pregnant right before senior year of high school was prob-ably worth a few fart faces. "So what are we going to do about Babygate? Like, do you even know or..."

"I'm fondly referring to it as the fetus. At least, mentally I am, and no clue." I reiterated my stance on abortion, that it was okay for others but I wasn't feeling it, pausing to ask her, "Is that dumb?"

She immediately shook her head.

"Not at all. It's a decision that's going to be hard for lots of people for lots of reasons. So, think about it, decide what sits right for you. No one gets to dictate your feelings about something complicated like this."

"I don't know what my mom's going to say."

"I'm betting, by the talk she gave me when I got here, she's going to support whatever you decide. She texted me, you know." When surprise made my eyebrows kiss my hairline, Devi nodded. "Yeah, she didn't know you'd called me. She asked when I was home and said she thought you could use some friends around, that you're going through some stuff. She wouldn't tell me what, though. I thought you'd appreciate that. Your mom was good about your privacy."

My mom was good about a lot of things. So was Mormor, when she wasn't throwing shoes or demanding vegetable service. I sat up in bed and swung my legs over the side, peering down at my feet. My toenails were blue with a pink sparkle. If I continued with this pregnancy—and I was feeling like I wanted to—I'd not be able to paint my toenails anymore, never mind see those feet for too much longer.

Fat Town, Population: Serendipity.

"So what did she say to you when you got here?" I asked, trying to distract myself from the idea of my imminent flesh expansion.

"Both of them assured me that you were okay, that they were taking care of you, but that you'd be super glad to see me. Which you were. You squealed a little." Devi hopped out of bed, immediately bending over to right Mormor's sheets and blankets. "I think they're gonna be cool about it. It's just a feeling."

"I hope so." I watched her work for a moment before clueing in that I might be pregnant, but that didn't make me useless, so I folded the afghan into a neat square. "I'm thinking adoption, maybe?"

"That's cool, if you don't want it. It'd make some other people really happy." She fluffed the pillows and peered up at me. Normally, she wouldn't be caught dead in daylight hours without some makeup on, but she'd come straight from Bubbe's, which meant she'd been clean-faced for over a month. I could see the ginger freckles on her nose. "But only if you don't want it. You're not obligated to give your baby up if you don't want to. I can't see your mom turning into a supervillain and selling your baby on the black market."

"She wouldn't, I don't think. I'm just not sure yet? Adoption seems like a good idea, but what if I figured out I was wrong after I gave it away? That I did want it? There's no take backsies."

"So you gotta be sure."

She was right, but I had no idea how to come around to that. A sit-down with my mother and grandmother would maybe give me some answers.

And, if not answers, an aneurysm.

Because Mormor.

"It's simple. I'll adopt it," Mormor said ten minutes later, after I'd presented my thoughts on abortion versus adoption versus ultimately keeping the baby. Both she and

Mom were very good through the listening, nodding and asking gentle questions to flesh out my thoughts on the matter. Mom kept rubbing her temple, and I was pretty sure I caught a waft of smoke in her hair, which meant she'd snuck off for a stress cigarette, but she was nice to me despite her strains. Mormor was direct and blunt and eminently Mormor-like.

"What? Ma, no." My mother's face contracted, her expression suggesting she'd like to put my grandmother's head in the garbage disposal. "That's not—"

"If she's worried about bringing it up, I'll bring it up. I have the time. You turned out fine," Mormor said. "Unless you think I was a bad mother."

"Ma," my mother groaned. "Don't. This isn't about you. If Sara wants to give her baby to a family, that's her right."

"But it's a Larssen baby," Mormor insisted. "I'd bring it up. If she's going to give it to a family, her own is just fine unless you know something I don't know about my parenting. So it's as much about me as it is about this baby. I'll raise it."

Devi looked at me across the table. She had that deer-in-headlights expression that suggested she had no idea what to do in the face of multiple generations of me arguing among themselves. I shrugged because I didn't know what to do, either. Arguing with Mormor was like wrestling a wolverine. I wasn't willing to go there, but I didn't have to, either, because my mom had my back.

"Sorry about this," I whispered to Devi.

Devi bit into her standard-issue tomato slice drizzled in balsamic. "It's fine. I just—"

"What do you want to do, Sara?" my grandmother interrupted. "Are you alright with the idea of me bringing it up if you don't want to?"

It. My kid is an it. I've been saying "it," too. Was that wrong? Weird.

Weirder: "my kid."

"You don't have to answer that," my mother shot back. "You're not required to make any decisions yet, Sara."

"Okay, cool. Yeah. I'd like to think about it more, I think." Mormor cast me a look like I'd betrayed her, so I immediately followed up with, "You're awesome, Mormor. If I decide to go adoption, I'd definitely consider it? I…mmm. I don't know. I don't want some weird V.C. Andrews situation is all."

"Isn't that the one about the kids locked in the attic and the crazy poisoner mom?" Devi helpfully chimed in.

"I'm not locking my kid in the attic, Devi. Or poisoning them." I frowned at her. She winked at me. How could you stay upset in the face of that? Devi was the best. I was in love with her a little then, and probably still am, which she knew but was kind enough not to make weird.

"The point is—I had a point before the poisoning—oh." I paused. "It's… I don't know that I'd want to lie to the kid and tell them that my grandmother is their mother or whatever. If we keep the baby, I want the baby to know they're mine. So we'd have to work something out if that's the way we go. Which I'm not sure of yet? But I'll think about it."

"We'll figure it out," Mormor insisted. "If you want to keep the baby, I say keep the baby. *We'll* keep the baby."

"That's Sara's decision, Ma, and you need to *back off.*" It was weird to hear my mom use Mormor's own tones against her, yet that's exactly what was playing out in Mormor's kitchen. Ice queen was being challenged by mini ice queen, woe be to those closest who would suffer their frozen wrath.

Which were me and Devi. We both wanted to hide.

Surprisingly, Mormor didn't retort. Instead, she startled when the toaster popped up two pieces of white bread, snagging them and smearing them with butter. The kettle whistled beside her and she efficiently whisked it away to pour a cup of tea. Both toast and tea were presented to me, the sugar bowl nudged over so I could "pollute perfectly good tea."

Mormor liked her tea with honey and only honey and anything else was inferior and wrong.

"You need to eat," she said matter-of-factly. "For you and the baby."

I frowned down at the buttered toast and tea.

"I might puke." I reached for the toast and nibbled on the crust despite the unpleasant gurgling in my belly.

Mormor stepped into the pantry to rummage around. She reappeared a minute later with a red pail that she slid next to me on the table.

"And this is why God invented buckets."

CHAPTER TEN

Two days later, I was at the OB/GYN, awaiting the arrival of a woman named Dr. Cardiff who was supposed to give me my first prenatal exam. I perched on the exam table, no pants, no panties, with a paper blanket over my lap. I eyeballed the counter, hardcore frowning at the implements of doom laid out beside the sink on a big blue pad. I could appreciate why the doctor's office did it; it saved time when it came to the actual exam, not having to run around and get all your supplies together, but seeing that shiny silver speculum next to a bunch of other doodads I couldn't name but that'd probably soon be inside of me? Not fun.

I hated the speculum. I hated it with the fury of a thousand starving raccoons.

Pelvic exams really *weren't* the worst thing ever, but the first time was traumatizing in that I-don't-know-what-to-expect way. After Mom figured out that Aaron and I were serious enough to bang, she took me to the doctor's to get me on the pill. That's when the "oops, sorries" and polite apologies happened as my doctor had nestled a speculum up into me so she could make sure my plumbing was fully operational.

It hadn't hurt, but it was uncomfortable in a foreign-pressure sort of way. I recognized after the fact, when Mom got me an apology sorry-for-the-cooch-check-up ice cream, I'd built the whole ordeal up in my head to be a lot worse than it actually was. At least my gynecological trials had yielded a prescription for birth control and a clean bill of health.

As evidenced by the new bean-sized parasite hanging out in my lower quarters, I had remained *extra* healthy.

Fertile Myrtle, that's me.

Now, you might be asking, "If you were on the pill with Aaron, why weren't you on the pill with Jack?" And the answer is side effects. Birth control pills came saddled with baggage, and my baggage was worse than most. My cramps were far worse on the pill than off. My mood swings were twice as bad while medicated, plus I was tired all the time. I tried three different pills over the two years I was on birth control to try to find one that wouldn't make me a mopey rage machine, but it happened with all of them to some extent. I suffered through it in the name of young love.

Screw you, Aaron. I want those years back without cramps, thanks.

When we broke up, I asked Mom if I could go off of it, assuring her I had no intention of riding the boyfriend carousel again because men were vile and ought to be launched out of cannons. She reluctantly agreed, knowing what the pill did to me. She was undoubtedly kicking herself for that decision these months down the line, but... well. It wasn't her fault. It was mine, as I assured her at least a dozen times the first day after my diagnosis of fetus.

She said she knew that, but I wasn't sure she believed it. The stress cigarettes told another story.

I could smell them on her, the smoke clinging to her hair, and I glared at her as she sat in the side chair in the office, rooting through her purse for bubblegum.

"You're smoking again."

"Not often," she said, frowning. She peered up at me. Her eyes were red at the edges, which meant she hadn't slept well, and that was probably my fault, too.

"If I have this kid and you get lung cancer, you'll feel bad," I said.

"I'll feel bad if I get lung cancer, anyway. It's cancer. Cancer sucks," she replied.

She had me there. She pulled out some peppermint gum, offering me a stick. Oddly, I was okay with that particular smell, and I'd been avoiding strong smells for a few days on account of the hormonal flux. I popped it into my mouth, trying hard not to think about the impending appointment. It was less the exam itself that bugged me, but more the embarrassment of having my innermost secret parts on display for a stranger.

When I voiced that to Mormor at brunch that morning, she'd scoffed at me over her bread topped with liver pâté.

"Do you know how many snipporna they look at in a day?" she'd demanded.

"…snipporna?"

"Yes. Vagoos. Vaginas. That doctor's life is looking at one snippa after another. Do you have teeth down there?"

"…Mormor."

"Well, do you? Teeth? Fire? Do you shoot fire from your vagina?"

"No! It's just—"

"It is no big deal to your doctor. It is only a big deal to you because you are young and stupid."

My mother took exception to my grandmother calling me stupid and the fight was on. I just sat there eating my toast while they fought, trying hard not to shudder because Mormor's liver pâté looked and smelled like cat food.

Which was how and why I was thinking about bubblegum, cat food and the Swedish word for *vagina* when my doctor entered the room.

Dr. Cardiff was tall and broad through the shoulders. She was probably in her thirties, with short-cut light brown hair, wire-rimmed glasses and a wide smile with lots and lots of white teeth. When she extended her hand to me, her doctor's coat rose up mid-forearm and I could see a sleeve of tattoos, the bottommost one a unicorn with a rainbow mane.

Okay, so, my OB/GYN is badass.

Cool.

"Hey there, Serendipity. Love the name," she said in greeting.

"Sara," I said. "But thanks. Gotta give my mom credit for that one."

"Good job, Mom. Dr. Cardiff, nice to meet you," my doctor said, extending that same hand for a shake to my mother.

"Astrid," Mom said. "Nice to meet you."

Dr. Cardiff sat down at the computer to my left and eye-balled my vitals. The nurse had taken them and, outside of a little high blood pressure because I had white coat syndrome, everything had looked good. The doctor perused a couple of screens, nodded and smiled. "Okay, so we're going to get some personal info out of the way before we jump into the pelvic. Can you state your birthday for me?"

From there, it was a series of questions about my period, my general health, family history that Mom had to help with and my personal life, which Dr. Cardiff explained as her ensuring I was safe and would be safe for the duration of my pregnancy. I had to admit to her, I had zero information on the baby daddy, which she gave me no crap for, but due to those gaps in knowledge, she did recommend the extended genetic-testing options so we knew exactly what we were dealing with. It was a blood test, she said, which she needed anyway for *other* tests, and what was a few extra vials?

The conversation wasn't too bad, taking about ten minutes total, and yielded an approximate due date on when the baby would exit my spew parts to join the world.

"Since you know the exact date of conception, we can comfortably say around February sixteenth of next year," she said. "You're eleven weeks along."

"Aquarius. I like Aquariuses. Smart and logical," my mom said, because she was totally into zodiac stuff and read her horoscope daily. This probably isn't so surprising, considering she was the woman who saddled me with the big-ass hippie name.

Dr. Cardiff smiled. "But with a hint of Pisces. They'll be creative."

That surprised me almost as much as her rainbow unicorn tattoo, but it also made me more comfortable with her, in general. She reminded me of my mom, only more butch and a little more badass because of the tattoos. When she asked me to scoot to the bottom of the table and drop my heels into the footy stirrup things, I complied, albeit awkwardly, and waited for the delicate pawing and coldness that had happened the first time I'd found myself in that position.

Mom reached for my hand and I gave it over. There was the squirt of lube as the doctor got ready to prod my no-no parts for the first of what would probably be many prenatal crotch delves.

Weirdly, the speculum was warm this time, and I looked at the ceiling with wonder that I didn't feel like she'd violated me with a Popsicle. That'd been my one takeaway from my last go-round with a gynecologist—that all medical implements were stored in freezers to make you as antsy as possible during your most vulnerable moments.

"It's not cold," I said, awe in my voice.

"That blue thing on the counter is a heating pad. You get a cold speculum up your wazoo once, you never forget it, or at least I don't, so I try not to use them," Dr. Cardiff responded.

I actually giggled at that, despite the little clicks of the speculum as she opened me up and swabbed me out. Again, it wasn't awful, just some pressure, an unfortunate draft where drafts ought not to be. She brought a bendy lamp in close so she could peer inside to make sure I wasn't harboring a cave troll down there and, deeming me "pink and perfect," pulled the speculum out. She adjusted the paper sheet for modesty and told me I could sit up.

"So I'm thinking we'll get an ultrasound ASAP. The bleeding the first few months warrants a check, and you're so close to twelve weeks, it's okay to peek."

I sat up on the table, glancing from the doctor over to my mother and back again. "Will we be figuring out if it's a boy or a girl or—"

"Not yet. That's usually closer to sixteen weeks, but I want to make sure there's a heartbeat and check our development."

The doctor washed her hands and moved over to the sink. I stared at her back, horrified at the idea of my kid not having a heartbeat. "So if it doesn't…"

"We'll worry about that if and when we get there," Mom said. "Don't borrow problems."

That was a Mormor-ism if I'd ever heard one. It was also

useless. I was already worrying, but saying so did nothing. Instead, I watched Dr. Cardiff sit back down at her computer. She glanced my way, offering me a bright smile.

"She's right. There's no reason to believe anything is wrong. Some women do bleed during part or all of their pregnancy. It's not super common, but no reason to panic. I'm more interested in other aspects of development, plus I want to be sure there's only one baby in there."

Only one baby.

Oh, God. Multiple womb goblins! I hadn't even thought of that.

I must have looked green, because Mom got up from the chair in the corner to come stand beside me. She leaned down to kiss my cheek, her smoke-stinky hair far too close to my nose to not make my stomach churn.

"We got this, kiddo. I promise. It'll be okay. Don't worry till it's time to worry, yeah?"

"Yeah," I said, collapsing back onto the exam table like I was boneless. I stared at the perfectly square ceiling tiles with their potted lights, blinking fast so I didn't cry.

Not worrying until it's time to worry.

Not worrying until it's time to worry.

Not worrying…

What a load of bullsh…crap.

CHAPTER ELEVEN

I was quiet post–doctor's appointment, so Mom did what lots of moms do and bought my happiness with McDonald's. It wasn't good for me—I was pretty sure I was eating actual plastic, like that fake Fisher-Price food kids play with—but it tasted good and was salty. Also, it was one food that hadn't become a toxic barf factory for me post-fetus, and for that I was grateful.

Grateful and gnawing on my second cheeseburger.

"Gotta pack up the rest of the kitchen," she said as we pulled onto the main route that'd get us home. I nodded and crammed about sixty billion french fries into my mouth because I wasn't proud. "I can't believe we're moving tomorrow. Are you ready for this?"

After Mormor's snippa lesson at brunch, the visit with the doctor and the unpleasant news that I had to visit my new school next week to do both course selection and talk to a guidance counselor because I was pregnant? No, I wasn't ready. Not for any of it.

But, of course, I was far too lazy to articulate that so I shrugged and ate more fries.

We got home. We packed. Most of the apartment was ready to go. Mom started carrying things down to the car, and when I bent to follow her and help, she tsked and swatted me away.

"Nope. No preggers carrying boxes. I love you, kid, but you're as useless as tits on a bull right now."

"I… Wait. What?"

"No heavy lifting. It's in the preggo contract."

"Oh." And so I had the unpleasant reality of watching my mother loading boxes into the car with no one to help her. It didn't seem fair, particularly with the amount of boxes we had to pack, her diminutive stature and the fact that my poor life choice had put us in the situation, so I did the only thing I could think to do in a dire situation.

Emotionally manipulate my best friend.

Wifey, I texted, my fingers gliding over the phone and smearing it with McDonald's grease. I dashed at it with a napkin but that only served to make bigger smears that'd require Windex or maybe a flamethrower.

Wut up.

Can you help my mom pack boxes into the car? Preggos can't lift.

There was a pause before I received, Kinda hate you rn.

I know. Please? I'll buy u a bcn double chzburgr.

Two chzburgrs but u suk.

"Devi's coming to help," I said to Mom. She frowned as she looped back around to pack more stuff.

"She doesn't have to do that."

"No, but she does 'cause she rules. She's the best bestie that ever bested, so. I'll be right back. Getting her bribery cheeseburgers."

Mom raked her fingers through her fine blond hair, a weary smile on her mouth. "Yeah, okay. She's a good kid."

"Yeah, she is. And don't smoke while I'm gone. I'll smell it. I've got a super sniffer right now."

"You're not my real mom," my mother said before sticking her tongue out. I climbed into the car with its first load of boxes and headed back to the golden arches, where I bought Devi not only her bacon double cheeseburgers, but myself another pair of regular cheeseburgers because apparently I and the fetus were really feeling them.

By the time I returned home, Devi was already there, talking to my mom. She loomed over her by a half a foot, looking taller than usual because of her cutoff jean shorts

and legs for days. Mom's capris and six-inch inseam didn't
stand a chance there.

I climbed from the car and jostled the bag Devi's way.

"I'm not fetching," she said. "It's pretty messed up that
you think I would."

"That's not what I meant!"

"I know." She grinned and swiped the bag from me.
Seeing the extra cheeseburgers, she asked no questions,
just taking her due and handing me the rest. I unpacked
another burger. Mom's brow lifted and she waved her finger at me accusingly.

"Hey, there, Miss Second Lunch. That's not much better than a cigarette. It's a food cigarette."

"In your butt," I said.

Which made no sense, but I was at a loss for words.

"No, in *your* butt," Mom replied.

Because I got the immature and stupid from somewhere.

"I'm eating for two," I reminded her before sitting on
the front step of the apartment building. It'd probably be
the last time I'd do so, and it would have been nice to be
nostalgic about the ten years we'd lived there. But it was
August and I was five feet from trash barrels that smelled
so bad I was pretty sure Oscar the Grouch had actually
died inside one of them.

"That's why you got two cheeseburgers earlier—one for
each of you, I thought." Mom cast me a smirk as she got
back to hauling. She'd brought some of the boxes down
to the curb while I'd been gone, and she proceeded to
drop them into the trunk, Tetris-ing them so she could
get as much stuff in as possible. Devi stepped in to help

once she'd sucked down her two cheeseburgers, using her jean shorts as a napkin.

"Classy," I said.

"Well, I wouldn't have to be so classy if someone had gotten me some napkins."

"Soz, wifey."

"Yeah, yeah. Soz."

The afternoon was filled with three-way chatter and jokes. Most of the furniture wasn't moving to Mormor's because Mormor had everything we'd need already. Mom had given it all away to friends and charity. The only big item to move was our TV, because Mom was pretty squarely over Mormor's ancient box TV with its rabbit-ears antenna.

"I'll bring my flat-screen TV," Mom had said during that liver-pâté brunch from hell. "It should fit in the TV cabinet no problem."

"Oh? Why do we need it?"

"Because it's two years old, and yours is older than Sara?"

Mormor had snorted. "Old things aren't good now? Why not, Astrid? I'm old, but I work perfectly fine, just like that TV. Should we throw me away, too?"

"Ma! Jesus Christ. It's just a TV."

Taking the lord's name in vain resulted in a Keds sneaker being launched from the pantry that hit my mom squarely in the shoulder—not hard enough to really hurt, but it was certainly startling. Mom jumped right out of her skin.

"I am a good Lutheran," Mormor said. "Leave Christ out of this discussion."

Mom picked up the shoe from the kitchen floor and whipped it back at the pantry. "Don't go chucking your shoes around, old woman! And don't think I didn't hear you just call the garbage man an effing idiot twenty minutes ago, except you didn't use effing."

"He always leaves my garbage lids on the curb. How hard is it to put them back where they belong! And I didn't say…effing idiot. Not exactly." Mormor stomped out of the pantry, carrying her freshly thrown shoe in her hand. "I don't like the garbage man."

"'Din jävla idiot' means—"

"I know what it means! But he is an asshole and I hate him. But that doesn't mean I want to hear it from my daughter's mouth, no matter how old she is. Do you want the shoe again?" Mormor waved the sneaker under Mom's nose before slipping it back onto her foot.

Mom wasn't impressed. "No, but you're taking the TV, whether you like it or not."

And there we were, packing the TV. Or there Devi and Mom were, packing the TV. I held doors open while they maneuvered their way outside with it and then somehow managed to fit it onto the passenger's seat. I'd be riding to Mormor's for the official move-in with Devi.

I glanced up at the side of our brick apartment building. It'd been home for a while, a good home at that, but I was ready to leave it behind, just like I was ready to leave the town and 99 percent of its denizens behind. No Aaron. No Samantha. No tiny little high school where everyone knew what everyone else was doing all the time. All the worthwhile things were coming with me to Stonington.

Devi. My mom. My stuff.

My fetus.

And a big-ass forty-two-inch flat-screen.

The move-in went exactly how Mom and I knew it would, which meant Mormor was a huge pain, barking orders about where everything should go and making those of us actually doing the moving and unpacking crazy. Dishes were to be put in the pantry and only the pantry until Mormor could go through them and decide if they deserved a spot among the Williams Sonoma elite inside her cabinets. Linens would receive the same scrutiny, so put them in the upstairs hallway until sorting time. Although she hadn't even wanted the new TV, its placement on the new wooden TV stand—which she had bought on her own because she didn't trust Mom to honor the farmhouse decor—had to be precise or it threw off her entire aesthetic.

"A little to the left, a little more to the left, a little more to the left" would haunt me in my nightmares.

Suffice to say, she'd talked so much during the move, she'd sucked most of the oxygen out of the house, leaving the rest of us gasping. By the time Devi brought the last of my stuff up into my new room, she was hot, sweaty and super annoyed.

"I think I owe you a few more cheeseburgers," I said sheepishly, folding my T-shirts and putting them in my new dresser.

"Yeah, like a few thousand. That woman needs an exorcism." Devi shoved a pile of my clothes up onto my pillows so she could sprawl out on her back on my new bed, her arms to either side of her body. "It's no different than Bubbe, though. Not really. I'm guessing with age comes lots of opinions."

"All of them. All of the opinions everywhere exist inside aging female bodies."

"Something to look forward to, I guess," she said. I couldn't argue it.

We went quiet for a few minutes, Devi catching her breath, me putting my clothes away. Downstairs, Mom and Mormor were bickering, which meant everything was fine. I'd have been far more concerned if they weren't fighting, to be honest, because it seemed to be their modus operandi.

"How are you doing?" Devi asked, her voice quieter and more serious than it had been a little while ago. "Like, with everything. You okay?"

"About the move? Sure. Living with Mormor will be interesting, but we visit so much it's not going to be too much different, I don't think."

"And about school? We go back in two and a half weeks."

"Fine, I guess. I'm not thinking about it too much. Well, I mean, I am—I've got a meeting with a guidance counselor and we're going to talk about what we need to do for delivery. I'll have the kid before graduation."

"Cool, cool. Good to have a plan. So, I told my parents."

I stopped folding to look at her, a Metallica T-shirt clutched in my hand. "And?"

"They were cool. Asked if there was anything they

could do for you. I probably should have talked to you before I said anything, but it...yeah. I haven't told anyone else. I wouldn't."

I wasn't exactly annoyed with her, especially not after she'd helped me out that day, but she was right—she should have asked me.

"Well, if you're going to tell anyone else—"

"—which I'm not."

"Right, but." I cleared my throat and went back to arranging T-shirts. "If you do, please ask me first."

"I will. I'm sorry."

"No sweat."

It was true for the most part, that things were fine, but she must have been worried that I was fronting because she got up from the bed and walked up behind me to hug me. Her chin dropped onto my shoulder.

"You got this. We got this. All of us."

"You sound like my mom and grandma." Just as I said that, the two of them got loud about something downstairs, each of them trying to out-bitch each other seconds before there was a hard thwacking sound, which was probably a shoe hitting the wall because Mormor was out of control. "Okay, maybe not exactly like them, but the solidarity thing, you sound like them."

"It's a new beginning. For you, for your mom and Mormor, and for the squirt."

"The squirt?"

"Yeah." She poked my belly. "This little thing. It's the CIIIIRCLE OF LIIIIIFE..."

"Oh, shut the hell up, Devi."

PART TWO:

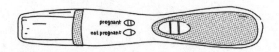

The cheeseburger queen,
my mom the Juggalo
and a leaf on the wind.

CHAPTER TWELVE

Mormor had been a plague on mankind for most of the day, but she made up for it by cooking ärt-soppa that night and inviting Devi to dinner. You can tell food is good when four people who talk as much as we do were silent for the duration of the meal.

Not a peep. It was darned good soup.

"You know, for Satan, she's a pretty good cook," Devi whispered right before she took off for the night. I waved at her retreating taillights and then went back to my room. Mom had left a couple more boxes of my stuff in my new room to unpack, but I was too tired. At least I had an explanation for my toddler-like need for all the sleep, forever. Who knew a newbie fetus could be so demanding already?

Now, imagine them at two and smearing poop on the walls. Poopcasso, the mural artist.

…am I ready for that?

Wait. Is anyone ready for that?

These were the thoughts that plagued me as I drifted off to sleep.

The sound of a lawnmower outside of my window plagued me the next morning.

A glance at my phone told me it was seven in the morning. When I shuffled over to the window to see what kind of weirdo started their day *that* early *that* way, I was completely unsurprised to discover Mormor riding a dinosaur-sized John Deere around, a brimmed hat on her head and her nose covered with a strip of that white sunblock stuff.

A pee, a hair brushing because curly hair and bedhead were the worst, a bevy of yawns and I went downstairs. Mom was in the kitchen, sitting at the kitchen island, her body huddled around her mug like she'd devolved into a coffee troll in the nine hours since I'd last seen her.

"She gets up at five, Serendipity," Mom said. "Who does that?"

"Mormor." I couldn't have the caffeine—doctor's orders that I had to limit my intake—so I started the water for decaf tea and popped some toast into the toaster. I wasn't super nauseated yet, but time would tell on whether or not my gut rebelled. At least I was on the cusp of the second trimester. According to the internet, that was the "good" time when nausea decreased and you got to "enjoy" the baby growing inside of you.

I wasn't sure enjoyment had factored into any of the baby business yet, but if the part about being extra horny was true, at least I'd be smiling a lot more.

Mom grumbled as she got up from her stool, shuffling over to the cabinet and preparing a teacup for me because she loved me. "We've got your ultrasound at ten. I guess she could have picked a worse day to drag me from the crypt early."

"Hey, just remember, you picked living here."

"No, our finances did, when I thought I was sending a kid to college next year."

Mom was just playing around, yet that stopped me cold. Her, too, for that matter. I glanced back at her, at her profile. Her brow was furrowed, the corners of her mouth dipped into a frown.

"Not that you can't go back to school after you have the kid," she added, trying to make it less doom and gloom.

Except you didn't go back to school after you had me. It was too much work because you were a single mom. Like I'd be.

I nodded and swallowed, my dreams of getting into an Ivy League school turning to ash right before my eyes. It's funny how that hadn't occurred to me until right that moment. "Right. And I might still go the adoption route and can maybe go a semester late or something."

"Right." The kettle screeched. Mom turned away from me so she could pour hot water over the tea infuser. "And if you decide to keep it—"

"If I decide to keep them," I interjected. "*It* feels weird to me."

"Okay, sure. If that's what you prefer."

I nodded, pulling my toast from the toaster and slathering it with butter.

"But what I was saying is single moms go back to school all the time," she said. "Maybe not right away, but they do. Programs at night. Or maybe even the day, somewhere local. Mormor certainly seems to want to help out. I can babysit at night. We've got some options."

"A state university or whatever. I mean, there's one fifteen minutes away."

"Sure! That'd work." Mom slid the tea my way, her fingers brushing mine. I looked up at her. The strain written on her face likely mirrored mine, but I couldn't blame her. It wasn't just one of us abandoning hopes of my going to an Ivy League.

Ten o'clock, in Dr. Cardiff's office, my pants waistband rolled down so far I was afraid someone would see my pubes, a sheet over my lap to ensure that didn't happen.

There wasn't a lot of dignity in medical care, I was discovering.

"How are you hanging in there, Serendipity?" Dr. Cardiff asked me, the ultrasound wand poised above my skin.

It was a fair question. I hadn't talked much since they'd squirted the cold conductive lube over my lower stomach. There were a lot of feelings going on, tangling up inside of me and stealing most of my words. I was afraid—feeling a little dread, even—because there was no going back after this. This was more "real" than the results of a pee stick test or blood test. No take backsies, no hiding from the truth. I was about to see irrevocable results of my truck fumbling.

"Okay," I said. "I'm okay."

"Cool. Let's do this."

Dr. Cardiff placed the monitor against my skin, on the side of my stomach. It was coldish, like the jelly had been, and I winced.

"There will be some pressure," she said, and there was. Not enough to make me run screaming from the room, but it was momentarily uncomfortable. I forgot all about that when she arced her hand around, pressed and found the magical spot.

There it was, on the screen. The jelly bean. I stared at it, my brain blanking much the same way it had when Dr. Bhatia had told me I was pregnant. It was too much to process for one meager mind, but then my mother gasped beside me, breaking my pseudo-trance.

"Whoa. They're kinda cute. Like a twitchy little alien blob," she said.

What I wanted to say but couldn't articulate quite yet was that this was *my* twitchy little alien blob, and that made all the difference in the world.

Literally.

All that cliché crap about having preggo baby feels? Yeah, it totally happened.

Something, something, papas and preaching.

Thank you, Mom's obsession with Madonna.

"Everything's looking good," Dr. Cardiff said. "All visual signs are a go."

"And there's only one kid! That calls for party hats," Mom said. "I love you, Sara, but if you'd made a litter, I'd have to sell you to the circus."

Still, I didn't say anything, instead absorbing every detail I could from the shivering image on the screen. Dr. Cardiff eyed me over the rim of her teal tortoiseshell glasses. She coordinated her glasses to her outfits, her button-down teal shirt, a black necktie circling her throat. "We good?"

"Yeah, I'm okay," I managed, voice thick. I hadn't planned on crying, but the tears happened anyway, wetting my cheeks and dribbling off my chin. There was a tiny person up on the monitor staring back at me. Okay, not really staring because I don't think they had eyeballs yet, but whatever. It was my baby. Me and some mystery guy named Jack had created a little ball of weird cells and that weird ball of cells would one day have hopes and dreams and maybe an appreciation of crappy T-shirts like their mom and F-150s like their dad because I knew pretty much nothing else about him other than the beer-and-truck thing.

My mom sniffled suspiciously beside me. I looked over, and she, too, was water-working it up looking at the jelly bean.

"...I cry at weddings, too, okay?" she said, defensively.

"What? I'm crying. It's fine."

Dr. Cardiff nudged a box of tissues our way, some parts kindness, some parts sparing herself having to look at two ugly criers, I'm sure.

"We ready for a heartbeat?" Dr. Cardiff asked.

"Yeah. Yes. Please." I smiled at her and blew my nose.

She turned a knob and seconds later, we heard the heartbeat. That murmur was in actuality tiny, inaudible, but thanks to the marvels of modern medicine, it filled the room. A strong, steady, surprisingly fast murmur that pounded in my ears. It was the sound of life that existed inside of my life. It was…lifeception.

Like an in utero Christopher Nolan–type deal.

More tears from both Mom and I, and she leaned down until our cheeks touched.

"Listen to that," she said. "That kid is thriving."

"Yeah, they are."

I must have had a weird look on my face beyond the rampant snot and ickiness, because she brushed my hair and whispered in my ear, "Happened to me, too, FYI. Wasn't sure what to do about you, abortion, adoption or whatever, but then I saw you on that screen and heard you. You were doomed to be my forever loin fruit after that."

"I… Yeah. I don't think I can—"

"It's okay. Whatever you decide is okay. And changing your mind is okay, too," Mom said.

Dr. Cardiff smiled at both of us before reaching toward the printer beside her. She produced a picture of the jelly bean and offered it to me. I accepted it, but my eyes were still fixed on the screen. "Weird," I said.

Mom sat up beside me and dashed at her cheeks with the butts of her palms. "What is?"

"The baby looks kinda like a chestburster."

"Oh, my gosh, from *Alien*? YES! But I can never say

that to my patients. They'd get upset, I think." Dr. Cardiff grinned. "You're cool, though. You can hang."

I found a smile, my thumb brushing over the picture clasped too tightly in my hand. I had to relax my fingers or I'd rumple the proof of my fetus.

"I can see the Larssen resemblance. Big head, tiny hands. That's our mutant superpower, you know. Ridiculously tiny hands. It's pretty useless in the vast scheme of things," Mom said.

Dr. Cardiff started laughing.

"Oh, my God. Mom!"

"Little tiny hands, one day pawing at your belly from the inside..."

"Will you please shut up?"

"Never, especially when it comes to torturing my kid and future grandkid."

Grandkid?

Oh. Right.

Holy crap.

CHAPTER THIRTEEN

The meeting with the guidance counselor turned out to be a meeting with both the guidance counselor and a school social worker. The presence of the fetus made the second a necessity, by policy. I could tell it made Mom nervous to have someone from the state there, but they reassured her they were there as a resource for future family planning. It wasn't some kind of state-led investigation into whether or not my oopsie reflected on Mom as a parent.

I felt crummy that it even occurred to her

that someone would think that way. My mom was pretty amazing.

There were a lot of questions about my home life, how safe I felt, how supported I was. There were questions about the baby daddy, too, which got handily squashed when I told them I didn't know his last name, where he was from and no, I promise, it wasn't sexual assault. My takeaways from the meeting was that Mrs. Wong, my guidance counselor, had pretty metal hair with a white stripe starting at her temple, that I'd be meeting with the social worker once a month for check-ins, and that they wanted me to enroll in some state program for teen moms that met on Saturdays.

I was dubious of that and told Mom as much as we walked out of the school, my enrollment packet in hand.

She wasn't keen on my skipping out.

"Do the crime, do the time, m'dear."

"But I—"

"We're not messing around with the school on this. They're being pretty reasonable about your end of year, all things considered. Take some time to think about it, but I don't want to push your luck."

She wasn't wrong. Since the kid was due in February, and I still had three months of senior year left, they determined I could effectively complete my schooling from home the last term without issue. Digital course loads and curriculums meant I could follow along at my own pace; the only time I had to bring my sad carcass in the flesh to campus was to take the finals with a teacher or counselor on hand to make sure I didn't cheat. One downside: it was possible I wouldn't actually graduate with my classmates. My ability to contribute to schoolwork might be diminished with a tiny human crap factory, and if I couldn't complete at the same time as everyone else, there'd be no cap and gown.

I was weirdly okay with that. I didn't know anyone in Stonington, and the important part was the diploma, not the horse-and-pony show. Mom seemed okay with it at first, but once we got into the car to leave the school...

"Well, I didn't want those graduation pictures, anyway. Much rather have pictures of you with baby puke in your hair," she said, strapping herself into the Jeep. "Sitting around in yoga pants, dark circles under your eyes, leaking through your bra and staining your shirts with breast milk. Much better than a cap and gown."

"Eww! Wait, what… Baby puke in my *hair*? Does it defy gravity or something?"

"You've clearly never held a baby who's spitting up. You were a champion barfer. Got great range. You've seen *The Exorcist*, right?"

"Oh, my God! Mom!"

"What! It wasn't green, more white because of the formula and milk, but you get the picture."

I appreciated what she was doing, but I recognized the jokes for what they were. Mom, for all that she was on Team Serendipity, used humor to deflect from conversations about hard feelings. The idea of not seeing her brainiac honors kid walk across a stage to get a diploma absolutely bothered her. She wouldn't have brought it up otherwise. So, of course, I silently committed to finish-

ing the course load on time, my spawn's pukey demands
be damned. Not once had Mom reamed me for getting
knocked up. The least I could do was provide her that
Kodak moment.

Mormor will hold the baby while I cross the stage, I bet.

It was the first time I'd really acknowledged to myself
that I was going to be a parent—that my life would ir-
revocably change. I'd known in the doctor's office after
seeing the jelly bean on the screen that I wanted to keep
it, but up until that point it'd still seemed like a nebulous
concept. Motherhood was part of my vocabulary, and
part of my reality, but…it hadn't settled into my bones, if
that makes sense. The thing about Mormor holding the
baby, though—that was tangible. Graduation would see
me wearing a big ugly gown, a flat hat and tassels while
my mother snapped photographs and my grandmother
held my kid.

My baby.

I was going to be a mom.

I hadn't articulated it yet to my family, or to Devi,
but…I was sure. The surety settled in as Mom drove us
back to Mormor's.

Now to just get the ovarian fortitude to fess up to it to
everyone.

"Penny for your thoughts?" Mom asked a minute later,
because long expanses of Serendipity silence were a rare
thing to behold.

"Hmm? Oh, just making a plan," I said, totally chick-
ening out. "I want to graduate on time for sure, though."

"Then you will. You can do anything you put your mind to," she said.

"That's kinda bullshit, though, isn't it?" I glanced at her profile. "We tell people that—you can do anything—but there are roadblocks. Like, I don't mean to be Debbie Downer, but I can't go to Harvard now, even if I got in. If I could do anything, I could do that."

The car rolled to a stop at an intersection and Mom cast me a shrivel-worthy side-eye. "Wow, breaking out the cuss words and everything. Someone's got feelings."

I wasn't really supposed to swear. I could, on occasion, and get away with it, but not in general. My fingers ran up and down the seat belt crossing my chest. I'd had to fuss with it four times so it didn't hit my aching boobs the wrong way. "Sorry, just... I dunno. I don't like sunshine and rainbows launched up my butt as a way to motivate me."

"Okay, sure, but what if I said you can still do Ivy League, but you might have to do it differently than you planned?" I glanced at her. "Night school, part-time classes. It's doable. Sure, it'll be harder if you don't live on campus, but you *can* do it. And to be clear, your goal is the Harvard degree, yes? It's not to live in a dorm room on a Harvard campus? Those are very different things."

"Ugh."

"What?"

"I hate it when you do that," I said.

"Do what?"

"Be smart. You're a jerk."

"I know, right!" Mom feigned a bright smile right be-

fore she put on her blinker so she could pull into Mc-
Donald's. "I'm so smart, I'm getting someone I know and
their little monster-bean cheeseburgers because cravings
are the devil."

I sat up in my seat, an eager beaver already longing for
tomato and salt between two plasticky buns. "Wow. I love
you so much right now."

She reached out to pat my knee, giving it an affectionate squeeze as she pulled up to the menu. "I know, kid.
Love you, too."

Mustering the courage to tell my immediate circle that
I was 100 percent on the keep-the-baby train took me a
couple weeks. Mom suspected as much at the appointment, but she never pushed me for confirmation afterward,
which I appreciated. Mormor, by contrast, was a nudge.
It was never direct, more in a roundabout way, talking
about things like shopping for cribs and strollers and baby
clothes, but I never rose to the bait, instead changing the
subject or finding a convenient way to leave the room.
She'd gnash her teeth about it awhile, but then leave it
alone for a day or two.

I'm pretty sure my mother threatened her with death if
she needled me, thus Mormor's atypical restraint.

Devi should have been the easiest one to talk to. She was
like Mom, never pushing, but I still couldn't go through
with it. It'd be real then—really real. No take backsies.
I wasn't ready to have the conversations that'd inevitably
follow the announcement:

"What color of a nursery do you want?"

"Are you hoping for a boy or girl?"

"Have you picked out names?"

I wasn't there. Instead, when Devi came over and sprawled out on my bed, we'd talk about Cap and Bucky and their super queer lovefest or Korean skincare or the next Doctor Who or…whatever dorky thing we were into at the moment. I promised myself I'd segue into it, but I never *quite* made it there.

It wasn't until the night before the first day of school, when Mormor was officially out of patience and clobbered me, emotionally, that I found the courage to speak up, and only because *she finally managed to piss me off.*

We should have been talking about the outfit I'd hung in the hall—some soft cotton leggings that would stretch while I stretched. A long flannel shirt. A belt. Some combat boots. Or maybe we'd talk about my book bag, stuffed to the brim with fresh notebooks and clicky pencils and pens. Or maybe my three AP classes: English, Calculus and Biology! But no, instead we were going to blow right by my first day of senior year at a new school and go straight to Babytown.

"We need to discuss Serendipity's situation," Mormor opened with. The three of us were seated at the dinner table around a platter of gravy-slathered meat loaf, mashed potatoes, green beans and homemade rolls. Mom and I had been more casual about dinner back at the apartment, but Mormor insisted on family meals every night. If you were silly enough to walk by the kitchen around five, she'd assign you sous-chef duties, making you cut onions or some other god-awful thing because she didn't want to do it.

"What about it?" My mother doled out her potatoes and handed me the bowl. I doubled up on it because I was ravenous. The nausea was still hanging around in the mornings, but by late afternoon, I'd become a walking, talking food vacuum.

All the food for the food hole!

"The baby. We have it on our fridge. Look at it. It looks like a Larssen." Mormor pointed over her shoulder at my black-and-white fetus photo, held up on the freezer by alphabet letter magnets Mormor bought me when I was three.

My mother frowned. "No, it doesn't. It looks like an insect."

"They," I corrected both of them. "They look like an insect."

"Don't be pedantic, Serendipity. Answer the question— do you still want to sell it? Them? Sell them?" Mormor sniffed. "I think we deserve to know."

My mother rolled her eyes. "She's not selling the baby to a circus, Ma. She's looking at maybe putting them up for adoption! And we talked about this—lay off."

"So why hang the picture? To taunt me?" Mormor's fork stabbed into her meat loaf, spearing it like she'd spear the cow itself before butchering it with her bare hands. Her ferocity knew no bounds. "To show me a baby that will not live here?"

"It's not about you," Mom singsonged. "We've been over this. A thousand times."

Which, if they had, they'd kept me out of it, and I was

grateful for that. Their bickering made them sound like those two angry old men from *The Muppets*.

I crammed a dozen green beans into my mouth and focused on my plate, pretending my grandmother wasn't staring at me from across the table. Every clink of her fork striking china, every one of her sighs seeming exaggerated.

Mom's foot nudged mine under the table. I glanced over at her. She winked at me and bit into a biscuit.

"Yes," I said, looking at Mom, but my words were for my grandmother.

"Yes, what?"

"Yes, I've decided."

"And?"

"I don't think I'm going to tell you yet."

That ill-advised proclamation, given in a moment of annoyance, hit the floor like a turd dropped from the roof of the Empire State Building.

"Excuse me?"

"Well, I asked for space and you haven't given it. Like, even a little bit. Mom's told you to leave me alone, and you haven't. And now you're demanding answers and I just...don't feel like telling you."

I shrugged. "Not yet."

Mormor's mouth opened and closed like a fish cast on the banks gasping for water. Eventually, she managed a "You can't be serious."

"She looks pretty serious," Mom said. "That's... I know my kid. That is Grade-A serious face."

If you've never seen a pale-as-paper person turn purple, you're missing out. Mormor looked like a silver-tipped eggplant, her eyes bulging from her sockets, her cheeks ballooning. She was the throbbing zit that needed popping, but I wasn't ready to relieve the pressure yet, so I just let her be an engorged rage factory of old lady and went back to eating my potatoes.

Which were delicious, by the way.

"Fine. Fine, we'll talk again when you're ready to talk about it. The disrespect of this girl." Mormor's hissed proclamations were followed by a long line of Swedish words neither Mom nor I understood. Mormor stood from her chair, collected her dinner and stomped out to watch *Fox News* in front of the new TV in the living room. For extra "screw you, Serendipity," she turned the volume up to ear bursting.

Mom glanced back behind her at the living room and then over at me.

"She mad," she said.

"Yep. You know what'd make her madder?"

"Eh?"

"She turned the TV up so loud, she won't hear me tell you I'm keeping the baby."

CHAPTER FOURTEEN

First impressions are lasting impressions, and my first impression of Stonington High School was that it was a huge metal wood tick of a building humping the ground. The center was a domed top—the gym, I'd later find out—with two stories of extending branches of classrooms to either side. The football, soccer and baseball fields were in the far back of the property, surrounded by a freshly painted green track. Tennis courts to the left. A large field of grass with dandelions to the right.

You could fit two of my former high school into the same space.

My initial meeting with Mrs. Wong had been at the superintendent's office, which was a separate building, so my first steps into the school were taken on my first day. Mom was at my side as we headed through the glass doors and past two impressive trophy cases to get to the main office. The floor beneath our feet was black-and-white tile. The walls were brick with oodles of bulletin boards with welcome-back banners.

Everything smelled like chlorine. It was not awesome on my roiling stomach. God, I love anti-nausea medicine.

On the upside? The school had a pool.

To the office counter we went. A middle-aged woman with brown hair came over, smiling at us. I presented my new student packet like I'd present a golden ticket to Willy Wonka. She eyed it and immediately pointed outside.

"Hi, Serendipity. Mrs. Wong is waiting for you. Two rooms down on the right."

"Thanks."

My mother walked me down the hall but paused outside of the guidance office door. "You want me to go with?" she asked, patting at imaginary lint on my oversize shirt. I wasn't showing yet, thank God, but I'd taken to wearing big clothes, anyway, just in case. She tucked a lock of curly black hair behind my ear for good measure.

"Nah, I got this."

"Alright. I haven't been this invested in your first day since kindergarten, but that was because you peed yourself in the car on the way there."

"Gee, Mom. Thanks for bringing that up."

"Hey! You're welcome!" There was a hug, a brief kiss and a whisper in my ear, "Don't let the bastards get you down."

"…it's high school. I think I'll be alright."

Mom waggled her fingers and walked away. The fact that a few of my probably-classmates checked out her pert butt in jeans as she left was not lost on me. I rolled my eyes and headed into the guidance office. An elderly woman behind the desk motioned at a long table wordlessly. I parked myself, dropping my backpack onto the floor and waited.

"Name," she barked a few minutes later.

"Serendipity Rodriguez," I said. "I think I'm supposed to see Mrs. Wong."

The secretary gave me a long assessing look before she picked up her phone. She was far more pleasant to Mrs. Wong than she was to me, continuing to ignore me both during and after the call. Fortunately, I wasn't waiting with Cerberus long, as Mrs. Wong exited her office with a sheet of paper in her hand.

"Hi, Sara. Good to see you again," she said.

"Hey. Hi." I stood up as she offered me the paper.

"I think this covers what we talked about at your first meeting for class assignments. We were able to get you into all your selections. Your homeroom is on the second floor, Room 212. I'll show you."

"It's fine," I said, because I was pretty sure I could find it if the rooms were numbered, but she ignored me, exiting the office and pushing through the busy throngs of kids excited to see one another. Some people turned their heads to look at me—Stonington was bigger than my old high school, but that wasn't saying a whole lot. I had a whopping fifty-five kids in my grade at Auburndale. Here, it was more like two hundred per grade, but that wasn't so big that new blood wouldn't stick out like a sore thumb.

I did my best to ignore the scrutiny, instead trying to acquaint myself with my surroundings. Everything at Stonington looked newer than Auburndale, from the lockers to the desks to the bookshelves in the classrooms and the computers in the lab.

"Is this place new?" I asked.

Mrs. Wong nodded, her smart heels still managing to click on the hard floor despite the din of the burgeoning school day. "Mmm-hmm. Three years old. The football field and track are actually built where the old school used to be."

That explained it.

A floor up and halfway across the building from where we'd started, Mrs. Wong stopped outside of a classroom and gestured me in. Everyone inside, including the teacher at the back of the room with a thick brown mustache and glasses, turned to look at me. The chatter quieted down.

"Mr. Ciullo, this is our new student. Do you prefer Sara or Serendipity?" Mrs. Wong asked, her hand on the small of my back gently but firmly pushing me forward. My boots shuffled over the floor, my eyes skimmed the sea of faces in front of me, most overwhelmingly white, because that's just how the burbs do in New England, I guess.

Great. I'm diversity-pamphlet material two schools in a row now. Fun.

"Sara," I said.

"Okay, everyone. This is Sara Rodriguez, newly transferred in. Be a helper, show her around." Mrs. Wong leaned in close to me. "Questions, always feel free to stop by. We'll be checking in regularly, but my door's always open."

"Thanks, Mrs. Wong."

"Hello, Sara!" Came a booming male voice from the back. I followed it to the source. He had black hair slicked back into a ponytail that was just long enough to brush his shirt collar. He was big—both tall and wide—with a fair amount of extra weight and a hell of a great smile. He was also darker than the other kids. I hadn't picked up on it on my first glance, but he would be accompanying me on my fateful journey onto the diversity pamphlet. He was brownish with deep chocolate eyes.

"That's enough, Leaf," Mr. Ciullo said. "Sara, come on in. Have a seat. I'll do roll call at the bell."

"Come sit next to me!" the kid named Leaf called out. "I'm friendly."

"Yeah, too friendly," a redhead in the second row said.

"You just love me too much, Bethy." Leaf grinned.

So much smile on one mouth.

But I did sit next to him in spite of Bethy Whatever's burn, and there's a simple reason why. He was the other "ethnic" kid. He might not realize I was in the category yet, though my last name was a huge clue, but we were different than the people around us, and being near someone who *might* get what that felt like was a comfort. It was a safety-in-numbers thing that white kids would probably never understand.

If your last name is Miller, no one asks you if you're Mexican with their lip curled, completely ignoring every other Spanish-speaking country existing in the process. If you're an Anderson, no one "jokes" about you being legal. And if you're a Smith? No one assumes your single-parent mother is on welfare until you prove otherwise. Of course, once they learn she's the Swedish parent, the narrative shifts completely, particularly when they discover my Hispanic father isn't around anymore.

"Typical," they'd say.

Hello, racism, my old friend. I've come to talk with you again.

White people, even well-meaning people that I legitimately liked, said some pretty heinous crap to me sometimes upon hearing my last name, and I was about as pale as paper. It wasn't such a long shot to think that the brown-skinned kid had it sixty times worse than I did.

"Hi," he said, leaning over his desk to offer his bear paw for a shake. I gave it. "I'm Leaf, like a leaf on the wind."

"Oh, like *Firefly*?"

"*Firefly*. That's a TV show, I take it?"

"Yeah. It's about space cowboys. Been off the air awhile. My mom likes it." I shifted in my seat, self-conscious that my grand opener at my new school was something super dorky.

"Ah. I should try it out, maybe. No, my birth name, Patrin, means leaf. Well, leaf trail, in Romani, but gadze screw it up and call me Patrick so I go by Leaf to make it easy."

"...what's a—"

"Non-Romani. I'm Stonington's resident Rom. Gypsy, but don't use that word. It's a slur."

"Oh, hey. Uhh. Cool." I hadn't known the thing about the G-word, but I burned it to memory so I wouldn't use it again. "Well, I'm probably their resident Hispanic so—"

"Probably! This school is pure milk. Pretty nice milk, though, so there's that."

Some other kids turned around to say hi to me then. A girl named Hannah with blue stripes in her long golden hair. A guy named Ryan who looked like a jock with glasses. Danielle, who had super short brown curls and big hoop earrings. I introduced myself to all of them, but any real chitchat was cut off when the bell rang and Mr. Ciullo took attendance. He seemed like a nice enough guy, cracking some pretty awful dad jokes as he checked us all off and gave us first-day instructions. These essentially boiled down to get to class on time, don't be a dick and remember that any and all cell phones spotted out during class would be confiscated until the end of class per school policy. They could, however, be used to take pictures of boards and homework assignments at the end of class, but had to be put away at the beginning of the next class. They were also allowed in the halls between classes and at lunch.

They were really explicit on the phone thing. Almost as explicit as they were on the fact that Friday we'd have what-to-do-in-case-of-a-school-shooter practice during our first two periods. They didn't mention shooters, instead saying "standard safety procedures" but this was not my first time on the high-school-panic-button bus.

Beware white dudes with guns, rehearsal at seven thirty.

The bell rang and I headed off for my first class, Advanced Placement English, hoping I'd read enough of *The Grapes of Wrath* on my skim to be able to talk about it. They'd assigned it and *The Great Gatsby* as summer reading for the AP curriculum, but unlike other kids who'd had months to get through the slog of old-timey words, I'd had less than a week. *Gatsby* had been easy enough, but I was so depressed a third of the way into *Grapes*, I'd done myself the service of reading online talking points and watching the movie with Henry Fonda.

This had been before the great baby blowout, so Mormor had been more than happy to be my copilot on the viewing. Too bad she'd talked through the whole thing, so my only takeaways were something-something-Rosasharn and everything sucks forever because Dust Bowl.

These thoughts plagued me as I got lost in the hallway on my way to my first class. I was spinning in a circle, frustrated I couldn't figure out the layout when everything was so plainly numbered, when Leaf came gallantly to my rescue.

"Where to, Serendipity?" He said my name like he was making music, exaggerating the syllables and playing with sound. It made me smile despite my usual knee-jerk reaction to correct him that it was Sara.

"Uhhh, Mrs. Weller's class? 233?"

"This way, down around the corner," he said, plucking at my backpack strap and leading me down the hall.

"Thanks. Appreciate it. Being the new kid sucks."

He smirked. "No problem. You read the books?"

"Arnold's boo—OH! Yeah. Sort of? I read *Gatsby* and sorta got through *Grapes*, but I tapped out because I had less than a week."

"You might be able to wiggle out of it on account of new kid," he said. "But if not, Weller's going to drop an essay on our heads right off the bat, guaranteed. She's kind of a hard-ass that way. It's not bad if you know the trick." Leaf paused in the hall and leaned down to whisper into my ear. I didn't exactly shiver, but I did rub at my arm like I was itchy all over. "Hypothesis sentence, list three reasons why you believe the hypothesis. Three paragraphs explaining each reason, closing paragraph. Five paragraphs total, formulaic, you'll get an A. Promise."

That sounded infinitely more pleasant than what I'd expected. I'd have said so but I was still quasi-distracted by his warm breath.

Maybe this is the second trimester Horny Horny Hippo thing.

"Cool, thanks. You've had Weller before?" I managed.

"Yep. Freshman Honors English, AP English Junior and now senior year. She likes organization in papers more than anything else. Style over substance, baby. Every time."

"…you just called me baby."

"I did, didn't I? Did you like it?" He winked at me and held out his hand to direct me into a classroom tucked around the corner. On one hand, I kinda liked it. Leaf was cute and friendly and big all over, which was a plus 'cause I liked big guys.

On the other hand?

I am knocked up with a stranger's baby.

CHAPTER FIFTEEN

Weller was crafty. After a short introduction and dropping a fourteen-pound syllabus on our desks, she passed a hat around the class and made us pick either a red or a blue paper out of it. I got red. She then announced that the people with red papers were writing about *Gatsby*, the people with blue papers were writing about *Grapes*, and yes, there was a first day in-class essay.

I glanced over at Leaf.

He winked at me again.

I shook my head and got scribbling, grateful that I'd survived round one of Weller. I took

Leaf's advice on formatting the paper, too, though I didn't need it as much. I hadn't exactly jumped for joy reading it, and the pool bit was a real downer, but I understood it fine and designed my entire paper around the last line of the novel, mostly because it was my favorite.

That was the only class I had with Leaf. After that was Contemporary American Issues, followed by Health, which was hysterical, because one of the lines on the syllabus was absolutely about safe sex, STDs and pregnancy. That was going to get awkward as hell fast, and I wasn't sure I wanted to subject myself to being an in-class demonstration-slash-moral tale. I made a mental note to bring it up to Mrs. Wong as soon as possible.

Three classes down and it was lunchtime, which was good, because the starving Hoover factor was in effect. I could and would eat anything, except eggs because they were still gross to me, and I loaded up my tray with a turkey sandwich, Tater Tots, a side salad, an apple, milk and cookies. The chips were a little overboard but I had no regrets. I was living my best life.

I was sitting by myself as new kids were relegated to do until someone took pity on them when Leaf called my name.

"Seeeeeeerendipity. Come here!"

Big voice filling a big room. One of the teachers whirled around and barked at him to sit down, but Leaf ignored her, standing up to wave me over. "Come here."

It was nice to not have to be off on Newbie-School-Kid Island by myself, so I picked up my tray and crossed the room. Leaf sat with two girls, one tall, reed-thin, with short red hair and gray eyes. She had freckles all over, a *Fraggle Rock* T-shirt beneath her plaid button-down and dime-sized red plug earrings in her ears.

The T-shirt was an insta-win with me for obvious reasons.

The other girl was shorter and rounder, more apple-shaped than I was, her hair done up in artful curls, her makeup and particularly her eyeliner perfectly applied. She wore a red-and-white-floral dress with a white shrug over top. Her hair was dyed black, but she pulled it off well, and her lips were fire-engine red. She had pretty light brown eyes with lashes for days, and a pair of black cat-eye glasses.

She was also, apparently, involved with the tall skinny redhead. Because the redhead pulled her in for a quick kiss on the top of her head, both of their eyes skirting over to the lunch monitor because I'm guessing that was an illicit cafeteria move.

Leaf motioned me to the bench across from him and grinned.

"Serendipity Rodriguez, meet my friends, Morgan and Erin."

"Hey. Trans-queer girl," Morgan said in greeting, eyeballing me warily. "So if that's not your deal—"

"Biracial, possibly bisexual but I'm not totally sure yet, girl-with-baggage," I said in return. "So if that's not *your* deal…"

It must have satisfied Morgan as she sat up straighter in her seat and dropped a smile. "I like to get it out there so I don't waste time on assholes."

"Fair," I said. "I have a pretty strict asshole-free policy myself."

The other girl, Erin, gave herself a once-over in her compact mirror before going at her lunch. "Hey, I'm Erin. Sorry Morgan lacks chill."

"I have chill! But we live in Stepford." Morgan motioned around her. "I have a theory that they reproduce by splitting in half, like amoebas. They're actually all the same person."

Leaf giggled. It wasn't what I'd expect from a big tall guy like him, but it worked. "There's a lot of good people," he said. "Some are jerks, but most are good people."

Erin nodded. "Morgan's just being sarcastic."

"Sarcasm is like breathing for me."

"Puns, too," Erin warned. "She likes puns."

"I love puns! And I'm good at them."

"That's debatable." Erin softened the dig by sharing a french fry with Morgan. Morgan snagged it between her teeth, play-snarling at her girlfriend. "Tell her the one you told me earlier."

"I can't just pun on command, you know. It's *punreasonable*."

"…what? No," I said, because Morgan had attacked me. Morgan had attacked me with puns and I wasn't having it. "You didn't."

"I did," Morgan said.

"And she'll do it again," Erin added.

"That's how Morgan does." Leaf unpacked his lunch, opening up a freshly microwaved Tupperware dish with beef and garlic and pepper inside. It smelled so good, my fingers practically itched to steal it. He must have noticed; he tipped the dish my way to taunt me with a whiff seconds before cutting off a piece and putting it on a napkin to slide it my way. "My father's a good cook. He loves to cook for people, too. You should come over some time. Have some good Romani food."

"Is that the cabbage thing he makes?" Erin practically swooned in her seat. "With the beef and rice and spices? It's *so* good."

"Oh, wow. I remember that," Morgan said. "Mr. Leon's a great cook."

I chewed what was effectively a spicy casserole wrapped in a cabbage leaf. It was delicious, and my yummy noises must have pleased Leaf, as he grinned.

"It's called sarma. And yes, it's good, but don't tell him that or he'll get a big head." Leaf chuckled. "It's spicy. I hope it's not too much. My grandmother taught my father to cook, and she's full Rom. I'm a little kinder with the pepper being a diddicoy."

For the second time since meeting him, I had no idea what a word he said meant.

"A diddicoy?" I asked. "And that was amazing."

"Biracial Romani," he said. "My mom was French. I learned to cook from both her and Dad. I'm not at Dad's level yet, but one day. I'm going to be a chef, I think. If you stick around, maybe I'll make you some of my famous honey tarts." He waggled his eyebrows at me as if the honey tarts weren't enticement enough.

He's flirting me up.

I'm letting him.

I'll drop the baby ball soon! But this is the first fun I've had since Jack and that was three months ago now. I can indulge a little bit, right?

I felt my cheeks go hot and looked down at my lunch tray. "I actually love spicy food. There's a Mexican place in my hometown that makes the best enchiladas. They smother them in a jalapeño sauce that's to die for. My mom and Mormor—my grandmother—are Swedish and they cook like Swedes—lots of sweet stuff. It's good! I like it, but I prefer the spicy stuff. Maybe it's in my blood. Thanks, Dad, wherever you may be." I gestured vaguely at the sky before cramming potato chips into my mouth.

"God, we have zero good Mexican places. Where are you from?" Erin asked. "Cause I'd be all over that."

"Auburndale. Just a town over. We moved in with my grandmother in August. I can show you sometime."

Erin practically glimmered. "Nice. We'll have to check it out."

Leaf pulled silverware from his lunch bag and very precisely placed them on the napkin on the table before him. There was some significance to the ritual of the thing, but I wasn't sure what it was, and it was probably rude to ask so I kept my mouth shut. "Will you miss it? Your friends?" he asked before tucking into his food.

"Not really? It's so close. Like, my best friend, Devi—she's super cool—she lives ten minutes away from my grandmother's house and I see her all the time. I'll miss her at lunch, but that was about the only time we got to hang out during school, anyway. I don't think it'll be that bad. Plus, I got away from a trash ex-boyfriend by moving, so that's nice."

Well, I mostly got away from him. I still occasionally got the random check-in text, which I'd ignore, but it was nice to know he was still out there, thinking about how he'd ruined my life. I wasn't going to blame the fetus sitch on him, but he'd played a part, in his own way. If he hadn't screwed around on me, I wouldn't have been boffing strangers in trucks as a way to purge him from my system.

Thanks, Aaron. You dong.

Erin groaned. "Ugh, those are the worst. Two tables back from you, kid with the green hair? That's my ex, Todd. Todd's a butt."

"I totally stole his girlfriend," Morgan said with a satisfied smile.

I lifted my chin and tried to do the casual glance. There was a table of skateboarders with wallet chains and colorful hair, and in the middle of them was a nerdy looking kid with ectoplasm green spikes on his head and an Anarchy T-shirt.

"You upgraded," I announced without hesitation.

"Yep, I like her," Morgan said.

Erin lifted a french fry in salute. "Same."

"I told you," Leaf said, after swallowing down a bite and dashing at his mouth with a napkin.

"You told them what?"

"That you could hang. I got a good feeling about you. Speaking of which, what are you doing Friday night? We get together and watch movies at Morgan's place every week. She's got a private movie theater."

"It's not a private movie theater," Morgan said with a sigh. "My dad's a football freak and got the reclining chairs and a big TV for Mantown is all. I hate it, but it has its uses."

"The TV *is* huge," Erin said. "Ridiculously huge. It might as well be a movie theater, babe."

"Dad really likes football. Patriots fans are kind of extra," Morgan said dryly.

I didn't answer right away, because I wasn't sure what Devi was doing that night and I didn't want to ditch her simply because I'd met new people. Leaf must have clued in that something was up, because he finished his food and motioned at me with his fork.

"Your friend, right?"

"Huh?"

"You said you miss your best friend. Bring her. If you like her, that's good enough for me."

"Oh! Yeah, I was worried she'd think I ditched her. What are you, psychic or something?" I smiled, thinking I'd just dropped some easy, forgettable banter, but Leaf's expression turned grim.

"Haven't you heard about gypsy fortune tellers? I see allllll."

I had no idea what to say to that because I wasn't sure if he was serious. Fortunately, I was spared the embarrassment of asking when Morgan reached out to whack Leaf upside the head.

"Stop it, you *ass*."

Leaf burst into laughter, not his earlier childlike giggles but a full-bellied roar of a thing that filled up all the space around the lunch table. "I'm practicing! Dukkering is a tried and true way to scam gullible gadze out of their money, don't you know?"

"You jerk." Erin rolled her eyes. "You like Sara!"

He picked up his milk carton and pressed it to his full bottom lip, his dark eyes fixing on me as he offered yet another exaggerated wink. "Oh, I do."

CHAPTER SIXTEEN

I walked into the house at half past two. Mom was at the day job, so it was just me and Mormor and would be until five thirty. Mormor had a thing about stuff that wasn't food on the kitchen table, so I swung my backpack onto the floor of the coatroom and kicked off my lace-up boots. Mormor stood by the sink, pulling the green hats off strawberries, with her back turned to me. She never looked my way.

When she'd said she wouldn't talk to me again until I told her what I was going to do with the baby, she meant it. She hadn't said a single word in days. On one hand, it was obnoxious and irritating and I recognized it for the emotional blackmail it was. On the other hand, if I was being perfectly honest, I didn't actually care. Mormor was famous for this kind of stuff, and if she wanted to tantrum, so be it.

Who am I to tell a sixty-something-year-old woman that she's acting like a turdsicle? At least she wasn't throwing shoes at me.

"It was a good first day," I said, making my way over to the fridge. I swiped a yogurt and some orange juice and a cheese stick for a snack. My lunch offerings to the womb overlord were apparently no longer sufficient because my lower quarters were gurgling like a backed-up garbage disposal. "I like my teachers. Met some cool new kids, too. One of them's Romani. His name is Leaf. I also met these two girls, Morgan and Erin, and I like them, too."

Silence.

"I ate with them and they were super nice. Leaf made sure I got to all my classes on time."

She rinsed the strawberries in the sink.

"Well, I'm gonna go upstairs now. Listen to some music backward and make an offering to my dark lord, then maybe ask Devi to come over so we can be lesbian witches together. Good talk, Mormor."

She made a strangled sound, almost like a cat with its tail caught in the door, but still she refused to speak. The fact that I nearly incited her to use her words was a victory in my book, and I climbed the stairs to my room, gnawing on cheese before my door was even closed. I texted Devi with a simple, Come over?

A minute later came, On my way. Chzbrgr?

Yas.

She was a good wifey.

I sprawled out on my bed, putting Pandora on mostly so I could drown out the sound of Mormor smashing things around in the kitchen in her frustration. I heard Devi arrive, heard Mormor greet her with a "How have you been, Devorah?" because Devi wasn't in the doghouse, followed immediately by "McDonald's isn't food, you realize."

"Yeah, but it's tasty not-food," Devi retorted before sprinting up the stairs. I didn't even bother getting off the bed, instead just moving over so she had room on the other side of me. She didn't fail to disappoint, sprawling out beside me within seconds of appearing in my life like a long-legged, cheeseburger-bearing unicorn.

"Oh, hi," she said in greeting.

"Oh, hi."

Talk was abandoned in favor of food, and it wasn't until I'd inhaled one burger and was onto the second that we got around to catching up.

You think I'm kidding about always being hungry when pregnant. I'm not. When you don't want to hork, you probably want to eat. Then you want to sleep. Reproduction is not elegant.

"How was it?" Devi asked.

"Good. Met some kids that don't suck. They want to hang out Friday. Invited you, too."

"Cool, I'm down. Same old, same old at Auburndale,

which means take me with you, please. I want to escape.
Got some good tea to spill, though."

"Oh?"

"Aaron and Samantha broke up."

That should have been satisfying on some level, and
months ago, I would have cackled at his misfortune, but
I just nibbled on a cheeseburger and shrugged. I couldn't
muster much in the way of caring, mostly because I had
bigger things to worry about. Maybe, just maybe, I'd finally sorta gotten over the guy who'd busted my heart
into a trillion pieces.

"I should block him," I said. "He still texts me sometimes, but—"

"It just happened today. Big fight in the cafeteria at
lunch, so maybe you should do that now, before he shows
up shivering and naked and sad on your digital doorstep."

I picked up my phone, expecting some of the familiar
hesitation to creep up on me when thinking about forever
thrusting Aaron out of my life, but it didn't come, and so
I did what I should have done months before:

I got rid of that trash.

"Good job, high five! About time, girl." Devi rolled
over to half sprawl across me, her leg draped over mine.
"How are you feeling?"

"Good. Hungry, pretty much always tired, but good."

I filled her in on the essay, the health class concern of being
their dissection specimen, and then I filled her in on the
keeping-the-baby thing. Which she took remarkably well.

"I'm gonna be an auntie," she singsonged, squirming
around on top of me.

"Not too loud. I don't want Mormor to hear, but yes."

"Oh, damn. She going to be difficult about it?"

"No. She wants me to keep them, but she's been so pushy about me making a decision, I'm making her wait for it. That's why she's not talking to me."

"Okay, so." Devi pushed herself up onto her elbows to peer at me. "You're kind of a douche, Sara."

I shrugged. "I'm okay with it."

Devi giggled and collapsed onto my chest. "I am, too."

I kept Mormor in suspense another whole day, the stubborn old woman refusing to talk to me despite repeated attempts on my part. Mom finally decided to intervene; she pulled me aside, freshly home from work, wearing a skirt suit, her bright white sneakers looking odd with her pantyhose.

"Okay, it's time to be the bigger person," she announced, gesturing at our dinners laid out on the table behind us. "I know this is terrible to hear, but I can no longer allow you, daughter of mine, to torture your grandmother."

"It's fine. I was getting ready to tell her, anyway." For all that Mormor had been a bully and a pain, she let us live in her house rent-free and she cooked for me every night, even if she wouldn't look at me or talk to me while I ate it. In fact, she'd pretty much set up shop in the living room in front of the TV during dinner so she didn't risk doing either thing. There was a distinct possibility she just liked eating in front of the news—that's how she used to eat when she was alone, before we moved in—but on the off chance I wasn't just a handy excuse for her to go back to her old routine, it was time to do the reveal.

Mom stroked my hair and then patted my belly. It wasn't really doing any rounding yet, though it was hardening. Belly fat is supposed to be soft, right? Except my stomach had gone from bread dough to iron skillet. My stomach felt how in-shape people's stomachs must feel!

Too bad it was the precursor to looking like I ate a basketball.

I wandered toward the living room. Mormor was tuned into *Wheel of Fortune* on Channel Seven, her finger accusingly pointing at a blonde woman on TV who'd incorrectly guessed the clue.

"That one is stupid. She is stupid, Astrid. I should do this show. I'd win a car."

Mom eyeballed me before slipping onto the couch adjacent to Mormor's chair. "That's cool, Ma. Hey, it's time we stop pretending our kid is dead, yeah?"

"I'm not doing any such thing. I simply don't want to talk to her until she respects me," Mormor insisted. "You can tell her that."

"I am literally standing three feet behind your chair."

Mormor didn't answer.

Mom looked over at me.

Be the bigger person.

"I'm keeping the baby," I said to the back of Mormor's head. "So, you know, that's cool, I guess?"

Still Mormor didn't say anything.

My mother scowled. "She told you, Ma. She's keeping the baby."

"Keeping the baby does not mean she is not selling it to some other family."

"Adoption's still not selling the baby! What are we, in the Twilight Zone? She's *keeping them* keeping them. Like, raising the kid. As a Larssen. Or, wait." Mom looked up at me. "As a Rodriguez? Your choice, of course."

That was something I hadn't considered. Would I give the kid the name of the bio dad I didn't know, who'd left me with so much angst about the half of me I wrestled to understand? Or would I name the kid after my quasi-dysfunctional grandmother who threw shoes and hadn't talked to me for days because she's an emotional terrorist?

"Dunno," I said, shrugging my shoulders. "I've got about six months to decide."

"Serendipity is a Larssen," Mormor announced. "The birth certificate is a piece of paper with a bad name. We raised this girl. She's ours. She's a Larssen. This baby is one of us, too. I told you the ultrasound looks like a Larssen. It's in the nose."

I looked back through the kitchen door, at the refrigerator. "They look like a legume from where I'm standing. A legume with eyes."

"That is incredibly creepy," Mom said.

"My great-grandchild is not a legume," Mormor insisted. "They are beautiful."

"It's a joke, Mormor."

"It's not a funny one. Do you want to be called a legume? Legumes are ugly. I ought to give you the shoe."

Mom sighed, raking her fingers through her hair. "Well, I guess things are back to normal."

CHAPTER SEVENTEEN

Weller proved to be the banshee of all my teachers. I was pretty cool with my calculus teacher,
my history teacher, even the health teacher who'd
be giving the moral lesson on how not to grow
up to be a Serendipity Rodriguez, but Weller was
hardcore, delivering not only the in-class essay,
but another at-home one on the *other* summer
reading that I had to turn in on Friday. At least
I could use the internet to my advantage; I was
pretty confident in my paper, despite only reading half the book.

The one downside to the week was how tired

I was during the day. I didn't nod off, but I came close a couple times, and I started chugging a bottle of Starbucks iced coffee between classes two and three to keep me awake. The doctor didn't say no caffeine, just limited amounts. That was my limited amount. It was enough fake energy to get me through midmorning.

Hopefully, it wouldn't scramble my kid's still-developing brain.

Sorry, kid. Mom really needed to get through Math.

Friday came. School happened. I sat with Leaf, Morgan and Erin at lunch that day as I had all week. Other kids had come to introduce themselves, and some of them were nice enough that I'd consider maybe hanging out with them, but I was still most comfortable in the corner table with the other "atypicals." We weren't Stonington's standard fare and we knew it. We were also blazingly okay with it, by all appearances, anyway.

"We're still on for movies tonight, right?" Morgan asked, wiping ketchup off her mouth with her sleeve. Erin tsked and shoved a napkin at her. Morgan looked at it, dashed at her already-clean lip and then threw it onto the table. "I already checked with the 'rents. Dad's taking Mom line dancing later so the house is ours."

Erin flinched. "Your poor mom."

"No, they like it, the weirdos."

"I'll be there with bells on," I said. "Devi, too. She's looking forward to meeting all of you. Anything we can bring?"

"Soda's always good. We'll have oven pizzas and chips and stuff," Erin said.

"Got it."

"I'm bringing some pastry tonight, I think," Leaf said. He was busy unpacking yet another amazing-smelling lunch, smiling all the while. I was leaning forward to steal a sniff when Leaf cut off a piece and slid it my way on a mini paper plate.

Like he'd done every lunch since I'd met him.

He winked at me.

"Enjoy."

"You don't have to keep feeding me!" I wasn't *really* complaining—the food was delicious—but I didn't want him thinking I was a dog sitting by his leg at the dining room table begging for food, either. It's not like he was feeding his other friends, too.

Leaf just shook his head and lifted his finger, reaching out to tap the tip of my nose.

"In my family, you always give food to appreciative friends. It's etiquette." I wanted to reassure him that I had plenty of food, to just look at my overloaded tray, but he simply nudged the paper plate my way a second time. "Eat, or you'll offend me, gadzo. And if you keep objecting, bad ideas will sail into your open mouth and take root."

It was again one of those moments when I couldn't tell if he was being serious or not, so I shut up and ate. I had no idea what I'd thrust into my mouth, but it was similar in flavor to the other Romani dishes I'd been lucky enough to sample. Some sweet. More spicy. Enough heat that the roof of my mouth tingled. There was tomato there, and garlic and pepper, but beyond that, I didn't even know what meat was in it.

I didn't really care, either, if we're being honest. Every bite was a treat.

"Lamb, this time," Leaf offered before pulling out his silverware. "Minced lamb."

"It's fantastic."

"My father gets up every morning to cook before work—for him, for me. He doesn't like to let food sit overnight. Leftovers aren't—" He paused, looking for a word. "They aren't something he's comfortable with. Rom can be particular about food. I'm not as strict as my father, and he's not as strict as my grandmother. She'd have never allowed me to eat food that had been sitting this long, but we break from some of her traditions."

I'd noticed that he had a different approach to food than other people, but it wasn't something I'd ever comment on because that was a culture that wasn't mine and I didn't like being rude. "It's all delicious."

"It is. He likes to cook with certain ingredients. Things that are powerful and make you strong. Big flavors." Leaf motioned at his Tupperware. "To him, this is why I'm tall and wide. The foods he makes. I keep telling him the wide is from my sweet tooth, and then he sighs and tells me I'm just like my mother. He's not wrong—she is half of me."

"Speaking of sweet tooth, are you making the honey pastries tonight? With the almonds?" Erin's eyes, lined again with her signature cat eye, swung my way. "They're the best. Like, to-die-for best."

"Raspberry instead of honey, I think. We have a fresh pint of berries from the market." Leaf paused to look at me. "It's like a baklava pastry, if you've ever had that? Layered pastry."

Oh, I had, and as much as I enjoyed that cafeteria pizza served plank-style with plasticky cheese and watery tomato paste, I really wanted that raspberry baklava stuff in my face, pronto.

"I am down like a clown," I said.

Leaf grinned at me over his food, his foot nudging mine under the table.

"Okay, clown. I'll be happy to see you get down."

Another wink and a slight curl of those plump lips as he ate his lunch.

...*wait.*

Was that dirty?

Six o'clock that night, I stood in Mormor's driveway next to Devi's black Ford Fiesta, a brown paper grocery bag full of two-liter bottles of soda and SunnyD because I was done with caffeine for the day.

"How do I look?" Devi asked with a delicate twirl. She wore a sundress with skinny straps and a sunflower print. Her toes were freshly painted. Her hair was covered by a soft gold cloth kerchief. There was makeup and hoop earrings and a pair of white Mary Jane shoes.

"Like a goddess. How do I look?" I asked.

"Like you're wearing your pajamas and flip-flops."

"Perfect!"

She wasn't wrong. I really was in a pair of checkered pajama pants, a plain black T-shirt with a pocket, and flipflops. At least I was wearing a bra, which was something of a feat when your nipples hurt for a minimum of six out of every twenty-four hours. But hey, that was a vast improvement over aching twenty-three of twenty-four hours every day, so we were making progress.

Second trimester, here I come!

We piled into the car. I'd just slammed the door closed when my mom, fresh off her workday, pulled into the driveway. Fridays were her casual day, so she was in jeans and a T-shirt…that was turned inside out, the tags sticking out in the back, the seams out and proud for the world to behold.

I rolled the window down.

"Menu shirt?" I asked, motioning at her getup.

Devi was confused. "Wait, what?"

"Menu shirt," Mom repeated, climbing from the car. "It's when you hit your shirt more than your mouth when you're eating and get stains, but no, not this time. I forgot about the No Logo'd T-shirts rule. Grabbed your Bucks T-shirt. Now it's an inside-out shame T-shirt."

"Well, that's fair. I mean, that's how most Starbucks drinkers should feel. Shame," Devi said.

My mom leaned on my car door to eyeball Devi. "You're such a New Englander."

"It's true. I'll probably die with a Dunkin' Donuts cup glued to my palm." Devi smirked.

"Okay, smart-asses, where are you off to?" Mom flicked at a lock of my hair that refused to stay inside of my plastic clip.

"Sara met a boy," Devi said, only she said it *that* way—

the rotten-school-kid way that totally warranted the jab I levied at her side.

"Oh, man. Don't we remember the last time you met a boy?" Mom asked.

"Good news, everyone! I can't get pregnant again yet, so no need to worry!" I snorted at them. "His name is Leaf and he's just being sweet. I'm sure he'll back right off when he learns about the fetus."

"His loss. You're a great girl. Whoever you're brewing in your belly's going to be great, too." Mom swooped in to press a kiss to my temple.

Immediately, I smelled the cigarettes.

Just like Mom. To keep a smiling face for me and then to freak out in the privacy of her own car with a pack of Marlboros.

"Stop smoking," I said. "You'll puke out your lungs if you don't."

"Going inside now. So I can get nagged by my other mother." Mom pulled away from the window and grabbed her day bag, slinging it over her shoulder.

"You smell like a chimney. A chimney's butt," I called after her.

"No, *you* smell like a chimney's butt."

"Love you, Mom."

"You, too, kiddo. Home by midnight or text me with a good reason why you're not here."

Devi started the car and we both watched Mom disappear into the house.

"The two of you are like two peas in a pod," Devi said.

"Right down to the teen pregnancies! Go Team Larssen!" I pulled out my phone to look at the directions. I'd been standing by my locker after school when Erin stopped by to give me cell phone numbers and an address. Morgan lived about fifteen minutes from my house, off a main road near the local movie theater, so it wasn't going to be a big deal finding it.

Devi was as cool as a cucumber the whole way there, but she was always laid-back. I was more worried about old friends and new friends intermingling. I also wasn't too proud to admit that the notion of Leaf trying to take it to the next level with me, beyond the flirts and casual touches, was going to require one hell of an uncomfortable conversation that I didn't want to have.

It was possible he wouldn't care, but I did. I cared. I cared what he thought of me, and what all of these other kids thought of me because they were cool and funny. What if their tolerance ended at "being seen with the pregnant girl"?

Devi clued in that I was fretting, because her hand left the shift and slid over to touch mine.

"It'll be okay," she said. "Promise."

"How do you know?"

She shrugged. "I just do. You're good people. Water finds its own level. Everyone will be cool because you're cool."

There were a thousand ways to poke holes in that logic, but instead I let it take the edge off, slumping into my seat and nodding.

"Thanks, wifey."

"You bet."

CHAPTER EIGHTEEN

"Pastry is bomb."

Morgan swiped another piece of Leaf's pastry from the tray on the coffee table, cramming it into her mouth and falling back onto the couch to kick her legs up in the air. Her head flopped back into Erin's lap, so Erin leaned down to kiss her forehead.

Morgan's outburst was understandable in the face of such culinary greatness. The pastries were buttery and sweet and nutty and tickled both me and the small human inside of me who vacillated wildly between "expel all food" and "I HUNGER." Fortunately, it was more the latter than the former lately, and I was curled up with a small plate of sweets and enjoying them greatly.

Devi sat on my left.

Leaf on my right.

"These are super good," Devi said to Leaf.

"Thank you! My grandmother's recipe."

Devi dashed crumbs off her bottom lip. "I'd like to shake her hand."

"She's passed away, but I'll shake your hand instead, if you'd like." Leaf grinned and leaned past me to offer a bear paw to Devi. She accepted it, his giant fingers enfolding hers. For a moment, I worried this was that thing that sometimes happened where, upon seeing my gorgeous best friend, I became second-choice slop, but no. Leaf immediately pulled away to fuss at me about taking another square.

"I think I'm actually full," I said, which probably didn't mean much to him, but it sure surprised me. The bottomless pit was not so bottomless after all.

"Good, good. I'm glad. But there's more. Pizza and snacks, too, if you change your mind."

Leaf got up from the couch to wash his hands in the kitchen. He'd done it quite a few times since we'd sat down to eat. I also noticed that he didn't share pizza with us, but stuck to his own personal-sized pizza. I hadn't asked why, but he had offered something of an explanation while we were eating.

"Rom are particular, yes? I mentioned that," he said. "It's complicated but I mean no offense. It's a cultural thing."

"Like eating kosher, right?" Devi said. "Food rules. I'm Jewish. My grandmother is particular, too. So are a lot of Jews."

Leaf nodded. "Yes! Something like that. The rules are different, but yes."

And then his focus was back on me.

"What kind of movies do you like?" He picked up a stack of Blu-rays from the dining room table and thumbed through. "We've got scary, action, funny, funny action—"

I plucked *Guardians of the Galaxy* from the pile and handed it to him. "This one."

"You've never seen it?" His dark brows lifted so high, they nearly kissed his widow's peak.

"Oh, she has. About six hundred times," Devi said. "It's her favorite."

"She has good taste! It's one of mine, too." Leaf left the couch to set up the Blu-ray player, pausing to glance back at Morgan and Erin, who were busy kissing and smiling and whispering to one another. Morgan was still sprawled across Erin's lap, so the kisses were upside down and awkward looking, but sweet all the same.

"Excuse me, lesbians, but are you alright with *Guardians*?" Leaf asked.

"Pardon me, straight, but sure, that sounds good to me." Morgan rolled her eyes up Erin's way. "You cool with that, baby?"

Erin nodded. "Team Drax for life. I think the second movie is around here, too?"

"Uh-huh." Morgan snuggled farther into Erin's middle, sighing contentedly. Erin stroked her hands through

Morgan's carrot-orange hair. She'd forsaken her usual glammed pinup thing for yoga pants and an oversize T-shirt. I appreciated her casualness; it meant I wasn't alone on Scrub Island.

I nibbled on the last of my pastry and went to the kitchen to throw away my garbage. By the time I got back, Devi had moved over to the sectional with Morgan and Erin, abandoning me to The Boy, who'd returned to his seat already. I stared at her across the room. She stared back. Then she grinned as she snagged herself another slice of pizza.

Oh, Devi. I know where you sleep.

The heat rose in my face as I sunk back into the couch. Not wanting anyone to see just how red I could get, I pretended to be interested in the Patriots football purgatory surrounding me. Blue-and-white banners, posters and signed photographs hung from the walls. Along the ceiling, there were decorative lights like you might see at Christmas time, only they were tiny football helmets with Patriots logos on the sides. There was a glass case with golden footballs and commemorative-issue Super Bowl rings. Jerseys flanked the almost-as-big-as-the-wall TV, framed and signed, one of which belonged to Saint Brady himself.

Erin's claim that it was a movie theater wasn't far off, if movie theaters were hosed down with puke-tastic sports memorabilia.

The credits started on the movie. Leaf leaned back over the opposite side of the couch. I was comfortable. I got more comfortable when I stretched out and he made room for me on the middle cushion. He glanced my way.

"You can put your feet on my lap if you want to lie down," he said. "I won't touch them. I know feet are a thing."

"Five-headed monsters," I agreed, because really, feet were ugly, but I took him up on his offer and there I was, totally horizontal on the couch, watching a great movie, with a nice-looking Rom volunteering to be my footrest.

I never moved during the movie, and he didn't seem bothered by it. His hand rested on my knee and never so much as twitched. There was no massaging or tickling or anything other than he had to put his hand somewhere, my legs were in the way, that's where it landed. What I liked? He asked me, quietly, "Is this alright?" before he did it. He didn't just assume and it scored him major brownie points.

I could have really liked him.

...if I was looking for that sort of thing. Which I wasn't. I was pregnant and that was trouble enough on its own, never mind complicating anything with a boy.

Those were the thoughts that plagued me between movie sprints—things along the lines of "what I deserved." I didn't deserve Leaf's attention because I had to be serious about my baby. I had to be an adult now. I had to realize that flirting was frivolous! Except...

I'm pregnant, not dead. I can still appreciate a good dude, right? Like, it's not selfish or stupid of me to do that?

I must have had a look on my face, because Leaf tapped the inside of my ankle to pull my attention. I stopped dead-staring at the TV and glanced his way. His smile was soft, but earnest; crinkly lines formed on the sides of his dark eyes.

"You okay?"

"Yeah. I think so? I... Maybe I need some air."

He lifted his hand so I could escape the couch. I trotted outside, pausing at Morgan's kitchen table to shoulder into my hoodie. The day had been warm with the last vestiges of summer, but the nights were taking on a chill that already sliced through clothes, boding poorly for winter. When I stepped outside, my breath turned into puffy clouds before my face.

While it was never pleasant to feel your snot freezing inside of your nostrils, it helped to clear my head. I paced back and forth in Morgan's driveway. Choices. I had choices. I could appreciate Leaf *or* I could take my baby seriously. Or...weren't both possible? I probably *shouldn't* jump into a relationship. That was irresponsible, particularly knowing Leaf would run when he found out about el bebé, but I could see him for the good guy he was. I could think about possible futures with him or really any other guy. A teen pregnancy didn't relegate me to a spinster life forever.

Mom dated. Sure, not till I was, like, five or six, but she dated.

It's just a long dry spell. I can handle that.

The clatter of Morgan's screen door made me jump. I turned around, expecting to see Devi there. But no, it was the tall dark boy with the very white teeth who'd been parading through my thoughts. He'd donned his jacket, his hands sunk into his jeans pockets.

"Devi said if you wanted her I could go get her," he said. "I just got up first."

"Nah. No. I'm okay." I managed a smile and looked down at my feet. Flip-flops. Oh, you'd seemed like such a good idea earlier, but now, with the cold…

"Anything I can do to help?" He was coming closer, nearing me. Fifteen feet separating us became ten, then five, then two. He didn't cross over into my personal space, instead lingering just outside of it.

"I've got something I should tell you." I eyed him.

He eyed back.

"Did I do someth—"

"I'm pregnant."

It was one of those moments in life when everything around you was almost too still. My voice, which had been whisper soft, somehow became a bellow in all that quiet.

"Oh." He blinked at me. "You have a boyfriend?"

"No, no. I did. I mean, it's not his." I frowned, never quite capable of looking Leaf in the eye. I wanted to explain but it was so hard to get it out. The words were stuck, like I'd have to hock a loogie just to expel them. "It messed me up, the breakup. Aaron broke my heart, and when he went to a party with his new girlfriend, I got stupid. Drank, met a guy, hooked up. Boom, baby. I don't even know where he is now. The baby daddy, I mean. Aaron is probably rotting in hell. Or, at least, I hope he is."

Leaf reached out a hand and gently placed it on my shoulder. "My sister had a baby at eighteen. That's a little older, but she's happy. My niece is great. Are your parents good?"

"My mom. I don't know my dad, but she's good. And my grandmother, she's good, too. I'll be okay." The last I added as an afterthought, mostly because I didn't want him thinking this was a pity ploy. No, this was worse in a way, because I was warning this nice guy who was interested in me away from liking me because I just so happened to be…you know.

Preggers.

"If you need anything, I'll help," Leaf said. "We all will. I don't think it'll change much."

"Thanks. I think I'll be okay. I'm guessing the kids at school will be weird about it." I shivered as another breeze shredded through my hoodie and made my bare toes curl.

Stupid flip-flops.

Leaf tsked, reaching for my elbow and gently pulling me back toward Morgan's house, his hand curled around my arm as he guided me up the porch steps. "You're cold. That's not good for you or the baby."

He smiled at me.

It was different. I couldn't tell you exactly *how* it was different—it wasn't in the way his lips tilted or in the slash of white against brown skin—but it was different. It was warm, but a different warm, like by announcing I was full of kid, I'd gone from potential girlfriend material to someone he needed to coddle. I'd literally lost all of my sex appeal with one declaration.

It's not good for you or the baby, he said.

He didn't mean it to be a slap in the face, but…

Well? My face stung.

CHAPTER NINETEEN

"Okay, queen of all that is dead cow and ketchup, I bequeath unto you a double bacon cheeseburger and a chocolate shake," Devi said, plopping a paper bag in front of me. I was sprawled out in my room, in the same clothes I'd worn to Morgan's house, my hair in a clip, a Jupiter-sized zit developing in the middle of my forehead.

I stared at the bag of fast food.

Devi nudged it my way.

"Guaranteed to cheer you up," she said.

On one hand, a depressed hunger strike was totally warranted.

On the other hand…

I am the cheeseburger queen.

I tore open the paper and did terrible, awful, unspeakable things to those double-beef patties.

I was in full Eeyore-mode, and had been since leaving Morgan's the night before. Leaf was ever-courteous, so nice! Very generous and caring all the way through both *Guardians of the Galaxy* movies. And very clearly *not* into me anymore. I thought at first I was just imagining it—being hypersensitive because of the ebb and flow of hormones—but no, Devi noticed it, too. When we climbed into the car, she asked about my long face.

"I told Leaf about the baby. He's done, I guess."

I almost cried saying it, which was dumb, considering I'd just met the guy, but he'd become representative of something bigger along the way. He was another missed opportunity thanks to Sara's Big Bouncing Truck Adventure—in the same category as my going to an Ivy League school post-baby. Possible, but not very likely because *things were going to change*.

"That explains it. He got quiet after you two talked." Devi pulled the car out onto the road to take me home. "But hey, he seems like a great friend to have, yeah?"

"Yeah, sure," I said, trying to sound positive, but I was hurting and she knew it. She dropped me off, let me sleep and the next day, as soon as I texted her in the morning to say hello, she informed me she was coming over to my house. So I should brush my teeth because morning breath was anti-friendship. Fortunately, neither Mom nor Mormor objected to the impromptu visit.

It didn't hurt that Devi primed that pump by bringing them coffee from Dunks and me a bag of Burger King.

Mmm. Burger.

The sandwich that would have normally taken me twelve bites to get through was devoured in five.

"He may just need a little time," Devi said, jumping right into it. She popped a chicken nugget into her mouth and chewed thoughtfully. "Maybe he just needs to think about it and figure out what he wants to do?"

I collapsed onto my pile of pillows. "I doubt it. He barely knows me. I'm just bummed out because everything's changing and there's not a lot I can do about it. Like, dude, check this out." I leaned back and rolled down the top of my pajama pants, pointing at my midsection where a gentle swell had had the audacity to ripen. Not a lot, just a touch, but I knew it was there—had noticed it for the first time that morning.

I'd blame it on cheeseburgers, but fat was soft. The Stomach was not soft.

Devi reached out to touch it, poking at my belly button.

"Yep, that's a kid," she announced.

"Yep." I rolled up my pants. "I tried to change before you got here but jeans fit weird. Too tight. So I said screw it and went back to my PJs. Fat pants forever, I guess."

"Hey, fat pants are the best. I own at least five pairs."

"Says the girl with no fat to speak of," I said.

"Don't hate." Devi crawled up beside me, her head *fwumping* down into the pillow beside mine.

I snuggled into her side. "I don't hate. I just wish I felt better."

"You will."

"You promise?"

"Yeah."

Except Devi was wrong. Not forever wrong, but wrong for a while, and most particularly wrong that next Monday. I was at my locker in the morning, trading my book bag for my folders just like I would any other school day, when it started. Six lockers down from me, a girl, who'd never even introduced herself to me, started talking about me. I think her name was Shelby, but for the purposes of this retelling, let's just call her Doucheface McAssBurger.

"She's *pregnant*," Doucheface said to her shorter thinner friend—henceforth called Armpit McButtSandwich—in a stage whisper. "Can you believe it?"

I'd never talked to either of these girls, but there they were, making my business their business and the business of anyone in earshot, which was everyone, because Doucheface's voice carried. I froze, staring straight ahead at my stack of books and papers, realizing that the soft din of chatter around me was probably all *about* me.

Oh.

The cat, it seemed, was out of the bag.

It was going to get out sooner or later, particularly with my starting to show, but knowing that the gossip rag had started with Leaf sucked. It sucked a lot. I'd been at the school a couple weeks, made three friends total and already one of them had thrown me under the bus.

My new-friend roulette hadn't paid off.

I glowered at Doucheface and Armpit hard enough that they stepped back, and I slammed closed my locker door.

My eyes stung. Stupid hormones made stupid crying more stupidly possible and I hated it. I managed to hold it together, swearing to myself that my hag classmates wouldn't get the satisfaction of seeing the preggo freak out. I was two steps down the hall when Danielle Hopkington, with her short brown curls, hoop earrings and barrage of freckles, called my name and fell into step beside me.

"Hey, Sara. Are you okay?" she asked.

"Yep."

That's not what you really want to ask, Danielle, and we both know it.

I kept walking. Danielle kept pace.

"I just heard you were in trouble, and like, I wanted to help."

"Don't."

It sounded bitchy. It was bitchy, but I didn't know this person well, didn't trust her as far as I could throw her and didn't give much of a crap what she thought of me. My upset at being outed was making way for anger, and anger meant...

Piss off, Danielle, was what it meant.

"Right, okay fine. If that's how it is," she said, sounding injured.

"It's how it is." I ducked into my class, leaving her standing there, stupefied, in the hall. I sat through the next hour of class growing more and more rage-faced. Leaf, this great guy, I'd thought, who'd shared lunches with me and talked about hospitality, and invited me out with his friends, had run his mouth with a story that wasn't his to tell. Who did he think he was? Did he think that was his news to share?

Was he adding the "lol Hispanic chick" angle to it, or would the other kids do that, 'cause it was bound to come up. "Hahaha, it's funny, the Latina—" which I wasn't, but nuanced discussions of Hispanic versus Latina weren't quite talking points for a lot of white people "—got knocked up." The jokes that'd follow would be about dudes not looking at me too long or I'd get pregnant. Or that I can't share Cokes or use a dude's toothbrush without getting a twin inside of me. The meaner comments would be about me being easy. Or ignorant. Or... Really, pick your trope, but they'd happen because no one knew me or cared about me in a new school. I was the weird outsider who'd just gotten a whole heck of a lot weirder and more outsider-y, which wasn't a word, but I didn't care.

I'd worked myself up into a full-blown snit by the time I got to Weller's class. I sat in my usual seat because I wasn't giving Leaf the satisfaction of seeing me squirm in front of him.

He promptly sat next to me and, without hesitation, pulled a Saran-wrapped pastry from his bag, sliding it onto the corner of my desk.

"Fresh batch," he said.

"Screw you," I said.

His surprise seemed real enough, but then I'd thought everything about him was earnest from the get-go. Maybe I'd misread him. If he was going to out me to the whole school as "that pregnant chick" maybe he'd played good guy at my expense from the very beginning. That red-haired girl on the first day *had* given me a half-hearted warning.

"What happened?" he asked.

"Like you don't know?"

Before he could answer, Weller stomped into the room and barked at us to clear our desks, which meant in-class essay time. Leaf kept desperately trying to catch my eye. I could feel the weight of his stare, but I didn't indulge it or him, instead keeping 100 percent of my focus on my paper all the way up to the bell ringing. I turned in my essay, grabbed my stuff, never looking back at Leaf, but he trotted up behind me and touched my shoulder.

"Sara, what happened?" He sounded sincerely baffled, and I stopped mid-hall to death glare at him.

"How many people did you tell?" I demanded.

The question took him off guard. "I…"

"How many?"

He grimaced. "One. Morgan."

"Okay, sure. Let's say I believe that. How many people do you think Morgan told?"

He looked away and cursed under his breath—a word I didn't understand, but the meaning was clear enough by his tone and the rigidness of his posture. "She cornered me after you left Friday night. Asked me why I didn't ask you out or kiss you or… She was telling me how much she liked you, and I said I liked you, too. I think she was trying to be encouraging, but she wouldn't let up on it, and so I told her about your situation. I asked her not to say anything. I wanted her to understand why I was giving you space…"

"Okay, that's great, and I even believe that your intentions were good, but now the whole school knows, so I'm going to guess that Morgan told Erin, and Erin might have told 'one other person' who then promised not to tell, but they went ahead and told one other person... You get me now? You see? 'Cause they know." I stopped talking to him to point at a cluster of girls standing near the lockers who were gawking at me. "You can't look at them and tell me they don't know. And sure, they'd have found out sooner or later, but I wanted that to be my choice. My reveal. I wanted to be ready, but today I walked into school and got a whole face full of suck and that's your fault."

Leaf spread his hands and looked down. He was ashamed. I could tell by the flush on his cheeks. Any other day, I'd have been sympathetic to it. Not that day. "It is my fault. I'm sorry," he said.

A whole lot of good that does me.

But I didn't say it. Instead, I went to class, and when lunchtime came, I went to the guidance counselor's office to eat by myself in peace, waiting for Mrs. Wong to see me.

CHAPTER TWENTY

Mrs. Wong listened. She was sympathetic, even. Or maybe that wasn't sympathy, but resignation that I had her held hostage in her office while I talked copiously, quickly and angrily. She nodded as I spewed venom and pushed her bowl of candies my way, probably in hopes that I'd cram one in my mouth and shut up.

It didn't work. I ranted for ten minutes straight before collapsing into her uncomfortable leather chair. My heart pounded. My pulse was up. The desire to cry was there, but I held it back because I was not going to let *any* guy milk me for tears.

"I'm so sorry this happened to you," she opened with.

"Thank you." I looked down at my legs, the left crossed over the right, studying the tip of my sneaker. I was embarrassed that I'd been so heated, but I felt better getting it all out there, even though my mom called emotional outbursts of this caliber "showing your butt."

I had, indeed, showed my butt. All of it. Full moon a-shining.

"I have a few thoughts," Mrs. Wong continued. "If you'd like to hear them? I can wait, too. I know you're upset and your well-being is my first concern."

Am I up for advice?

It's gotta be better than going back to class and getting stared at.

"Sure. I guess."

"We have a few options. The first is we could do sensitivity education regarding health—"

"No," I interrupted. "I don't want to make everyone sit through sensitivity training. They'd hate me."

Mrs. Wong nodded. "I was getting to that. On one hand, it'd improve some things, but it'd also leave you vulnerable in other ways. I understand how high school works, I like to think." She paused. "You aren't required to tell anyone your situation. You can tell them to mind their own business."

"Oh, don't worry about that. I will be doing that a lot. Often. And if they get too obnoxious, I'll..." I didn't finish the sentence, which was in actuality the worst thing I could have done in the situation—I just didn't realize it at the time. Mrs. Wong was already concerned about me, but hearing that, she went into hyperdrive. A straight-A student with monstrous SAT scores, one of the few diverse students at her curdled-cream high school, sounded like she might, maybe, drop out of school.

There was only one thing she could do.

Reach into her drawer and produce a pamphlet.

I don't get the thing with guidance counselors and pamphlets but they must have a club.

"I'd still like you to consider this program. It meets on Saturdays, there's a meeting one town over, from nine to two. It's for teen mothers trying to finish their educations while having a baby."

I stared at the sea of faces on the front of the pamphlet. It was pale to dark, left to right, diversity accounted for with white, Latina, Asian and black girls. All smiled. All were transposed over a black silhouette of a girl's body with a baby bump. Words like "friendship" and "support" and "resources" were in big pink block letters. It was inspiration porn, preggo-style.

"Thanks, but no thanks." I pushed the pamphlet back her way.

She frowned. "It's worth considering, Sara. The reality is, you're in a high-risk demographic, and I know your classmates finding out will challenge you for at least the foreseeable future. The teens in this program will know what you're going through. The counselors talk to girls like you every day—"

Bitterness flooded my mouth. It was like she'd grabbed my jaw, unhinged it and poured lemon juice straight into my face hole. "Oh, really? Girls like me? I have an almost perfect GPA. Are my SAT scores the best in the school, or top two or three? I had five Ivy League schools on my wish list and a good chance of getting into a couple of them. So are they really like me? *Really?* Because I'm betting there are some distinct differences that matter."

Mrs. Wong hesitated a moment before speaking. "Sara."

"Yes?"

"I mean no disrespect, of course, but—" she sighed and shook her head "—this class isn't about GPAs or Ivy League or anything to do with your privileges. You're all young people who are very likely not prepared—emotionally or financially—to bring a child into the world. You need to make a plan. Maybe focus less on what makes you different from the other pregnant students and look at what makes you similar."

Privileges.

She actually said that.

…and she's not wrong. I'm no better than anyone else.

The tears I'd promised myself I wouldn't shed rained hot against my cool cheeks. It was too much—Leaf's betrayal, Aaron and Jack the stranger, my own stupid choices. And now? Mrs. Wong pointing out in a very polite, roundabout way that I sounded like a spoiled, self-inflated brat. I jerked my head away so I didn't have to look at my counselor's pity face. She said nothing, just slid a box of Kleenex my way.

"I'll talk to your mother. We'll make a plan, the three of us. I want to help in any way I can," she finally settled on. She pulled the pamphlet away and tucked it into her desk drawer without another word.

"What is wrong? You look like someone punched you. They didn't, did they? If they did, you punch back."

Mormor was at the sink washing dishes when I came home. She had a dishwasher, she just didn't feel like it got the dishes clean enough, so she'd run the dishes through a dishwasher cycle and then spend an hour hand-washing them, too. I had no idea what the point of the first cycle was, and when I asked her about it, she hissed at me like a cat and kicked me out of the kitchen.

Mormor was particular. I chalked it up to her personal flavor of weird.

"No one punched me."

"Then what is it? You're upset. It's not good for the baby. Sit." She turned off the sink, dried her hands and went to the bread box in the corner. I watched her, irritated and sullen and refusing to talk, but then she produced the pepparkakor—Swedish ginger cookies. They were a common Christmas cookie, but Mormor tended to make them year round. Both I and fetus perked up. I reached for the plate before she even peeled the Saran wrap back, snatching a cookie and cramming it into my maw. She left me to my feeding so she could put on the electric kettle, producing two cups of tea just a minute later.

I doctored mine. She stirred hers. Staring.

Ever-staring Mormor. Like one of those lizards that only blinks once every two minutes.

"The kids found out," I finally managed. To reward myself for conversing like a human, I grabbed another cookie.

"Ah." She nodded. "Yes, that would be hard."

"One of my new friends told them. Well, told one person, who then probably told one person. I'm thinking they're not my friends anymore."

"That's too bad, but I understand why. It wasn't their business to tell. Were the kids terrible to you?"

"Not directly? They just looked at me a lot. One girl tried to get me to talk about it." I sipped my tea, my free hand going to my temple, which had started to pound. "I talked to Mrs. Wong at lunch. She told me I didn't have to tell anyone and then tried again to get me to go to some weekend program with other knocked-up teens. I'm like, 'no, thanks.'"

Mormor peered at me over the rim of her teacup. "Oh? Why?"

"I don't know."

And I didn't, really, beyond my gut saying that it was a waste of time. I had Mom and Mormor. I had Devi. It was something I'd have to wake up for on my precious sleep-in Saturdays. Etcetera, etcetera, etcetera. It was a whole long list of etceteras, none of the excuses really holding much water and boiling down to a toxic case of "dunwanna."

Mormor knew it, too.

"I'm going to tell you a story about my grandmother, your great-great-grandmother, Astridh, the woman I named your mother after," she said.

I didn't exactly want to hear a story about great-great-grandmother Astridh at that moment but the presence of pepparkakor said I could be bought. "Okay."

"Your great-great-great-grandmother, Elsa, got pregnant by a local boy. This was before people had safe choices about babies. She had the illegitimate baby—Astridh—

and lived at home until she met her husband at twenty. He was good to her, but not to Astridh. He didn't want her. The only children he was interested in were the ones he fathered."

She reached for a cookie, probably because she could see her cookie-less future if she let the preggo keep noshing on the baked goods.

She nibbled thoughtfully. "It was not easy for Astridh growing up in a house like that and it never got easier, so when her stepfather offered her a one-way ticket to the United States, she took it." Mormor paused. "She was fourteen years old."

That stopped me in my tracks. "...wait. You mean *by herself*?"

Mormor nodded. "Mmm. She was desperate to get away from a family that didn't want her, and they were desperate to be rid of her, so she got on a boat and immigrated. There were Swedish colonies in Maine, and opportunities for work. Astridh found housing with some other young women and worked at a shoe factory until she met and married my grandfather."

Mormor had never talked about any of that, and my initial disinterest gave way to a tremendous amount of respect for a woman I'd never gotten the chance to meet. "Wow, great-grandma times a billion was badass."

Mormor's lips twitched. "Yes, she was. Now then, why would I tell you about her now? You're a smart girl. Be smart for me."

"Because she was fearless and I should be fearless?" Admittedly, it was more a question than an answer, but after the day I'd had, I wasn't super willing to play games with Mormor. I didn't have a lot of gas left in my care tank.

"Not quite." Mormor shook her head. "She was terrified, and rightfully so. New place, new people. They didn't send her with money or valuables. She showed up to this country with the clothes on her back. No, the reason I tell you this is she got through her ordeal because of her community. She found her people. They took her in when she came here. They housed her, fed her, clothed her, found her work. They were the only people who understood what she'd gone through and what she'd need to prosper here."

Mormor looked at me pointedly.

I looked down at my cookie.

"I have you and Mom. And Devi," I said. I sounded petulant. My bottom lip was probably so pouty it protruded six feet from my face.

Mormor was unmoved.

"And none of us are going through what you're going through. Your mother was pregnant twenty years ago. Times have changed. We can empathize, but these are kids living your reality right now." She tapped the table and stood up to go back to her overachiever dish-washing routine. A moment later, her back still to me, she said, "I would consider the program, Serendipity. It doesn't sound like such a terrible idea to me."

My reply was to grunt and eat another cookie.

CHAPTER TWENTY-ONE

"I still think it's a great idea."

Those words, said by my mother over dinner about the Saturday morning teen-mom thing, were Brutus-on-Julius-Caesar-level betrayal. I gawked at her over my meatballs, her knife twisting between my shoulder blades.

"Seriously? You want me to go to preggo patty-cake meetings?"

"Mormor makes a great point," Mom said. "We had kids young, but it was different back then. Social media bullying, cell phones, networking—we didn't have any of that to deal with. This program will know how to navigate that stuff. Plus, there will be counselors you can talk to about things you're not comfortable talking to us about. Like gross biology stuff."

"I have Devi to talk to when I'm freaking out," I insisted.

"What does Devi know about delivering a baby?" Mormor asked. "Nothing. She hasn't done it. These people will educate you on the important things."

"Like the pooping on the delivery table thing," Mom said.

"...excuse me?" I looked down at my meatballs with gravy. I looked back at my mother. "Say what now?"

"Later," Mormor chided my mother.

"Later? Why later? Oh, God. What?" I looked between them. They were smiling at one another, like they were in on an I've-spewed-writhing-life-from-my-loins-and-you-haven't-yet power kick.

"It's not appropriate dinner conversation," my mother warbled, her bottom lip quivering.

"Okay, but you don't get to just drop that bomb—"

"Oh, it's a bomb alright," my mother murmured.

That was it. Both of them gave up on the pretense of not being wildly entertained by my poop trauma. Mom burst into laughter—big peals that bounced off the walls and ceiling to fill the room while my stoic, usually dour grandmother tittered into her napkin. Instead of making actual noise, she pretended to cough, but I knew what was up. I knew whose team she was on.

"It's totally natural," Mom managed. "Everyone does it. Almost. There's a lot of pressure down there."

Mormor pointed at my mother, nodded in agreement, but refused to look at me, too dignified to indulge such base humor.

Except she wasn't at all. She was laughing so hard, her shoulders were shaking.

I'm onto you, old lady.

"No," I said.

Mom quirked a blond brow. "No what?"

"NO, I REFUSE. I AM NOT POOPING ON THE DELIVERY TABLE."

"Oh! She refuses! Yes, okay. Well, you refuse, Sara. That'll do something, I'm sure," Mom said, stuffing meatballs into her mouth and smiling. I could see them there, smeared on her teeth, all brown and gooey.

"I'll talk to Dr. Cardiff at the next appointment," I said. "And you look like you ate poop, just so you know. I hope you're happy now."

"Mmmm. Delicious. I think I'll have more."

She stuffed another meatball into her face.

Disgusted, I grabbed my plate and stood to leave the dinner table. Mom reached for my elbow and Mormor pointed at my chair.

"Sit, please. I'm sorry." Mom dashed gravy off her bottom lip and got up to give me an awkward plate-between-us half hug. "We're being awful. Please stay?"

"Okay fine, but I don't want to hear the word *poop* from you again. Now or possibly ever." I took my seat and dug into my meatballs. In the wake of our conversation, I should have been way more disgusted about the food's sloppy brown appearance, but I was hungry, and Swedish meatballs are delicious, so down the hatch they went.

"When's your next doctor's visit?" Mormor asked, steering the conversation ship into safer waters.

Well, safer-ish waters. It got choppy fast.

"It's coming up, I think?"

Mom nodded. "Friday. Hopefully sprout will cooperate and we can gender them."

"Oh, good. I told my gardening club I think it's a girl, so let's see if I'm right." Mormor looked *too* smug, and I had visions of those over-the-top gender-reveal parties with people shooting colorful exploding canisters. The idea of it bugged me, and I was afraid my grandmother, in her Larssen pride, would bake forty billion blue or pink cupcakes post sonogram to celebrate.

"We're not going to make this a big deal, right?" I eyeballed them. "I'd prefer not to."

"What do you mean by big deal?" Mormor gave me a not altogether friendly look.

"I wanna keep this chill. No parties, no colorful cakes, or pink or blue confetti."

"Why?" she demanded.

I frowned. "Because I think it's weird to celebrate genitalia."

Mormor looked mutinous, which usually prefaced aerial shoes and squawking, so Mom sprung into action, her hand snapping out to grab Mormor's bicep and holding tight. "Wait, Ma. Can you explain, Sara? I don't think we're catching your drift."

I didn't want to explain, particularly not with Mormor

looking at me like she wanted to pummel me with the meatball dish, but I did because I'd opened up that can of worms. Might as well own all of its wormy goodness.

"Okay, so Morgan—" Saying Morgan's name made me tense up because I'd liked her, a lot, and what had happened hurt, but I cleared my throat and pressed on. "Morgan's a girl. If her parents had one of those parties, they'd have popped a blue canister or eaten a blue cake. But she's a girl. Those parties celebrate dicks and vag, not people."

"We don't say dick at the dinner table," Mormor snapped.

"Can the language, Sara, but I get what you're saying." Mom looked over at Mormor. "We can respect that reasoning, right, Ma?"

"Mmm." Mormor shook off my mother and took the dinner plates to the sink, her back to us. Her earlier good mood had evaporated all because I'd suggested she shouldn't make cupcakes.

Screw today.

"I'm going to head upstairs," I announced. "Unless you want my help cleaning up?"

Mormor didn't answer me, which meant the silent treatment was back in effect. Mom rolled her eyes. She got up from the table and walked me to the stairs, and then up the stairs, tagging along behind me. When I ducked into my room, she ducked in with me and closed the door behind her.

"She'll get over it," she said.

"I know. She's old and set in her ways." I plopped on my bed and grabbed my phone from the end table. Devi had texted me, which was a relief. I'd sent her a message after school to complain about Leaf and company but she'd been busy at cheerleading practice.

"Yep, and it's no excuse, but you're probably not going to change her mind. You gave her a fair explanation, though. If she chooses to ignore it, that's on her, not you, but it'd be really weird if she threw a gender-reveal party and neither baby nor Mom were there. You've got her by the short and curlies, kiddo."

I was about to start texting Devi, but Mom sat on the end of my bed and plucked the phone from my hands. I didn't want mother-daughter bonding time, not after everything I'd been through that day, but it seemed like I'd been overruled.

"Are you okay?" Mom asked. "Like, for real. Mrs. Wong called me at work convinced you were going to drop out. I told her you wouldn't make that decision without me. I wasn't talking out of my butt, was I?"

"No? No." I shook my head. "I'll finish. I'm just pissed that my new friends outed me. I'm pissed that I spent lunch in Mrs. Wong's office and then had to run from class to class so people wouldn't stop me in the hall to get the scoop. I'm pissed I had to avoid eye contact with everyone or I'd see everyone staring at me. I'm pissed I don't know stuff about what's going to happen to me and my body, and about this Saturday program thing, and at Mormor. I'm just… I'm mad."

Mom nodded and reached out to pat my stomach through my pants, her palm rubbing over it in circles. It felt nice, and a microscopic amount of tension eased out of me. "Pissed is better than sad, but pissed can become sad. You know I'm here. I'm listening. I don't want you to do the Saturday program if it's going to make you unhappy. That said, I don't see the harm in trying it for a couple weeks. Say, three weeks. And if that sucks, whatever. I won't bring it up again. What do you think?"

I thought it sounded like a nuisance, but she was being reasonable and it was hard to argue with reasonable, particularly when you were tired and miserable and wanted her to go away.

"Yeah, sure, okay," I said.

"Alright! Cool. I'll call Mrs. Wong and let her know. Maybe she'll stop panicking. She was really worked up."

So was I when I was in her office, I thought, but I didn't say it because saying it would encourage more dialogue and I was dialogued out. Mom leaned over me and pressed a kiss to my forehead, her pale hair sliding past my face. I forced a smile for her and she turned for the door. Just before she left, she paused and pulled her silk short-sleeve shirt aside to show me a circular patch on her upper arm. It took me a minute to recognize it as a nicotine patch.

"I'm listening," she repeated. "Seriously."

Before I could answer, she stepped outside and closed the door.

CHAPTER TWENTY-TWO

By the time I got to texting Devi, I was tired of talking about my day. I'd shown my butt to Mrs. Wong, Mormor and Mom, in that order. A fourth set of ears wasn't going to make me feel better. It was beating a dead horse with a broom immediately after you'd beaten it with a stick.

I kept the conversation brief.

Devi's ever-loyal response was, "I hope they get eaten by marmots."

I kept her around for a reason.

The constant fatigue of incubating a human plus the emotional fatigue of *existing* meant I went to bed doing half of my homework and leaving the rest to the YOLO gods. Somehow, despite ten hours of sleep, I was still dragging the next morning. Complicating it was the fact that I simply did not want to go to school and face more of my classmates' rubbernecking about my pregnancy. Staying home was tempting, but I was afraid if I did that, Mrs. Wong would send out a SWAT team to find me.

I pulled on a pair of leggings and a tank top before shouldering into a red-and-black-checked flannel that didn't button quite how I wanted it to anymore so I just left it open. Combat boots, a quick brush of the hair, a clip and I was downstairs foraging for food.

I was awaiting the pop of the toaster when something significant occurred to me.

It was my first morning without morning sickness.

"Heeeeey, thanks for not making me wanna paint the world with barf," I said to my stomach. In response, the passenger yowled for sustenance, so a bagel in half the bites it ought to have taken and I was off to the pit of despair known as school. My heart raced as I approached the front double doors, my shoulders so tense I trembled, but a few long, deep breaths and I forged ahead, wearing my very best "Just Don't" face, which was really just me borrowing Mormor's 24/7 resting bitch face. It came in handy every once in a while.

Once again, I navigated the gauntlet of horrified-slash-curious classmates, managing to dodge four conversations with kids who'd collectively talked to me for six seconds total since I'd started at Stonington but who suddenly wanted to be my closest confidantes. It seemed everyone wanted "the scoop."

What they got was a scoop full of nothin'.

Lunchtime, to maintain whatever chill I still had, I snuck off to the library. No one was supposed to bring food or drink in there, but a quiet inquiry to Mrs. Wong about needing refuge from my circling classmates and she'd called in a favor to the librarian. Five minutes later, I had a nice table by a sign that read Periodicals, except there were no periodicals, just computers lined up on desks against the wall. It was chicken salad and an ebook on my cell phone and a whole lot of much-needed peace and quiet.

Until Leaf, Morgan and Erin showed up.

They didn't come immediately, probably because they were hunting me through the school like a pack of hounds, but a few minutes into my lunch, they appeared, backpacks strapped to their backs. Morgan and Erin were shoulder to shoulder, frowning at me, Morgan's crazy orange hair slicked up to stand on end, Erin plain-faced with no makeup in a dress reminiscent of Wednesday Addams. Looming in the back, Leaf had his hands in his jeans pockets while he stared at the industrial carpet beneath his boots.

I blinked at them, unimpressed. My tongue lashed out to rid my lower lip of chicken salad smear.

"It's my fault," Morgan started, stepping away from Erin's side to whirl a chair around so she could straddle it, her lean arms laid across the chair back. "I'm really, really sorry. After you left, Leaf told me what happened and

I went in to tell Erin. My parents had come home. My mom overheard me. She's friends with half the neighborhood, so then they knew, and it went from there. I wasn't careful, but I promise I didn't tell anyone other than Erin. I'm just loud and stupid."

"And I didn't say anything, I promise," Erin said. "Like, I'll swear on my cat and I really love my cat."

You really love your cat?

Okay, weird thing to swear on but I guess I get the point.

I sighed and put my phone aside, looking from Morgan to Erin and back again. "You guys screwed me. I know you didn't mean to, but—"

"I know, and I'm really, really sorry. But I think you're cool and I just—I'd like to fix this? I'll crotch punch anyone who gives you shit about it, I swear. Crap. Sorry." Morgan glanced over her shoulder to see if the librarian had overheard, but Mr. Chekowitz was busy reshelving books across the room. Morgan turned back my way. "I really don't like to hurt my friends, and I'd like to think you're my friend? I'm serious about the crotch punching for anyone who messes with you."

Thanks, I think?

"I feel awful," Leaf murmured. When he looked at me, it was with the puppy-dog sad eyes. Aaron used to do that to make me less mad, like if I felt sorry enough for him, I could push my upset away and focus on what *really* mattered in the situation, which were his guilty feelings. I must have scowled making that parallel because Leaf took a step back and cleared his throat.

Maybe he's being sincere?

Or maybe I'm being an idiot because I caught an easy crush.

"Leaf likes you," Morgan blurted.

"Morgan!" Leaf barked at her and shook his head, his brow knitting. "Leave it alone."

"Dude, I may have ruined everything for you and that sucks." She looked from him back to me. "So. Yeah. He likes you and don't blame him for me being a jerk. I pushed him into telling me. I'm a crap friend on two accounts."

"Three," Erin corrected. "You just totally outed him to the girl he likes."

"Okay, fine, three, but if it makes anything better, it was worth it." Morgan got up from her seat to stand in front of Leaf, her back now to me. She was tall, but he was taller, and they stared at one another. "She's cool. I'm sorry to screw that up, man."

Leaf rolled his head back. He looked tired and stressed and pretty miserable. When he didn't say anything, Morgan reached for Erin's hand and tugged her along out of the library, both of them mumbling goodbyes. That left me with a guilty-looking Rom who couldn't *quite* look me in the eye.

Likes you, Morgan said.

Not liked. Likes.

Maybe…

Uggggh. Why is this so hard?

"I'm not sure what I'm supposed to say beyond I'm sorry, I broke your trust and I won't ever do it again," Leaf said. He gestured at the chair across from me that Morgan had just vacated—it was a question, to see if I'd welcome his company. I nodded. He shucked his backpack and turned the chair back around to sprawl, or try to sprawl, a big, heavy guy in a plastic wreck of a seat shifting his weight as he tried to get comfortable. He ran a hand down his face and then through his hair, tugging on his black ponytail. "She's not lying. I do like you. This is so uncomfortable."

"Yeah, it is," I said. He glanced at me, his worry on full display. I managed a small smile for him in spite of it all. Yes, he'd pissed me off, but I was warming up to him again because, in part, I'm a sucker for punishment, but also, can you really blame me? My micro-crush had just admitted to micro-crushing back. Morgan's explanation certainly painted Leaf in a better light, and in Leaf's shoes, maybe I'd have done similar.

Slow down, Sara. Slow down.

He's still new. You need to be smart about this.

I cleared my throat. "I mean, it's not okay what you did, but I don't hate you or anything. I'm mad, but that's mostly because everyone around here is acting like they've never seen a pregnant chick before."

"They haven't because she dropped out," Leaf said. "Got her GED instead. She didn't want to deal with the garbage. She was one of three brownish girls in her senior class, and people were crappy to her already, never mind with a baby coming, so she went to night school instead. I hope you have a better time of it than she did."

"I hope so, too." While his sister's path wasn't one I particularly wanted for myself, acknowledging it existed if things went topsy-turvy—or topsier and turvier, if that was possible—was a comfort. Well, it would be if everything turned out okay for her, anyway. "How's she doing? Your sister?"

Leaf smiled, the strain on his face evaporating as he talked about his family. "Miri's great. She lives with her husband, Eric, and my niece, Elana, at a military base in Florida. Just got stationed there. We'll see them again during the holiday, or we'll go see them if he can't get time off. I'm not sure how that works with the army but I'm excited. I miss her."

"That's cool."

Leaf nodded and reached into his bag for his phone, promptly producing a zillion photographs of a toddler with black hair and dark brown eyes. I could see a little bit of Leaf in her nose and chin.

"She looks like you. Right here, the jaw shape in particular." I tapped the screen of his phone.

"The poor kid."

I snorted. "Hardly! You're cute as hell! She's a lucky kid."

The words spilled out before I could think better of them. Heat flooded my cheeks, my eyes darting up to his face. He was peering at me, his head cocked to the side. "You think so?"

"Well, yeah. Different circumstances, sure." The silence between us was heavy, like sediment, and I squirmed in my chair, devolving from teenaged girl to a worm on hot pavement in two seconds. "I know you can't really date a pregnant girl, though."

"Oh? Well, not if she doesn't want me to, no." He

reached for his phone, and I slid it into his big palm, my fingers grazing his.

"Oh," I said. "I thought, after we talked the other night, you were all set with me that way. I suspected you liked me, but you got different after I told you about the kid."

"I was worried about what my father would think more than anything," he admitted. "I think I told you that some Rom have strict beliefs? My grandmother was a traditionalist, and I was afraid—well. It doesn't matter what I was afraid of because my father was good about it. He said you're like Miri, if she hadn't been lucky enough to find a good boy. He told me to consider that it's extra responsibility to support someone in your situation, but I'm okay with that if you are."

It sounded almost *too* easy. Wasn't it supposed to bother him more? Or bother me that people would judge him because of me?

"Would you like to go out with me on Friday?" he asked, gentle and quiet and unassuming, which was not a side of Leaf I'd seen before. He was big and brash and loud, but this was none of those things. "If not, I completely understand, and I'd be glad to be your friend, either way. I really don't want you to hate me."

"I don't hate you," I said.

Anymore.

Earlier, I kinda wanted to light you on fire, sure, but who's counting?

He eyed me from under a fringe of thick inky lashes. "There's a movie playing everyone's talking about. A comedy. Really funny, I guess? I'd cook for you before, maybe?"

That sounded way more awesome than it should have. Where was all that irritation? Where was my righteous indignation?

Did Aaron teach me nothing?

"I'd love to," I said.

Nope, nothing.

"Good. Great. I... Thanks, Sara." Leaf stood from his seat, smiling and reaching for his backpack. "I won't let you down. I gotta go now, though, if I want to catch something to eat before the bell." He motioned over his shoulder at Mr. Chekowitz. I hadn't noticed until then that he was eyeballing us, probably to inform me that his leniency regarding my lunch didn't extend to my friends, too, without explicit permission.

That's just how adults do.

"Okay, thanks. I'll see you later," I said.

In class.

And then on our date.

Holy crapsicles.

CHAPTER TWENTY-THREE

"He probably thinks you're easy," Mormor said.

"Mom! Will you just...talk less. Okay? Talk less."

Both my mother and grandmother glowered at one another over a pile of potatoes. I, meanwhile, shoveled food into my maw. Sure, what Mormor said was screwed up, but when you expected very little of people, they rarely disappointed you.

It was how I survived living with Mormor most days.

"What? She *is* pregnant! There is only one way for that to happen." Mormor snorted and poured gravy over everything on her plate. "I love Sara, but we cannot avoid the truth that she had intercourse to get here. Now, this boy is probably thinking he can have plenty of it with her without consequence."

Is that what I did in that truck? Have "intercourse"? 'Cause it felt a lot like fu—

"Or maybe he's a decent kid and that didn't occur to him at all." Mom grabbed a roll from the basket for herself before lobbing one my way. It bounced off my head and onto my plate, splashing gravy across my shirt and making me look like a Jackson Pollock painting. My care cup was empty. I bit into the roll and eyed my grandmother while I chewed, slow and deliberate, not unlike a cow with its cud.

"She can still get the AIDS," Mormor announced, swinging her watery blue gaze my way. "You will need to practice safe sex regardless."

"Great dinner conversation. Really engaging. So glad I brought up that I have a date," I said. "I love it when we talk about The AIDS over meat loaf."

Mormor snuffled. "You have a baby to think about now is all I am saying."

Mom looked like she wanted to crawl under the table and die. Instead, she grabbed my hand and squeezed my fingers. "This is her way of worrying about you, I promise. On the bright side, aren't you glad your mom is a functional adult most of the time? The weirdest thing I ever did was have an abbreviated Juggalo phase and name you Serendipity."

"Are those the murder clowns?" Mormor demanded. "I hated them. That was terrible. You looked like a demon slut."

Anything I could say—about Leaf, murder clowns or The AIDS—would turn into an argument I didn't want to have. I kept to my food and minded my business. My mother hadn't told me I couldn't go out with Leaf, so I was keeping my plans. If in some weirdo parallel universe he really was just going out with me because pregnancy equated to *easy* in his mind, he was going to be really, really disappointed.

Jack was the exception, not the rule. It took Aaron a year to go spelunking in my undies.

The conversation shifted from me to Mormor's bridge quartet, Mormor complaining about her friend Florence's insistence on cutting the crusts off her finger sandwiches. I took that as a cue that I was clear to take off and, finishing my dinner, I loaded the dishwasher before excusing myself to study. I pulled out my review packets for an exam I had the next day, but I also pulled out my phone and immediately messaged Devi.

Wifey. Guess what.

What, she sent back.

Date with Leaf Friday.

NOWAY. She followed that up with, What time I'll do your face. lol do your face get it.

I snickered.

pervy ace friend is pervy. no idea on time yet.

gray ace perv thx. see you after school Fri. :) :)

I put the phone aside and concentrated on my homework. There wasn't much to review that I didn't already know, so I finished before eight. I slid out of my school clothes and into some light cotton pajamas. Sprawled out in my bed, I played phone games, overcame a preggo hormonal surge by wanking myself stupid and then passed out. The early nights were becoming habitual, as were the mornings where I woke covered in sweat, my discarded pants lying in a heap on the floor beside my bed. Hormones had turned me into a furnace.

A shower to rinse my gross body, and it was back to the grindstone: dressed, breakfast, heart palpitations as I approached the school doors and trudging down the hall with my head high, eyes not meeting anyone else's.

I was almost to my first class when I heard *the voice*.

"Hey, Mamacita! How you doing today?"

I turned toward the kid, blinking slowly, my hand gripping the nylon strap of my backpack so hard I thought I'd tear it off the main satchel. I didn't even know his name. He was tall and handsome and wearing a Patriots' Brady jersey, which immediately added to his pecker-head quotient. I was fine-ish with other players, but Brady was an insta-eyeroll.

"What'd you say?"

He glanced at two of his friends, grinned and shrugged. "Just saying hey."

"No, you said mamacita. Why?"

He blinked at me. "It was a joke."

"Oh? It's funny? HAHA, sure, okay. Super funny. Are you Spanish? Latino?" I closed in on him, until I was less than a foot away, my head tilted back so I could look him right in the eye. His eyes were pinched at the corners, mouth flat, smile evaporating.

"Me? No. I'm Irish." Again, he looked away from me, color rising in his cheeks. "It was just a joke."

"Pointing out I'm pregnant and Hispanic is a joke? Wow. You're a comedian. Super funny. Like, I nearly peed my pants." I turned on my heel and stomped away, shaking my head. "I'm going to be laughing all the way to first period, whatever-your-name-is. You are one funny guy!"

He was braver now that I'd put distance between us, and called out, "You don't have to be such a bitch about it."

Which was promptly answered by Mr. Hayes, one of the chemistry teachers, shouting out "MICHAELS, GET IN HERE, NOW!" from the doorway of his classroom.

Bagged, asshole. Enjoy your detention.

There was some satisfaction there, but not enough to overcome the sheer WTF-ery going on in my brain about the situation. I got through my classes like a zombie, not seeing or hearing, not really keeping with the program beyond shuffling along and groaning every once in a while. When lunchtime came, I debated where I should go to eat—to the library for some peace, or to the cafeteria to sit with my no-longer-so-estranged friends.

As much as I'd have liked to stare at Leaf awhile, appreciating that he had not two dimples but only one on the left side, the library won out, particularly after Mamacita. I settled in with a book and my packed lunch, inhaling my tuna fish with not a small amount of indelicacy. I would regret this choice mere minutes later when none other than my Friday date himself presented himself on my proverbial doorstep.

I smelled like a haddock.

Awesome.

"Hey," I said, eyes sweeping over his jeans, new sneakers, T-shirt and a plaid shirt he'd left unbuttoned.

"Hello there, Serendipity." He had such a nice voice, rich and deep, and he played my name like an instrument. It made me wriggle all over like an excited puppy.

…most things did. The hormones were intense.

"Hey." I glanced over at Mr. Chekowitz. His gray head was dipped forward as he filed books on a cart. "Not sure I'm supposed to have company? They made an exception to the rule to let me eat here."

"Don't worry." Leaf winked at me before sauntering over to talk to the librarian. I couldn't hear their exchange, but Leaf smiled a lot, motioned at me, and Mr. Chekowitz nodded his grizzled head. The charming boy had charmed someone else. Not surprising, and I pushed aside my book bag at the table so Leaf could sit beside me.

"We have to be quiet. I promised," Leaf said in a conspirator's whisper before plopping down into his seat and unloading about forty tons of home-cooked food.

"Whoa, what is this?" I poked at the red top of the plastic.

"Deliciousness." He doled out portions, halving everything. I eyed my brown-sack lunch, half of it gone already.

"…I kinda ate."

"You're not hungry?"

"No, I am. I always am lately. The kid likes their food. I just feel bad."

"Don't. Eat or I'll be insult—mmm. I should explain." Leaf produced a pair of plastic forks and motioned at me to dig in. "I told you many Rom have food rules, right?"

"Mmm-hmm." I could have argued more with him about whether or not I should let him throw food into my facial garbage disposal. Or I could enjoy the bounty before me.

Bounty it was.

Leaf continued. "I don't like to use the word superstitions, but we have certain cultural beliefs. Things are pure or impure—impurity is bad. The word my family uses is mochadi. It means dirty, essentially. We strive to not be mochadi." He paused. "Mochadi is much more than just a physical thing. It's spiritual, too, and the rules about how to avoid it change depending on which Romani person you talk to. Even the word changes, because we were run out of most places we tried to settle.

"When we finally got somewhere we *could* stay, we assimilated. Our traditions are melting pots of our culture and local customs. Where we live, our religion, how many other Romani people are in our communities will determine how we judge things as mochadi. My grandmother was more strict upholding those cleanliness standards than my father. My father is stricter than me. Me and Dad are Americanized, but my grandmother was a refugee from the Holocaust during World War Two. Many Romani people were killed by the Nazis. She was very—the rules were like granite for her. I think in a way they anchored her when she fled to the United States with her family. They were few Rom in a sea of gadze. What they knew were themselves and their traditions."

I'd stopped eating, not because I was full—I wasn't sure I'd ever be full again with a human growing inside of me—but because I was interested. "That's really cool."

"It is and it's not? It's just like anything else, really." He frowned. "My father brought us to this town because it was near the hospital where my mother was being treated when she got sick. There aren't any other Rom here, which means many people don't have our standards for cleanliness. And our traditions—you can catch mochadi almost like a cold. That's why we wash our hands a lot. There are strict rules about food preparation and dishes. There are even strict rules about leftovers. But like I said before, it's not all about the physical stuff, either. It's about spiritual stuff, too. My grandmother wouldn't talk during meals at all because she believed ill thoughts and bad luck would creep in through her open mouth while she ate. That could lead to uncleanliness. And etiquette—to breach our etiquette rules—could make you mochadi."

He tapped his fingers on the lid of his Tupperware. "This is a long way of saying one of our customs is to feed our loved ones. If I give you food, it's because I am showing my appreciation of you. To not accept is a slight—if you were Rom and rejecting my food, you could be suggesting I'm mochadi. While I know you, Sara, aren't accusing me of being mochadi by refusing, I always wince. It's how I was brought up. I mean no offense."

"No, I totally get it. Well, I mean, not totally because

that was an abbreviated version but I can see why you'd flinch." I paused. "Do you want me to go wash my hands? I did a little while ago, before lunch. I don't want you to get mochadi cooties from me."

"No! No, oh. Oh, Sara. I don't mean to say—" He frowned and shook his head, reaching for my hand. He looked at it, then up at me. "Look at this hand. It's wonderful. Exactly as God intended it to be. I don't think you're impure, or that you can make me impure. Truly, I don't. I just wanted to give context. I know I act different sometimes, but you are perfect as you are." As if to prove his point, he lifted my hand and proceeded to press his soft, dry lips to the pad of my pointer finger. And then my middle finger. And then my pinky. His eyes fixed on mine, and for a moment, my heart stopped. He had a beautiful mouth, truly, with the delicate arch in his upper lip, and that flurry of kisses—to show how mochadi he thought I wasn't—pretty much destroyed me.

Aaaaand maybe destroyed that resolve I had about not screwing around again.

I'm a slut, maybe.

Totally okay with it.

"Yeah," I said, because a poet I am not. "Yeah, totally. I get it."

He let go of my hand, albeit reluctantly, before going back to his meal.

"Good. I am glad."

So was I.

CHAPTER TWENTY-FOUR

Devi texted me Thursday night just before nine, when I was deep in my evening PJ sprawl. There was a half-eaten jar of Nutella beside me and no knife. That's right, I finger-swipe ate half a jar of Nutella and there were no regrets.

I was living my best life. Even if that much Nutella translated to never pooping again.

Hey, got permission from Mom btws, she sent.

I didn't know what she was talking about.

For?

To go with you tomorrow. She's dismissing me at one.

My brain immediately went to, *On my date?* but then I remembered the other momentous occasion on my plate, which was finding out the flavor of the belly sprout. I didn't recall ever inviting Devi along, but I wouldn't mind having her there, either. I just had to make sure Mom was okay with it.

And I had to see if Mormor planned to go. Devi deserved fair warning. She could wear some Kevlar or maybe a magical medallion to keep the evil away.

I tromped downstairs. Mom and Mormor were in the living room, both knitting. Mom hadn't been a knitter before we'd moved in, but she'd picked it up as an activity she could do with her mother that *usually* wouldn't devolve into arguing or shoe throwing. Mormor was big into crafts and kept her stash of craft stuff in the spare bedroom upstairs. It was thirty years of accumulation, from pastels to paints to stencils to yarn to woodcrafts. She had wall-to-wall craft cabinets that made Michaels look pretty amateur hour.

I'd been given glimpses of the place before Mormor had quite literally locked me and everyone else out of her she-cave. She hoarded acrylic craft paints like Smaug with his gold.

Mom's knitting needles clicked furiously. She glanced my way, tossing her head to get her too-long blond bangs out of her face.

"Hey there, peaches."

"Hey. Can Devi come with us to the ultrasound tomorrow? Her mom gave permission."

"I don't see why n—"

"Am I invited?" Mormor interrupted. I flinched. I'd figured Mom would have already brought it up to her, but apparently I'd figured wrong.

"Of course you are," I said.

"Why didn't anyone tell me sooner? I'm very busy you know," she said.

"Because reading *Better Homes and Gardens* can wait an hour while you come see your great-grandkid," Mom replied. "I was supposed to invite you and I forgot, but I also planned on you going, so…"

Mormor sniffed. "Maybe I will, maybe I won't."

"Can you not, Ma? Don't punish Sara because I screwed up." Mom's eye twitched. That was the precursor to loud noises and verbal bombardment. Maybe instead of aerial shoes, there'd be aerial knitting needles, which sounded a lot more dangerous.

Like tiny javelins.

"We'll go tomorrow, it'll be cool," I said, trying to keep the peace before someone got murdered. "I'd like you there, Mormor."

It was a lie. It was *such* a lie, but what else could I do?

Fortunately, it appeased the beast. Mormor relaxed, her knitting returned to a craft and not a potential blood sport. "Well, I have to go then, if you'd like me there. No need to get testy, Astrid. All you had to tell me was Sara wanted me there. Why wouldn't she want her Mormor there?"

If looks could kill, Mormor would have ceased to be on

the spot. Mom had her laser stare going. I reached out to squeeze her shoulder. She tapped the backs of my knuckles with her knitting needle. "Don't leave me here. When have I ever forsaken you?" she whispered.

"Sorry, gotta sleep, yo. I do as the kid demands."

"Damn you, grandchild of mine. Damn you. Tell Devi we'll pick her up at half past one." Mom swooped in to brush a kiss to my temple.

I trundled upstairs, tired, but my brain was on fire, too. I kept thinking about Leaf. Even as I texted instructions to Devi about pickup times, I thought about Leaf. When I turned off the light, I thought about Leaf. I kept mentally replaying that moment when his soft lips met my fingertips. I'd get no rest until I sated the horny brain beast, so I relieved myself of some pent-up tension. It was never glamorous to wank oneself to sleep, but I never claimed to be glamorous in the first place. I passed out with my head in the pillow, my hand still stuffed down the front of my pajama pants.

You know you're tired when you don't even bother to hide the evidence of your most private deeds.

I slogged through the next school day, my head feeling like a bowling ball. Leaf sat next to me in Weller's class as the old lady holler-lectured for an hour straight.

Leaf brushed my hand with his before he parted for his next class. Again, I was reminded of the fingertip kisses from the day before. Again, I had a reaction in the pants parts because that shit was intense. I'd overcome it by the time lunch came and shifted my focus to deciding between eating in the library or the cafeteria. In the end, the cafeteria won; I couldn't be the Periodical Troll forever. Besides, everyone had left me alone all day. What happened with that butthead kid, Michaels, and his Mamacita comment must have gotten around.

"I was thinking of cooking tonight," Leaf said, sitting next to me. Erin and Morgan sat across from us. "Then maybe we could go to the movies?" He glanced at Morgan. "I'm missing hangouts tonight, by the way. Sara and I are going out."

Morgan grinned at me from behind her Capri Sun. "Fiiiiine."

"Sure. What time should I come over?" I asked.

"I can pick you up if you need, or—do you have a car?"

I shrugged. "Access to, most of the time, but Mom'll probably dump me off at your place so she can escape my grandmother. She goes out for drinks with her work friends on Fridays. She says she drinks to keep Mormor pretty."

Leaf chuckled. "I can see where you get your fire from. And that'd be perfect. I can drive you home after the movie."

"Awesome."

I smiled at him. He smiled back.

Morgan gagged.

"You guys are so gross," she said.

Leaf snorted and waved his fork in her direction. "Says the girl who spends half her time diving for Erin's lungs with her tongue."

"Those are exceptionally sexy lungs, thankyouverymuch." Morgan winked at Erin. "I love your lungs, beautiful."

Erin poked herself in the side of the boob. "Yeah, you do. You love them a lot."

"I didn't even mean *those*!"

"Maybe not this time you didn't." Erin blew Morgan a kiss. Morgan pretended to catch it midair and devour it. It was pretty weird, but Erin giggled, so I guessed that's all that mattered.

"You two excited for tonight?" Erin asked.

My cheeks went hot. Leaf shrugged.

"I'd say so, yes," he said. "But, even if it's just a friend date, we'll have fun. We get along. I think it'll be a good time."

I nodded, swallowing past a lump in my throat that was not Leaf's shared lamb and rice. "Yeah. I—yeah," I said, because that's all I could manage.

Morgan's smile was slow and wide.

"You're grosssss," Morgan replied. "Soooooo. Verrrrry. Grosssss."

What was also gross was cold goopy jelly smeared over a belly sporting new dark hairs that weren't there the week before. Body hair in itself wasn't a problem—razors existed. I was comfortable with the de-furring that went along with being a pale-ass Swede with thick black Hispanic hair. However, hair you didn't notice until your pants were rolled down, when you had a doctor, your mother, your grandmother and your best friend gathered around you all staring at it? That was an issue.

I wanted to reach down and pluck them out one at a time. Alas, the pushy wand was there, cold and insistent as it skimmed over my firm, slightly rounded midsection. I was doomed to remain yeti-like until I got home.

"You know, this would be easier if you weren't looking like you," I said to Devi. "Like, here I am all lumpy and furry with my pants rolled down and you're standing there being perfect. Be uglier, please?"

She smirked, but she really did look like a supermodel, with her cashmere sweater and designer jeans and who-knew-what-designer brown leather shoes. Her hair was covered by a beautiful purple scarf with gold medallions. Her ears rocked diamond studs she'd gotten for Hanukkah from her grandparents the year before.

Devi rolled her eyes.

"You look fine! You're at the doctor's office. No one's pretty here."

"You are, I bet," I said. "And do you have weird belly fur? No, no, you do not."

"Hair growth is normal during pregnancy." Dr. Cardiff rotated the wand around and dug it in halfway between my belly button and pelvis. I winced, but she just kept right on pressing.

"My nipples got hairy," my mom offered. "During breast feeding, so that's something to look forward to. Chest hair like a gorilla."

What.

No.

"You're lying." I swung my gaze to Dr. Cardiff's profile. "Tell me she's lying?"

Dr. Cardiff shrugged. "Sorry to say, I can't help you. It happens."

"Oh, God, that's balls." My hands went to my boobs and gave them a preemptive sorry-little-buddies squeeze.

"Don't swear," Mormor said, flicking my ear. "It's un-ladylike."

My would-be brilliant retort about social expectations thrust on young women in the guise of words like *ladylike* fizzled when, up on the screen, appeared not a legume-slash-alien like my last ultrasound, but a real tiny human. With arms and legs. With eyes and a chin.

Oh, my God, the baby looks like a baby.

I stared.

"There they are," Dr. Cardiff said, adjusting her teal glasses on her nose. She pointed at the screen, tracing the outline of my kid's face with its bump of a nose and giant fivehead. Yeah, the kid got a big forehead, just like their mother, but no worries, I'd teach them an appropriate comb-over technique as soon as they had hair.

Hair like my sad stomach, and my soon-to-be sadder nipples.

"That is a Larssen," Mormor said, nodding. "Look, the profile is just like yours, Astrid."

"The poor kid," Mom replied.

"Did we want to know the gender?" Dr. Cardiff asked, probably hoping to ward off another Larssen-fest.

"Uh, yeah." Devi looked down at me with a huge grin. "This is so cool. You want to know, right? I mean, that's why we're here?" She squeezed my hand. I squeezed hers right back.

I nodded, breathless, and Dr. Cardiff grinned. "Looks like you're a superfecta, ladies. It's a girl."

…a girl.

Wow, it's a girl.

I hadn't considered the gender thing too much, not beyond telling Mormor she couldn't make colored cakes or give out cigars, but hearing that the kid was a girl was a relief. I knew how to girl. Sort of. And what I didn't know, Aunt Devi did know. Or my mom knew. Or, God forbid, Mormor knew. And if it turned out none of the girl stuff was for my kid, when they had the wherewithal to determine their own gender, okay, cool. That gave me extra time to figure out how to bring up a boy or a non-binary kid.

"Rad," Devi said, stealing my word for her own. "That's totally rad."

"Yeah it is. Now Sara doesn't have to worry about training a kid to not firehose the bathroom wall with urine." Mom ruffled my hair before pressing a kiss to my forehead. "Grats, kiddo. Let's hope our periods don't all sync up."

Mormor, in typical, stoic Mormor fashion, waved at the monitor. "I knew it was a girl. Larssens have girls. Do you have a name figured out yet, Sara?"

"Cass," I said, without hesitation, surprising me as much as everyone else in the room. "Cassiopeia."

CHAPTER TWENTY-FIVE

"What about Cathy?" Mormor suggested. "Catherine, Cathleen. It's a lovely, traditional name. You could pick—C or K."

I sat in the back seat with Devi while Mom guided the car into the fast-food line at McDonald's. Mom answered the call of the wild—aka my needy kid growling inside of my stomach—with the golden arches. Mormor sat beside her in the front seat clutching her handbag.

"I like Cass," I said.

"Agnes is a traditional Swedish name. I had an

aunt named Agnes. My mother's name was Iris. That's pretty, too."

"I like Cass," I repeated.

"Two double bacon—two, Sara?" Mom asked from the front seat.

I nodded. "Yes, please."

"Make it three. I'm going to solidarity-eat bacon," Devi said. "You can nail me to this cross. Soz, Christians. Too soon?"

Mom and I weren't practicing anything so we didn't care. The only one who went to church was Mormor, but she was too caught up in the baby-name debate to defend her Lutheran savior.

"What about Brita?" Mormor pressed.

"That's a water filter, Mormor. No. I like Cassiopeia, like the constellation."

Mormor looked appalled. "That poor child is going to have to spell that in kindergarten."

"Leave it alone, Ma. Sara figured out how to spell her name eventually. She was sixteen, but I'm still really proud of her. Do you want anything?" Mom asked.

"I want her to name my great-granddaughter something normal."

"Okay, that's not really your call. A cheeseburger, however…"

"No. I don't eat this garbage. I could make you a perfectly good cheeseburger at home."

"I'm sure you could. Sara's hungry now." Mom rolled up to the intercom. Fortunately, after Devi and I acquired our newest round of hot grilled garbage, Mormor was sullen and stopped talking. I was okay with that. The cheese-burger was far more pleasant, anyway.

Back to the house we went, Devi in tow so she could do my makeup pre-date. Mom didn't ask many questions about my plans with Leaf beyond what time I'd be back—which was midnight, I promised, and no later. She accepted it without another word, which was weird. Normally, she was all up in my business, giving me warnings to protect myself from all sorts of awful stuff, but not this time. Maybe she figured there was less to lose with me already knocked up? Except that wasn't true at all. I could get diseases or abused by weird dudes on the bus or mauled by bears if I wandered too close to the zoo.

Had things changed so much? Did she think I had the wisdom of ages because I was going to birth a baby with a fivehead?

I chewed on my lip thinking about it all the way home. I thought, maybe, I was just worrying too much and it'd die down, but as we climbed from the car, Mormor going first to unlock her front door and disable the security system because she was convinced our mailman was going to steal the flat-screen, I called for Mom.

"This is going to sound crazy," I said.

"Oh, I like the crazy. It's where I'm most comfortable." Mom leaned on the hood of the car, peering at me, her arms folded before her, keys clasped in hand.

"You're not giving me fifty billion warnings before my date like you usually do. You didn't say *anything*. And it's weirding me out."

Mom's eyes jerked away from me and she stared off at…a wheelbarrow? Maybe? I followed her gaze and she was fixed on the shed and the garden and the wheelbarrow Mormor had left outside, which was odd because Mormor thought the mailman was going to steal *that*, too. Devi clued in that my question was more than just a little innocuous, so she hustled to go inside and help Mormor, giving us some privacy with a reassuring waggle of her fingers.

The front door closed, Mormor chattering Devi's ear off about my name choice, Devi looking like she only wanted to die a little.

"It's a fair question. I hadn't thought about it, really." Mom sighed, her chin dropping to rest on her forearms. "The lectures—I gave them. Give them. It's not like you're gonna get off the hook all together, right? I'm serious about being home by curfew, and if you blow it, you're grounded. But I also warned you about safe sex and it didn't do a whole lotta good. I'm not saying that to hurt you, but… I guess I figure you're old enough that you're going to do what you're going to do. You've heard it all by now, and you'll either hop to or ignore it."

It was exactly the answer I had been afraid of.

"You're giving up on me," I said, my voice thick. "Because I got pregnant."

"Nope. I didn't say that at all." Mom turned her gaze back my way. "Should you drive drunk?"

"Well, no."

"When do you carry your cell phone with you?"

"All the time. And bring an extra battery. Okay, I get it, b—"

"Do you do heroin? Touch people in inappropriate ways? Ignore people who need help?"

"…no."

I shuffled my weight from foot to foot.

Mom smiled. "Exactly. You know this stuff. And you'll take my advice or you won't. It's not that I don't care, Sara, or that I gave up on you or whatever maudlin horse crap you invented. It's that you *know* all of it. You're old enough to choose to follow it or not. What you did with Jack was a choice. Not stopping to get a condom was a choice, too. Funny enough, inaction has bigger consequences than taking action a lot of the time."

She came around the side of the car and slung an arm over my shoulder. I settled in against her, appreciating the kiss she pressed to my temple. "I'm going forward with the understanding that you'll follow the rules. If you want to live for free in my house—or Mormor's house—with your kid, you'll do all the stuff you're supposed to do, which includes being home on time, being honest with me, and not putting yourself and your kid in harm's way. If you screw a guy, you wear a condom. Fastest way to put your pregnancy at risk is to get an STD. I won't stand for you being irresponsible and hurting my grandkid, Casspee-yuh."

"Cassiopeia," I said. "Like the constellation."

Mom smirked and threw open the front door of the house. "Oh, I know. I'm just being a turd."

"Thanks, turd."

"You are *most* welcome, turdlet."

"You look awesome," Devi said, standing behind me to fuss with my hair. "That cat eye is rocking."

It was similar to Erin's, with bold thick lines and a flirty flick at the end. Devi had gone lighter on the other stuff, not a lot of shadow or blush, because she wanted the focus on my eyes, she said. It was the right call. It and a little shimmery lip gloss and I looked Kardashian glamorous.

If Kardashians could be glamorous while pregnant and wearing combat boots, then so could I.

"I'm not changing them," I said, answering Devi's earlier call for a change in footwear.

"Oh, come on. You own cute shoes! It's not *too* awful to wear sandals in October. I guess."

"He likes me how I am. Including combat boots."

"I'll give you a pedicure!"

"Thanks, but no thanks."

"You are the worst." Devi sprawled on my bed and eyeballed her phone. "I suppose I should get going, too. You're not the only one with plans tonight."

"Oh?" I glanced her way, my brow raised. "That's news."

"Not really. It's a video-game hangout. Some guy I've been talking to on my message board. He's ace and I'm discovering I like his non-creepiness, particularly as it pertains to killing demons."

"I hope you have a great demon-killing time together."

"People who slay together, stay together, I guess?" Devi grinned and hauled herself up. "You ready for this, buttercup?"

"No, not really, but I'm going to go, anyway, because I'm stupid."

We headed downstairs. Mormor was knitting in front

of the TV. Mom was running around looking for her second shoe, the first already donned. She had a tendency to walk around the house kicking them off wherever, so most days leaving the house involved her searching for the other shoe while Mormor berated her for being irresponsible this far into her thirties.

Eventually, she found her other oxford, and we were out the door. Devi was dropped off first, leaving me with a kiss and a pinch for good luck. I gave Mom the directions for Leaf's house straight from his text message. He lived about fifteen minutes away from me, in a single-story yellow ranch house with white windows. We'd know it was his house, he'd said, by the blue-and-green flag with the red wagon wheel hanging next to the doorway.

Mom pulled into a short empty driveway. The garage was dead ahead of us, the entrance to the house—the side door, Leaf had said—wedged between the garage and the house body. The shrubs were tidy, the grass recently trimmed with no evidence of the brown and orange autumn leaves polluting my own side lawn. I grabbed my phone and my purse from the back seat of the car and turned to go. Before I left the car, Mom snagged my wrist.

"You need anything, you call me, okay?" she said.

"Okay."

"Do you want a token lecture for old times' sake?"

"...Mom. No. You dink."

"Oh, he's *handsome.*"

"Who—oh!" Leaf stood in the front window of the house smiling out at us, all six feet something of him, dark hair pulled back, his thick body covered by a...pink frilly body apron with *Kiss The Chef* stitched on the front pocket.

"So are you gonna?" Mom asked.

"What?"

"Kiss the chef?"

I groaned and climbed from the car. Mom leaned over the passenger's side seat to shout at me. "I love you. Don't get doubly pregnant. Mormor might make you live in the shed if you defy science."

I slammed the door shut. I could hear her laughing as I walked up to Leaf's side door. Suddenly, the nerves about our first date weren't so bad. Anything was better than listening to my hag mother continue doing her hag thing.

At least, that's what I told myself as he opened the door to welcome me inside.

"Hi," he said.

CHAPTER TWENTY-SIX

I didn't know the name of the French food goddess who'd birthed Leaf, but I wanted to offer her tribute. He was a gift unto normal people when it came to kitchen technique. We sat at a small, tidy square table in his kitchen, shoes off, sock-clad toes bumping into one another below. I devoured my thin strips of steak sautéed with green and red peppers and onions. I inhaled my flatbread and spicy rice and a squash side dish full of garlic.

It was incredible.

Stinky, but incredible.

If I kiss any chef, it's only because I know he reeks as bad as I do.

"This is so good," I said. "Like, I can't even boil water without burning it."

Leaf beamed. "Thank you! I take pride in my cooking. One day, I'd like to have my own restaurant, I think. What about you?"

"You wouldn't want to eat at my restaurant. My daily special would be hot boiled garbage."

Leaf chuckled and spooned rice onto his flatbread, wrapping it up and tucking it between his lips. "Do you know what you want to do for a living, I mean? After school?"

I ran my napkin across my lower face before replacing it on my lap. Soon, there would be no lap, only the bulbous protrusion that was my growing offspring. "I dunno. I thought I'd go to an Ivy League, maybe become an English professor because I'm a cliché. But with the kid, I may look at a state school. Way cheaper, accessible for mom hours. Boston's a long train ride."

"I could see you being a teacher. You could be Weller Junior."

"I'm not that mean," I said. "I don't *actually* lure children into my gingerbread house to eat them."

"If you try hard and believe in yourself, anything is possible," he retorted.

I stared at him.

And then I laughed. He joined in before reaching over to pat the back of my hand.

We finished dinner a few minutes later. Leaf cleared the table, talking more about Romani customs, including how he washed his utensils separate to avoid contamination—

they went in his mouth, other dishes did not. I asked if he wanted any help but he declined. There was a ritualistic aspect to handling china, he explained, and I assumed it had to do with that term he'd taught me in the library: mochadi. I'd do more harm than good messing with things, and so I sat at the table, my fingers toying with the lace edging on the pink apron he'd folded and put on an end table.

"Was this your mom's?" I asked.

"Hmm? Oh. No. Not exactly." He shook his head and smiled, his towel swirling over a plate before he put it in the stack with the rest. "It was supposed to be, but she died before I could give it to her. It's a keepsake. We don't—it's bad luck to keep the possessions of the dead, so we tend not to hold onto much. Photographs, but other than that, we gave her things away to Goodwill."

I nodded, eyes skimming the small house. We were alone, Leaf's father was working that night as a security guard at a nearby factory, but the guitar leaning against the wall was his, Leaf said, as well as the stack of video games. "I don't play," Leaf said. "But Dad's a COD monster." There were family pictures on the wall with Leaf, his father—whom he resembled not only in features but in stature—his sister, Miri, and his niece, Elana. There was also a picture of Leaf's father with a tall, willowy pale woman with auburn hair.

Leaf had her nose.

Her name was Michelle, he told me.

The furniture was well cared for but mismatched—a striped armchair next to the fireplace, a floral couch with a stack of colorful blankets on one cushion pushed against a teal-painted wall. Braided rugs, a bookshelf with fantasy novels, a leather ottoman and a coffee table filled the rest of the space. The flat-screen TV was held up by brackets, the wires hidden behind a shallow entertainment center housing the PlayStation, DVR and DVD player.

A solid collection of Blu-rays filled the bottom shelf alphabetized for easy plundering. I got up from my seat and walked over to crouch before them, pulling out *Young Frankenstein* and holding it above my head.

"Is your dad home at all tonight?" I asked Leaf, who was on the other side of the half wall in the kitchen finishing dishes.

"Not till midnight. Why?"

"Do we want to skip the movies and hang here? You've got a lot of good stuff. I'm cool with going to the theater, too, if you had your heart set on it. It's just, we can talk here."

Leaf towel-dried his hands and moseyed out to the living room, plucking the DVD from my grip and grinning. "This is one of my dad's favorites. Mine, too."

"Same! I'd be down if you are."

"Sounds good. Great, even." He paused. "I didn't make a dessert, though. I figured we'd be getting popcorn."

"That is what convenience stores were designed for," I said, standing up and heading for the kitchen to grab my sweatshirt from the back of the chair. "Onward, to victory. And by victory, I mean crap food."

An hour later, crunching on Doritos and drinking root beer, we were situated on Leaf's couch, our feet side by side on the ottoman, a stash of disgusting food piled up between us. *Young Frankenstein* played on the flat-screen. We hummed along to the violin theme. We neighed when Frau Blücher's name was said. We giggled at Marty Feldman's Igor. By the time the "Puttin' on the Ritz" song and dance routine was up, the junk food had been packaged away for another day and we were sitting side by side, holding hands.

He didn't even mind my orange cheesy fingers.

"I feel like we've been doing this forever," Leaf said quietly.

"Huh?"

"Hanging out." He turned on the couch to look at me, smiling softly. "You're an easy person to get comfortable with, I think."

That surprised me. The ex-boyfriend had said the opposite—that I was prickly and hard to warm up to. Of course, Aaron had said that after he'd asked if Samantha could hang out with our group of friends and I'd pushed back. I'd known early on that she had a thing for my boyfriend; that's why she wanted to hang out. But Aaron made me feel like I was being a bitch and wasn't giving her a chance, so I'd relented and she'd become part of our circle despite my never really liking her.

We know how that all went. Apparently, though, the idea that I was prickly had lingered long after Aaron had made his exit.

"I can be kind of a douche," I said. "Devi says that all the time."

"Hardly. You're funny! But it's not mean funny. You're just sarcastic, that's all. I like that type of humor. I like you."

He reached up to finger a curl of my hair, pulling it long and watching it boing back up into shape. He did it again.

I let him.

"I like you, too," I said. "I'm just worried that this whole baby thing will be too much." I paused, then frowned. "I don't mean I'm looking for you to take responsibility or anything. Just that I'll have to sink a lot of time into being a mom, so I'm hoping that won't be a problem for you. I won't be around as much as other girls."

He nodded over at the picture on the wall of his niece, Elana. "I think I'd be more put off if you didn't take it so seriously. Do you know how angry I'd be if my sister neglected Elana? They're babies. They need parents who love them."

It was *such* a sweet thing to say, my breath hitched. Leaf's gaze dropped to my mouth. Mine dropped to his. He had a ridiculously pretty smile, higher on one side than the other, thick-lipped. I just wanted to—

Him? Yep, okay, him. We're clear. All systems are go on Leaf.

"Can I, uhh. Can I kiss—" I managed to get out, but then he was there, his head tilting my way. His nose bumped mine as he closed the gap between us. I could smell his breath, sour from dinner and snacks, and I didn't care, not one bit as he pressed his lips to mine. They were warm and full. They felt good. We were interlocking in a totally organic, lovely way. Not vacuum sealed. Not slurping on one another. It was light touches of soft skin. Brushes. It was a gentle push, a light suck. Nothing wet until he flicked his tongue at me and I opened up and then it was wet, just a little, and then *I* was wet because apparently second trimester hormones were no joke. I went from zero to hornball crazy in two minutes.

My whole body was warm. I thrummed in all the fun places. I had to ball my hand into a fist to keep myself from going too fast—from touching without permission. The kisses were perfect. Sublime. Letting myself enjoy them at a leisurely pace was so, so difficult but also so, so rewarding.

Leaf's big hand cupped the back of my head, his fingers threading through my hair. I reached for his ponytail, giving it a gentle tug, and he groaned into my mouth, pulling me closer. Chest to chest, heartbeat to heartbeat. He leaned back, taking me with him as he notched his body into the corner of the couch, the armrest at his back. I was sprawled out on top of him. I liked his size and how small it made me feel. I liked how it felt when his hand settled in the small of my back to hold me close, too.

I liked how he looked when he pulled away from me, with a flush in his cheeks. With his eyes big and glassy. With his pulse pounding.

"You are beautiful," he said quietly, his fingers tracing across my shoulders. "Your skin. Your hair. Your nose. I like the tilt of it."

"You are, too," I said, then quickly corrected. "Handsome, I mean. Even my mom said so when we pulled up."

He nuzzled at my hair. I willed my frantic heart to quiet. I wasn't ready for anything more with him yet, despite the screaming of my quivering bits. Lucky for me, Leaf wasn't *looking* for anything more, either. He was content holding me against his body, stealing occasional kisses and whispering how pretty he thought I was. We spent two and a half movies like that, twined together like cats, until I dozed off on top of him, comforted by his warmth.

And when my phone beeped at eleven thirty to remind me to *go home, stupid, your curfew is at twelve*, he woke me up from my nap and piled me into the car like a sleepy toddler. We pulled into my driveway ten minutes early, so we spent ten minutes kissing and making plans for Saturday, at his place again, with more movies and cuddles.

I walked into the house in a daze. It had been, without a doubt, the best date of my entire life.

PART THREE:

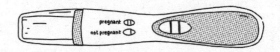

Fat pants,
Oops Redux and
"Twinkle, Twinkle, Little Star."

CHAPTER TWENTY-SEVEN

One date became two. Two became three. Three became four. Four became officially a couple. We rejoined our friends at Morgan's house to watch movies on Fridays—Devi was brought into the fold easily—while Saturdays became "our night."

"Our night" consisted of dinner at his place followed by more movies, which became a bunch of kissing, over-the-clothes groping and me falling asleep on him because incubating a tiny human was hard work.

It was pretty simple.

It just didn't stay that way.

Because.

"Are you ashamed of us?" Mormor asked over dinner, ever combative.

"What?" I looked up from my plate and stared at her. "Where is this coming from?" We'd been talking about my impending Teen Mom social group for most of the meal, but apparently, Mormor had something else she wanted to talk about, and she broached the subject with all the grace of a bull elephant.

"You have a boyfriend. You've met his father, but you've not brought the boy here."

It was true. I had met Mr. Leon the previous week, before he was out the door to go to his security job. He was as quiet as Leaf was chatty. He seemed really nice. The only problem was he was a listener instead of a talker, to the degree that I felt the need to fill the quiet with noise because, otherwise, he was just looking at me and smiling a lot and it made me nervous.

So I talked about the baseball card collection I'd started at seven. I'd collected for two years, and then promptly lost the binder at school and was so emotionally traumatized I'd given up baseball for good. But that was okay because I'd organized the cards by which players I found the cutest and not by any stat that any real baseball fan would care about, so I wasn't a "real" fan, anyway, apparently.

Mr. Leon had apologized to me. For misplacing what had been basically a binder of pretend boyfriends.

…it hadn't been my finest moment.

Bull elephant runs in the family.

"The boy has a name, Ma," my mother said. "It's Leaf."

"Leaf. Yes. Now invite Leaf over for dinner," Mormor said. "Unless you are hiding us away like some dirty secret. Is it because I'm a Republican?"

"What? No. It's not—I don't know if he likes Republicans, but he's never said—I just hadn't gotten there yet is all, Mormor. I'll invite him when I talk to him later."

"Good. You are a good girl. I'm simply interested in the boy who may end up being near my great-grandchild is all. Little Star can't fend for herself yet."

"Little Star" was the nickname Mormor had taken to using in lieu of my chosen name which, on one hand, was incredibly insulting because it disregarded my wishes about my kid's name. On the other hand, it was possibly the cutest nickname ever so I was willing to let it slide.

"She really can't." Mom winked at me and slid the potatoes over so I could take my seconds. She was good about the changes going on in my body, realizing not only was I eating like a horse, but the night sweats had turned into day sweats, too, so she didn't give me garbage about how I was dressed at the dinner table. She'd warned Mormor off giving me any trouble, too. We were careening toward a Massachusetts winter, complete with frost on the plants in the morning and puffs of clouds emanating from our mouths when we talked. But there I was, walking around in a tank top and shorts with my hair up because I felt like I was cooking from the inside. It didn't do a lot to hide my big fat butt or my expanding midsection, but I didn't care. I was comfortable. Ish.

The kid was a presence, always.

I hadn't really "popped" yet, but Dr. Cardiff said it was

imminent when I asked. My stomach was no longer a simple swell but domed, and soon, it'd protrude, and maybe my bellybutton would do that weird innie-to-outie thing. My jeans were packed away for less-pregnant days, and even my leggings were straining under the growth. My skull leggings, for example? The stretch was so intense, my smiling sugar skulls had morphed into that creepy dude from *The Scream*.

Mom said we'd hit the maternity section soon, to look for stuff to get me through my last trimester. It wouldn't be my most fashionable shopping adventure, but it'd be the most comfortable.

Or else.

"Saturday," I said. "I'll invite him over Saturday."

Mormor nodded, pleased. "Good. I'll make kok korv, I think. We hear so much about his Romani dishes, we should have some good Swedish food for him to try."

"That'd be pretty cool, eh, Sara?" Mom asked.

Except, was it? Leaf had customs about food, strict ones even, and I wasn't sure if he'd be *able* to eat kok korv or really anything we prepared. "I think so, but—okay, he has rules about food. Kinda like kosher eating rules," I said, using Devi's parallel because my mom and grandma might understand it better that way. "I want to talk with him tonight to see if food's an option or if it'll be hella awkward."

"If food's a no-go, we'll do kok korv another night, the three of us, and we can just hang out with him," Mom said, heading off any of Mormor's accidentally-racist-but-no-less-irritating commentary. "You get out of your group at two on Saturday. If he can't do dinner, we'll shove some food at you, then have him over during the day to talk."

"Cool. Yes. Thanks." I packed away the last of the potatoes and pushed myself up from the table to wash my dish in the sink. Three steps in, I stopped dead, my eyes going wide. I nearly dropped my plate on the floor because *my stomach was fluttering.* It was the only way to describe the sensation—like I'd swallowed butterflies and they were flapping around inside of me. My free hand went to the left side, where it seemed the most intense.

"Everything okay?" Mom asked, obviously concerned. She rose from the table and came to my side, her hand going to the small of my back. I jerked my head her way. She was concerned; lines creased her forehead, her blue eyes were narrow.

"I'm okay. I think I can feel the baby. It's like...a twitch, maybe? Or bubbles inside?"

"Oh! Oh!" Mom's worry evaporated and she put her hand over mine. "That's totally normal. You felt like buzzing bees at first. It wasn't until later that you used my bladder like a hacky sack. Which is why I sometimes pee when I sneeze."

"There's a shelf life on guilt, Mom. We're pushing twenty years. Move on." I pushed my fingers into the spot on my stomach to see if I could feel anything through the skin, but not yet. The baby was being shy. "It's— really weird. But cool, too."

Mormor came to my other side, her hand going over mine. There was nothing to feel, but she smiled all the same. "This is good. She's healthy in there. She's strong."

Because she's a Larssen, my brain filled in automatically.

Which is how and when I decided that my baby was not going to hold my name—the name of a man I barely remembered—but my mother's maiden name.

Cassiopeia Larssen.

The conversation about Saturday night with Leaf had to wait until the next school day because I laid down for a "little nap" post-dinner and woke up when my morning alarm went off. I slogged into school, gray backpack attached to me like a weighted wood tick. Black leggings, a long hoodie sweatshirt and one of my more forgiving T-shirts went along with slip-on sneakers. The boots weren't as feasible anymore because bending was getting more ungainly. I could do it, but it just felt weird and would only get worse.

My homework was done-ish—enough that I'd get credit for doing it, not enough that I could say it was my best work. I spent each of my classes furiously finishing what work I could because the early nights were a danger to any and all productivity.

Leaf kissed my cheek as we went into Weller's class. The other kids didn't notice. In fact, after the incident with Mamacita and detention boy—whose name was Shane Michaels I found out later—everyone backed off. No one exactly warmed up to me, either, but that was okay. I'd found my friends and they were enough for me. I hadn't been interested in the social-climbing aspect of school before, I certainly wasn't sweating it in Stonington, either, particularly not with a bun in ye olde oven.

Class was a blur. I was having trouble focusing lately, which was less the shiny new boyfriend—he was nice to have around, but I wasn't ridiculous over him, either— and more pregnancy brain. I'd asked Dr. Cardiff about it at my last check-in. She assured me that, though there's not a lot of medical science that delved into the subject, preggo brain was widely recognized as a thing that settles in between the second and third trimesters, and sometimes continues on after the baby is born. The brain is overloaded with hormones that makes it work differently.

I sincerely hoped my brain righted itself after the kid was born. I was already tired of what I'd titled The Dumbs.

I threw my backpack into my locker and trudged to lunch. I didn't bother bringing my own food anymore; Leaf insisted he'd take care of me so I let him. The argument wasn't worth it. When I pointed out he did way more for me than I did for him in return, he simply shrugged and said, "It's not about receipts. It's about happiness. Feeding you makes me happy."

How do you argue with that?

You don't, is the answer. You let your boyfriend spoil you to death with good food and snuggles.

I sat down and waited wordlessly for him to produce the Tupperware. He didn't fail me. Instead of rice, there were noodles and veggies and meat. I thanked him and shoveled food into my slathering food hole, not knowing or caring what was actually in my meal, because Leaf had earned my trust over the few months I'd known him.

About food and in other ways, too. He was the most considerate guy I'd ever met.

Morgan and Erin sat with us, Morgan carrying their shared lunch tray. She'd recently shorn her hair off above her ears and dyed it lime green, creating a stark contrast with her red hair. Part of me envied the bareness of her neck beneath the buzz. Sure, I'd have looked like Mrs. Potato Head similarly fashioned, but she was likely much, much cooler than me, buried beneath a couple pounds of black curls as I was.

"What's shaking," Erin said, reaching for food.

"My mother and grandmother want to meet Leaf," I replied. "They've decided if he's going to be near Cass, he needs to meet their approval. Which is valid, I guess."

"I'd love to," Leaf replied, his hand squeezing my knee beneath the table. "When?"

"Saturday night? They invited you for dinner, but if you can't—"

"Looking forward to it," he interrupted.

"You are?"

My surprise birthed his. "Of course I am. Why wouldn't I be?"

"Your food rules," I admitted. "I wasn't sure if you could eat out."

"Oh! Some Rom might not, but that's the more insular type. I follow tradition when I can, but that doesn't mean I can't enjoy a night out. You're sweet to consider my feelings, though," he said, brushing a kiss to the backs of my knuckles.

"Yeah, like gag-me sweet," Morgan said. "You're making me look bad, dude."

Erin snorted. "No, he's not. We're as bad as they are. Maybe worse."

"Well, yeah, but what kind of friend would I be if I didn't give them loads of crap." Morgan winked at her before turning her head my way. I noticed that, along with the hairdo change, she'd swapped her earplugs from her trusty reds to rainbow colored ones. "Also, hey, the kid's name is Cass? You hadn't mentioned that before."

I hadn't? I could have sworn it'd come up, but maybe that was only with Leaf, who had been true to his word about not spreading any of my news to anyone else without explicit permission.

See previous comment about most considerate guy ever.

"Yeah. Cassiopeia. Like the constellation."

"Huh." Morgan chewed thoughtfully. "Cass is gender neutral-ish. That's cool. Also can go to Cash in a pinch pretty easily. Not that you were, like, thinking along those lines but."

"Not about the name, not really," I admitted. "I figured they could change it later if they wanted to. I have been pretty vocal about making sure I didn't drown my kid in pink or traditionally girly stuff, though. My mom seems to be on board. I don't trust my grandmother but I'm going to keep an eye on it."

Morgan nodded, pointing her french fry at me. "Good call. There's nothing wrong with pink stuff, but—" Morgan paused for a minute, thinking. "Okay, so my dad… God. You know how much I hate that downstairs room where we watch TV? With all the football stuff?"

I nodded.

Morgan rolled her eyes. "When I was little, Dad signed me up for football. I liked playing—I love sports—but it got stressful fast. There was such a focus on being little men with all the baggage that went along with our idea of 'being little men' that I couldn't get into it."

"Toxic masculinity," Erin chimed in, and Morgan nodded.

"Yeah, that. So, you have all this toxic masculinity in football, and there I am figuring out my gender still. I didn't *belong* there, you know? But I love my Dad a lot so I sucked it up for years, hating it the entire time. I felt obligated to act like all the boys and it just wasn't me.

"It got so bad, looking at the shoulder pads started giving me panic attacks," Morgan finished. "In ninth grade, my therapist backed me up when I told my dad I didn't want to play football anymore. He only sort of got it, only sort of gets what me being trans means at all, but the point is a lot of stuff for kids follows that pink-and-blue thing. Your kid might like pink stuff, and that's totally cool! But if they don't, it needs to be real clear that's okay, too. Kids will do *a lot* to make our parents happy even if it's at our own expense."

I understood what she was saying, but we weren't at the point where my kid *could* make choices yet. It was on me, and I...kinda didn't know what I was doing? Supposedly, that's what the Saturday class was going to teach me, but I doubted they'd touch on gender politics and infants. If they did, super cool, but I was pretty sure they were focusing on Baby 101, like "how not to put your infant in a microwave" and "don't drink Clorox and breastfeed."

"My kid'll be a loud, fleshy cabbage the first year or so.

They're not exactly going to have an opinion," I said. "And I really don't wanna mess her up before she can even talk."

"Fleshy Cabbage—album or band?" Erin asked.

Morgan smirked. "Band, definitely. And you won't mess it up, dude. Just get the kid all sorts of toys and let them decide what's fun for them when they get old enough to have opinions. Same thing with clothes. A baby in a dress isn't going to make or break anyone, but if they get to the point they don't like dresses? Don't force it on them. But that's just my take, too. I'm one trans girl. There are lots of other takes."

I nodded. "Thanks. I hope I wasn't being weird asking."

"Nah, we're friends. You can ask me anything." Morgan smiled at me and then, without a word, took Erin's empty water bottle up to the fountain to refill it for her. She took care of her girl, always.

"What time on Saturday?" Leaf asked, handing me a napkin and motioning at his lip. It took me a second to clue in that I had food on my face, and I cringed and swiped it away.

"Sorry. I need a feedbag. Let's say five? I should be home by three but knowing me, I'll need a nap. And you're warned, Mormor's intense. She's…very. Very what, I don't know, but she's very."

"Not too worried about it. Five works for me." Leaf glanced over his shoulder at the cafeteria monitors and, seeing them chatting and ignoring the kids, pressed a quick dry kiss to the corner of my mouth. "I look forward to it."

Glad one of us does.

CHAPTER TWENTY-EIGHT

At nine o'clock on Saturday morning, I was in a classroom at a community college thirty minutes from home, seated next to a girl named Erika who, after five minutes of small talk, I discovered was almost exactly as pregnant as I was, except she was huge. Like Sputnik huge. It made me appreciate my conservatively rounded paunch more; the longer I could put off the carrying-a-basketball phase, the better. I was hesitating on wearing the maternity jeans Mom had bought me with the belly pocket and stretchy waistband because denial is NOT just a river in Egypt.

Erika was not so lucky. She was well into her maternity pants because, apparently, her kid was going to be the size of the Hulk.

The poor thing.

Erika was sixteen and went to school four towns over from me. She had dark brown skin and dark hair as curly as mine that she wore under a red cloth headband. Seeing that my last name was Rodriguez on my Hello My Name Is badge, she peered at me.

"¿Hablas español?"

I shook my head. "Nah. Dad took off when I was little. Didn't get a chance to learn."

I braced for the usual pushback—the value judgments made about being bilingual in Latinx and Hispanic communities, but Erika was cool about it. She shrugged.

"Mi padre left, too. I get it. That sucks, but what you gonna do, right?"

"Pretty much."

There were nine girls in the room, who all looked as unenthused to be there as I felt. There was me and the Hannahs—Jones and McGovern, respectively, who were as fair-skinned as I was but with far lighter hair—an Asian girl, two Latinas, two black girls and Erika, who was Afro-Latinx if surnames were to be believed.

Hers was García.

"Where are you from?" I asked her, thinking I was asking about her hometown.

"The Dominican. You?"

Oh. I meant Stonington but…

"Spain," I said, which was a bit of information that

didn't always go over so well because it translated to "Colonizer."

Super white colonizer at that, thanks Swedish mom.

Erika nodded but said nothing else. I left it alone— she'd talk to me again if she wanted to. There was a lot going on among Hispanics and Latinx, power dynamics centered on colonialism and colorism. It was complicated stuff that I only sort of understood, so my approach was to be friendly with people sharing my label but *not* pushy. I was always Hispanic, and no one could take that away from me, but I was also a walking, talking example of what made the community so messy in the first place. I tried not to take it personally when people didn't warm up to that. It wasn't about me so much as it was about what I represented.

Erika would be okay with me or she wouldn't. I wouldn't sweat it either way because I wasn't in the class to make friends. I was there to...

Put diapers on a bag of flour, I guess?

The two women who taught the class were licensed social workers, both closer to Mormor's age than my mom's. They seemed nice. There was blonde, perky, white Amanda with the cherry-print top and red capri pants and executive bob haircut, and quiet, black Marie in the cotton workout pants, velour sweatshirt and pink Nikes. Marie spoke in such a low tone of voice we had to lean forward as much as our pregnant bellies would allow to hear her, but what she said was supportive, and more importantly, informative. She mentioned Lamaze classes as a thing we should sign up for ASAP, that there were classes online we could take. She talked about state benefits to teen moms that made those classes free or discounted at certain hospitals and birthing centers. She answered questions about getting GEDs for the people who wouldn't be able to finish high school traditionally with a baby around, but also advised there'd be a whole class on that, so sit tight. She told us there'd be sessions about health benefits and medical resources for both pre-birth and post-birth. There were practical knowledge things, too.

Like the whole flour bag, disposable diaper and cloth-diaper-with-the-pins *thing*.

The disposable diaper was easy. The cloth diaper—not so much. After the third time I stabbed my bag, I was convinced Cass would look like a busted piñata within a week of being born. Amanda and Marie assured me it was okay, to try again—and I managed eventually, but it's odd to know you can do advanced placement calculus but not baseline baby stuff like diapering your pretend flour kid. Even with Amanda's help, my diaper looked lopsided and weird.

"It gets so much easier with practice," she assured me.

Maybe that was true, but did it get easier before or after I and my child lost a quart of blood to the diaper-pin gods?

We took a break for our bagged lunches and then we did what was, essentially, a group therapy session talking about the various challenges each of us faced with our pregnancies. It was…eye opening. One of the girls, Maria, a Latina from a Boston neighborhood, was already working two jobs on top of school to try to save money for her and her baby. One of the Hannahs? Her baby's father was a friend of her father's—a married man—and she hadn't told anybody because she was afraid to. And Erika was contending with a man who had other children with another girl—something she hadn't found out about until she'd gotten pregnant herself.

When it came time for me to talk, I didn't feel included, like Mrs. Wong or my mother had so desperately hoped I would joining this group of fellow preggos. I felt ridiculous because my story was so *banal*.

"I had a bad breakup so I got drunk and screwed a guy at a party," I said. "It was dumb. I should have used a condom. I'm lucky to live with my mom and grandma who are supporting me so I can finish school."

It wasn't a contest of tragedies, and I realized that, but the thing I'd built up in my head as earth shattering and catastrophic...was still huge, but I definitely had it easier than some, too. The perspective was good, I supposed, but also uncomfortable.

People were quiet around me, either expecting me to talk more or for Amanda or Marie to speak. It probably wasn't a very long silence, but it felt like forever as I fussed with the strings on my hoodie and stared at the floor. The circle had lots to say with the previous three girls, but not so much for me. It was Wei, the Chinese girl with the long-sleeved pink T-shirt and almost polite micro–baby belly, who saved me from melting in mortification.

"My boyfriend and I thought you couldn't get pregnant if you pulled out," she admitted, shyly. "So, if you're dumb, so am I. I'm going to be living at home, too."

"Kinda the same," said the other Hannah. "I thought

me and my boyfriend were cool because my period was really regular so I could work around ovulation, but I screwed up the math by a day or two."

That led to a third girl, Janeen, a pretty, petite black girl with elbow-length box braids and a red pullover hoodie nodding in agreement. "I didn't want to ask my mother for condoms 'cause she would have flipped on me. I should have gone to the free clinic but I was lazy. So if you're dumb, I'm real dumb."

"I hate that word, *dumb*. For lots of reasons," Marie said, smiling at all of us. "But people make mistakes. It's part of growing. Maybe you made a choice you'd do differently if you could turn back time, but that's not how life works. You're young people conquering something a lot of people don't have to worry about until later, when they're more financially independent and have a little more experience under their belts. But just because it's hard doesn't mean you can't do it."

Amanda smiled at all of us. "Because you can. Marie and I teach this class because we had babies young, too. Life isn't over. It's just out of order from most everyone else, and you might need a little more help than other moms, and that's okay."

That minute, right there, with tears popping up in my eyes I really hadn't asked for, was when I knew I'd stay in the stupid flour-diaper-baby class after all.

"When you say you stabbed the flour baby a lot, do you mean on purpose because it made you angry?"

Mom grinned below the pink-framed sunglasses that

ate up half of her face. We were on the highway, heading home from group, the windows cracked in the car
because New England was weird. Two days before it had
been thirty-six degrees. It was almost seventy and I was
sweating to death. I peeled off my sweatshirt, not caring
that my *Legend of Zelda* T-shirt was stretched so taut over
my belly that Link looked like Jabba the Hutt.

"Very funny, smart-ass," I said.

"Hey! Be nice to your mother. It took thirty-seven and a
half hours to push you out. I sincerely hope Cass is kinder
on your hooha, pumpkinhead."

"You're rude." I fished around in my hoodie for my cell
before throwing the sweatshirt in the back seat. Phones
were forbidden during teen preggo class for obvious reasons, which is how I missed the party that had started in
my messages at twelve past one in the afternoon.

The party being Devi's near frantic texts.

girl

srsly grl

where are you

call me now

Sara

Serendipity.

Dude.

I FOUND JACK. BABY DADDY WORKING @ GAS STATION ON CORNER OF ELM AND NORTH IN CHESHIREVILLE. IANELLI'S GARAGE.

Cheshireville was the town next to Stonington, not ten minutes from Mormor's house.

He'd said he wanted to work on cars with his dad. Of course they owned a garage.

I couldn't make my fingers work on my smartphone. I couldn't really speak, and the squeak I did manage was swallowed by the rushing whir of the car's open windows. I stared at Devi's texts, then glanced at Mom's profile, my heart pounding, my head spinning. I tried to say something, failed and instead shook my head, pulling up my GPS on my phone and typing in Ianelli's Garage. It took four tries thanks to misspellings, but I found it in the list and set our course.

"Exit fourteen," I managed to say, sounding choked.

"What about it?"

"Get off there? Devi found Jack."

Mom's brow crinkled. "Jack who?"

"…truck guy. Cass's dad."

Mom's mouth fell open. She looked as shell-shocked as I felt, but she quickly nodded and moved the car from the center lane to the right so we could get off the highway. We were wordless as we made our way to Cheshireville. A few times Mom looked like she'd talk, but she shook her head and licked her lips instead.

GPS said we were four minutes away from the garage by the time I replied to Devi. Omw w/mom.

Devi's response was to call me. I picked up and cleared my throat, hoping the frog would vacate so I could actually say something. I needed the practice; it wouldn't do me a whole heck of a lot of good to go see the sperm donor and not have the capacity for speech. I mean, the belly was conversation enough if he knew how to do math, but it'd be nice if I could manage *anything* beyond the obvious, too.

"I almost crapped myself," she said in greeting. "We stopped for gas after picking up Dad's dry cleaning and Jack waited on us. He didn't recognize me, though, and I didn't know if I should say anything? So I kept my mouth shut. I hope that was the right thing to do."

"I—mmm. It's fine," I said, because really, it wasn't her job to do that work for me.

"You okay?"

How was I supposed to answer that? On one hand, it was nice to know Jack's last name. He was as responsible as I was for my Jabba-the-Link condition. Without his efforts, there'd be no diaper pins or diminishing line of sight on my feet. On the other hand, ignorance had been bliss, too. What if he wanted custody? What if he got mad at me that I hadn't aborted? What if he—

"Hi, Devi," Mom said, effectively stomping out my panic before it set in.

"Hi, Mom," Devi said back, forcing me to repeat it.

I sucked in a breath and sighed.

"I'll be okay, I think? I dunno. Depends on how this goes, I suppose." Mom put her blinker on and the GPS voice told us to go a mile and Ianelli's would be on the left. "I hope he's still working."

"He was when I texted you. At least you know how to get in touch with him, either way. Call me after, okay? If you need company or whatever, I'm yours."

"Yeah, sure. Leaf's meeting Mom and Mormor later, though, so I should be okay until then? But I'll let you know."

"Cool. I'm here. Love you."

"Love you, too, wifey."

We hung up right as we pulled the car not into one of the lanes to get gas, but the small parking lot beside the garage. It was a white building with three pits for cars, the big aluminum doors lifted to reveal a pair of SUVs on mechanic lifts. Red-and-green lettering announced that I'd arrived at Ianelli & Sons Garage, the sign spinning in slow circles. I couldn't see any people milling around at first, and I sat there in the idling car with Mom, steeling myself for whatever was to come next.

A blue Corolla pulled up for gas.

The door of the office opened and out walked a tall, thin guy with black hair and a crooked nose wearing a navy blue jumpsuit with his name stitched in white on the left breast. I couldn't read the letters from where I sat with Mom, but I knew what it said despite the distance.

Jack.

CHAPTER TWENTY-NINE

"Do you want me to go with you?" Mom asked.

Mom's presence was support, but at the same time, she had that hole in her face that insisted on making words and noise and that could go so wrong so fast.

"I got it."

"You sure?"

"Yep."

Mom frowned.

"Good luck, peaches. Signal if you need help. If you light him on fire, I'm assuming he was a butthead."

"Thanks, Mom."

I fussed with the seat belt, grunting at the stretch of right arm looping over round belly to unlatch myself on the left side. I walked from the car, my hand going over my bump with the distorted cartoon T-shirt face. Jack was either going to assume I'd gotten fatter, or he was going to figure it out pretty darn quick. It was a highly localized protuberance, shall we say.

Thank you, Mrs. Weller, for that fifty-cent vocabulary word.

Jack finished with the Corolla and spun around to greet me, hearing my feet shuffling over the loose gravel of the parking lot. At first, he didn't recognize me. People got that glassy eyed, vacant look with strangers, kinda like dogs trying to do physics, but then something clicked in his head. He blinked. His head tilted just slightly, and his mouth tipped up taller at the ends.

Of course he was smiling. The last time he'd seen me, I was bouncing on his weenie like it was my own personal trampoline.

"Sara, right? From the party?"

"Yeah, hey, Jack. My best friend came to get gas earlier and said you were around. Devi? She was at the party, too." I managed my own smile but I felt like I was going to barf on his work boots. "I. Uhh. I was looking for you for a couple months after we hooked up, but no one could find your number or knew your name." I pointed up at the family garage sign. "Know it now, though."

He nodded. "Same, yeah. Didn't help that I couldn't remember your bigger name? I knew it was Sara-something but not the rest of it. And there are a lot of regular Saras around, come to find out. I'm dating another one now, actually."

His smile was sheepish. His hand went to the back of his neck.

He was so cute.

…look, just 'cause I'm on a diet doesn't mean I can't look at the menu. Jack was a good-looking guy. That in no way impacted my fondness for Leaf. If anything, it made me happy that maybe our kid wouldn't be uglier than a bucket of rocks.

"Cool! I've got a boyfriend, too. His name's Leaf," I replied. "And I'm Serendipity. It's not an easy one to re-member."

"Nice! And yeah, that—sorry. I tried. On the name."

Awkward silence.

More smiling.

I kept waiting for him to notice my belly. Heck, I kept patting it in circles to draw his gaze downward, but he kept right on looking at my face. The one time in my life I wanted a guy to give me that lazy perusal and he wouldn't comply.

Going to have to do this the hard way, I guess.

"So I'm pregnant," I blurted. "About six months."

"Whoa. You are?" That got him to look down, and when he got there, staring at my distorted Link-faced midsection, he wavered on his feet. "That's…so. Is it…"

"Yep!"

I probably sounded too cheerful, like Barbie on ste-roids, but in reality, I was panicking, my body hot, my toes curling inside my sneakers. The tummy flutters that indicated the child was awake increased. When Mommy was twitterpated, so was Little Star, apparently. We were going down the anxiety trail together—our first Mommy-and-Me adventure.

Jack couldn't stop staring at my belly.

"I'm sure. Really sure. We can do testing if you want, but I hadn't been with anyone else and haven't been since. Not even with Leaf yet, but…that's TMI. Sorry. I'm babbling. It's just—I'm thinking of naming her Cass? But we can talk about it if you want to be involved. Dr. Cardiff said the baby will be born with a vagina so I'm assuming she's a girl. But I'll be down if she determines she's not later. That's…yeah. I'm babbling," I finished weakly.

"Oh, shit. Oh, shit. My old man is going to *kill* me." Jack glanced over at the garage, his hand covering his mouth. I followed his gaze. A tall, thin man with graying temples and a mustache worked on one of the SUVs, his hands twisting inside the guts of the machine. Jack was built like him and dressed like him thanks to the uniform. It was like looking at a second Jack, before and after a time machine.

"I didn't want to tell my mother, either. It's hard, I know." I felt like crying again, but to be fair, I'd gotten weepy at a tampon commercial the week before thanks to hormones, so it wasn't out of character.

Watching Jack process—the flicker of emotions from shock to sadness to anger and frustration—felt weirdly invasive, like I was peeking at his diary. I hadn't been able to process the anvil dropping on *my* head in private, either, and I didn't want to do that to Jack if I could help it.

I grabbed my phone and pulled up my contacts list, keeping my eyes averted from him so he didn't think I was gawking at his expense.

"You've got to think about it, and talk to your parents and stuff. So why don't we exchange numbers and you can get back to me? If you want anything to do with the baby or—well. Talk to your parents, I guess, and then text me? We can maybe get together?"

It took Jack a minute, but he nodded and pulled out his phone, too. He was sheet-white as he typed in my number. His voice warbled as he gave me his. I felt sorry for him, to the point I leaned in to give him a fierce hug. I hoped he didn't think it was weird, but I'm pretty sure when you've exchanged bodily fluids and made a baby together, a hug was a fairly innocuous thing to do.

"I'm sorry," I said. I wasn't sure what I was apologizing for, but it felt like the right thing to say.

His arms closed around me and he squeezed tight. "I'm sorry, too. I'll get back to you quick. Promise."

I pulled away and nodded, walking my way back to Mom and the car, aware that he was watching every step I took.

"But you're okay?" Mom asked for the fourteenth time since leaving Ianelli's.

"I think so."

"I want to support you," she said.

"You can support me by getting me home so I can clean my room before Leaf comes over," I replied.

Mom nodded. She accelerated five whole miles more per hour.

"I'm just worried he won't call back. What if it's a fake number?"

Mom was *fretting*.

"…we were at his dad's garage. With the family name on it. I'm pretty sure he wouldn't do that, anyway, but if he would—he's real dumb and I'm sorry to my kid for saddling her with his inferior gene pool."

Mom cringed.

"Point! I'm nervous. Sorry."

"So am I."

After I'd given up on finding Jack, I'd abandoned the idea that my child would have a father. Truthfully, I'd been okay with that. It was what I knew. All the major milestones: Mom and Mormor. School plays, graduation from middle school, my spelling bee competitions—my mother and grandmother had been there. My father was a ghost in my life, a concept that people told me existed but I never actually saw. Sometimes, Mom got child support when my father worked somewhere that his wages could be garnished, but that was rare. Mom said he did odd job construction under the table, probably to avoid paying for me.

He never called or asked for pictures. There were no birthday or Christmas cards. He was nothing to me. I wasn't even mad about it because how can you be mad at nothing?

The notion of dealing with things like support and custody and weekend visitation because a dad wanted to be around was foreign territory. And it was *scary*. What if Jack talked to his parents and they wanted to take my baby away from me half the time? They probably wouldn't but…what if?

I'd said I was okay but it was a lie. Mom knew it, too, if her glances were any indication. We pulled into the driveway without another word. I shuffled into the house, feeling tired and achy and vaguely like I had to pee. Dr. Cardiff said that'd get worse throughout the third trimester as the kid's weight pressed on the bladder. While I was still compact-ish, the pressure was mounting. I could only imagine what month nine was going to look like. I'd be spewing urine like a lawn sprinkler.

I mumbled a hello at my grandmother. The house smelled like food—she'd started cooking early in preparation for Leaf's big entrance. Pots, pans and the slow cooker bubbled like witch cauldrons, their contents more sweet than savory and all delicious.

"Hello," Mormor said, standing by the sink, washing her hands, paintbrushes and a paint tray drying on a towel beside her. Cooking hadn't been the only thing on her day's agenda, apparently. She'd changed into her overalls—an ancient denim pair she used for all of her various household projects. The last time I'd seen her in them, she'd been stenciling the foyer with cardinals and twisty branches.

"It didn't go well then?" she said to my retreating back.

I ducked into the bathroom with a shrug.

The front door slammed. Mom stomped into the house.

"Is she okay?" Mormor asked.

"I guess? Group was good, but she found Jack."

"Who's Jack?"

"The kid," Mom said.

"What kid?"

"The baby's father. He works at his dad's garage in Cheshireville. Devi stumbled across him getting gas earlier. Sara and I stopped by after class. They exchanged numbers. I don't know what's next, but she's—we're—weirded out by it."

"Why?"

"Dunno. I guess I didn't plan on having him around. It's change. Change is bad and scary. Boo change."

Hearing Mom say that was comforting in a way. I supposed if anyone would get it, it'd be her, though; she knew the familiarity of an all-woman family. Her father had died when she was twelve, years before I came along. It'd been her and Mormor, and then her and Mormor and me until Mom married my father and moved away.

Knowing they were talking about me, I didn't want to go back to the kitchen, but I had to. I couldn't get to my room otherwise. Two sets of Larssen blue eyes followed me from bathroom to living room. They were so *present*. So *expectant*. I hovered on the threshold, my eyes rolling toward the ceiling.

"I'll be fine," I said.

"Of course you will," was Mormor's immediate reply. "You have us."

"I know. I just don't know what's going to happen and it's making me nervous. He might not want anything to do with the baby. And if he does, he has a girlfriend now and I have a boyfriend and I don't know if we're supposed to drop everything to try to be together for the baby or—"

"No," my mother and grandmother said, in tones eerily similar to one another.

It was a relief. I didn't want to uproot my life simply because Devi found Jack. Jack hadn't made overtures suggesting he'd want to do that, either, to be fair, but I knew how some people thought, and some people thought parents should stay together for the kids. Not only did I not love Jack, I didn't even know if I particularly liked Jack. How the heck was I supposed to think along lines of forever with someone I didn't know, regardless of the womb fruit?

"I'm just worried, I guess," I finished quietly. "This stuff is confusing."

Mom and Mormor shared a look.

Mormor turned on her heel to pull plates from the cabinet. "Are you hungry?"

I glanced over at the stairs and considered. My room was clean-ish, and there was time yet to tidy up before Leaf came over. I didn't really want to do a feelings fest, but Mormor was a great cook and I was willing to take comfort in the false promises of Swedish meatballs. I claimed a stool at the kitchen island. Mom sat next to me. A minute later, we were merrily stabbing gravy-covered meatballs with toothpicks and rifling them into our mouths.

Mormor turned on the electric kettle and sat across from us, her gray hair pulled back, a smudge of blue paint on her upper cheek. "You do not love this boy, right?"

"No," I said. "I met him the night of the party."

She nodded. "That makes it easier. Sometimes people

meet and they immediately fall in love and manage to keep the flame burning forever, but that is rarer than the storybooks will have you believe, Serendipity. Relationships take work." She doctored her teacup with honey and set her bag, her fingers idling while she talked. "I told you I had an abortion in Sweden when I was younger. I did not, perhaps, tell you about the baby's father. I loved him dearly. More than I've loved anyone else in my life. You will notice he is not here with me. He's in Stockholm with his wife, whom he met years after he and I fell apart. They had six children together. We exchange letters sometimes. And sometimes, it still hurts."

Mormor assembled two more teacups for me and Mom. I knew she was in serious mode because she never mentioned our sugar-and-milk pollution of perfectly good Earl Grey. "But, back then, we were inseparable. Until the pregnancy. Hardship can destroy new love. It can whittle it down, until there is nothing left. The good is harder to see when you are expecting a baby and your parents will not support you. When there is no money or place to go. When work is not so accessible because people dismiss you because of your age. That shiny love dims in the face of so much adversity.

"It is not impossible, mind you," she said, "but you need to be realistic, too. If you want to be serious with this boy, or any boy, including your Leaf, it is something you work toward. Slowly. Together. I think when you are young, it is easy to fool yourself that ignoring problems is okay because everything will mystically work itself out. It doesn't. Problems come back to bite you later on."

The kettle rumbled that it was ready. Mom waved Mormor off and poured our cups, her fingers holding the teacups in place so they wouldn't skid over the countertop. "She's not wrong. I married your father because of you," Mom said. "I was Not Prepared. Like, at all."

"I know," I said. "You've told me."

"Ehhhh. I've told you some." Mom's smile was tepid. Her tea was not. She sipped and winced at the burn, smacking her lips together and putting the cup aside to cool before climbing back onto her barstool. "Look, I really don't think you're going to try to run away with Jack. You're not, right?"

I shook my head no.

And ate more meatballs.

"Good. 'Cause forcing a relationship because of a kid doesn't work. If Jack wants in the baby's life, okay fine. He helped make her and he has that right. But *your* life, he has to work for the right to be there. Trust me, I stayed with a physically abusive man for two years because his family told me I ought to for your sake. It was crap."

I'd stopped eating meatballs at the word *abusive*. Mom had indicated things weren't great with my father, that they'd fought a lot, but she'd never mentioned that he'd hurt her *that* way before. By the pained expression on her face, she wasn't chomping at the bit to discuss it much again, either.

"I had no idea," I said. "About Dad. Sorry."

She shrugged. "Don't be. It's not your fault. Your father's family was very traditional and some of those traditions weren't great. He treated his mother like gold and his wife like garbage. When I asked his mother what to do after he'd smacked me around the first time, Maria told me that it's just how their men did. And when I told *my* mother about it, she dragged me out of there and told me I deserved better. She was right. I did. So did you. You didn't need to grow up seeing that. No kid should. My example is extreme—Jack's probably not an abuser—but the point stands that a happy home makes for happy kids. You and Jack can be great parents apart, without faking it till you make it. If a relationship comes in time, cool. If not, well… Leaf sounds great, too."

"He is great," I said, sipping at my tea. "Really great. I really want you to like him."

Mom smiled at me. "I'm sure I will."

"And maybe I will," Mormor said.

…because, of course that's what she said.

CHAPTER THIRTY

Five o'clock that night, I sat on the bench on Mormor's front porch, watching the road for cars in anticipation of Leaf's arrival. It was not lost on me that the dog across the street, a black lab named Remy who they had to tie with a harness because he was completely unhinged, did the exact same thing, only he barked while vigilant. I just fidgeted and sighed and glanced back at the house, at Mom and Mormor who were co-knitting in the living room while watching the Game Show Network.

Five past five.

Ten past.

I was just about to text Leaf to find out where he was when his dad's car appeared. I stood, my hands skimming over my shirt. I'd changed out of the Link T-shirt and into something that fit better, and by better, I mean more loosely. I didn't like calling attention to the baby bump in Mr. Leon's presence. Leaf assured me his father understood, that judging me meant judging Miri, too, and Mr. Leon wouldn't do that, but I still fretted.

"Slut shaming," Erin had told me once at lunch. "It's a thing. It messes with us. Don't let the bastards get you down."

I loved Erin and her feminism.

Leaf exited the car and waved at me. Wine-colored long-sleeved shirt over a black T-shirt. A black leather belt. Jeans. New sneakers. His hair was pulled back into its usual sleek ponytail. Mr. Leon waved at me from behind the steering wheel of the car. He was in his work uniform, his walkie-talkie thingie attached to his shoulder already.

I waved back and watched him pull out of the driveway. Leaf eyeballed Mormor's house, smiling at the colorful potted mums still clinging to life on the front steps.

"This place is niiiice," he said.

"Mormor's kind of a fanatic about her house, yeah."

"Should I take off my shoes?"

"Nope, that's fine. You ready for this?"

"Sure am."

I threaded my fingers with his. He lifted my left hand to his mouth and pressed a kiss to the backs of my knuckles. I pretty much melted into the porch. We'd been taking it slow, and I knew, logically, it was a smart move—for me, for the baby. That didn't, however, mean that my rampaging pants parts weren't a factor. A good portion of my second trimester had been me furiously quenching the fire raging in my preggo veins.

I led him into the house with the Swedish she-wolves I called family. Mom was frowning at a misshapen sock she'd been trying to assemble with circle hooks, her hair wound tight with a floral scarf. Mormor was sliding a stitch marker into what I was guessing was going to be a blanket of some kind. It was navy blue with a fancy yellow trim.

"Hello," Leaf said in greeting.

Mom grinned at him, tossing her knitting aside and offering him a hand. "Hey. I'm Astrid. You can call me that or Ms. Larssen if you're inclined. This is my mom, Mrs. Larssen."

"Mormor will do," Mormor said. "It's easier."

She didn't stop knitting. Instead, she eyeballed Leaf over her stitches, her eyes narrowed like a sun-swollen cat.

Leaf was not deterred. "Your home is beautiful, Mormor. Like something out of a magazine. I love it." People often threw compliments that they didn't mean, especially when they were nervous, but Leaf... The way he delivered his lines was *everything*. He wasn't really looking at my grandmother so much as at the art with the crackled paint frames. At the stenciling she'd done herself along the top border of the walls. At the antique curio with the glass front and the country-flavored knickknacks inside. At the Americana swan on top of the TV cabinet.

Leaf meant what he said about enjoying her aesthetic. And it made all the difference.

Mormor *melted*.

"Thank you! I've worked hard to get it to my liking." She went from wary predator to purring kitty cat in three sentences. I knew my boyfriend was charming, but I was pretty sure that was some kind of record and he might actually be a brilliant supervillain.

"I can tell. Thank you so much for inviting me to dinner."

He grinned.

Mormor nodded her approval, tutting quietly.

"Well, let's eat, shall we?"

Ten minutes later, Leaf had his first Swedish smorgasbord, or really, American-Swedish smorgasbord. Mormor told me fish starters were standard at home, but a lot of Americans weren't big on cold herring and eel, so instead it was two types of bread, soft cheeses, sweet butter and egg dishes, including quiche. There were cold sausage cuts and hot ones, too, with the kok korv. She'd made ärtsoppa for me because she loved me, and the meatballs, and a bunch of hot and cold vegetable dishes. She'd made sweets, which would come later, after we'd digested the mountains of food.

Mormor didn't bust out the big meals often, but when she did, we had leftovers for weeks.

Leaf tried everything. He even tried it how Mormor told him to try it, meaning a lot of Swedes eat ärtsoppa by dipping their spoons into a sweet mustard first before taking a mouthful of soup. Each new food was considered, savored and at one point, he dropped the ultimate compliment on her meatballs.

"I'd love to learn how to make these, if you have a recipe."

Mormor bloomed.

"I can write out the recipe for you, but you will want to come over and learn. It's nice to see someone appreciating good cooking. It is a dying art form. My girls don't care much."

"That just means they need their men to cook for them." Leaf flashed a pearly smile at my mother. "I cook for Sara. I love to cook."

"She told me. Sometimes she makes me drool a little." Mom sipped her coffee. "Of course, I drool for fun on Wednesdays, too, but I swear this time it's about your food."

Leaf chuckled and got up to rinse his dishes in the sink. When Mormor started packing up the extra food, he insisted on helping, ladling things into Tupperware and meeting Mormor's small talk with his own, the two of them bonding over cooking. They were getting along almost too well. Mom's eyes met mine and she pointed at them, mouthing, "Do you see this?"

I did.

My boyfriend was the best.

Inspired by—okay, let's be real, guilted by, because that's the truth of it—Leaf's easy willingness to help clean up, I started loading the dishwasher. Mom was on make-room-in-the-refrigerator-for-the-extra-everything duty. It took us a good half hour to get the kitchen back to a working state, but we managed it. Leaf told Mom and Mormor about his sister and her baby, showing them pictures of Elana in her holiday dresses on his phone. His most recent shot was of her in her Halloween costume, which was a lobster, 'cause I guess if you're from New England that's how you did your kids dirty.

…I made a mental note to be sure I found something equally as ridiculous for Cass the following year. Maybe a frog. Or a unicorn onesie.

Heck, I wanted a unicorn onesie.

We could be twinsies.

"Alright, you two are off the hook for spending time with the old people. I'll call you down for dessert in, say, an hour-ish?" Mom glanced at the clock. It was only six-thirty. "Make that two hours. I think I ate an entire horse."

Leaf slung an arm over my shoulders. "My father has a saying—the older the violin, the sweeter the music. I'm having a great time—down here, upstairs. It's all good to me."

Mom's eyes widened. "Oh, you're trouble. Good trouble, I think, but trouble. Go on. Get out while the getting's good. If you stay in the kitchen too long, she'll find more work for you to do." Mom waved her thumb in Mormor's direction. "Or maybe she'll throw a shoe. She does that for fun sometimes."

"Astrid! I would never. He's been very helpful. Far more helpful than my own family," Mormor protested. "But yes, go. We'll take some time before dessert."

Leaf snickered and guided me toward the stairs. I ducked in front of him, holding his hand and bringing him up to my room. The other rooms upstairs were closed save for the bathroom, where Mom had done the customary there's-a-guest-in-the-house lighting of the candles. It was the only time anyone actually burned candles, ever. The rest of the time, they gathered dust waiting for their next round of usefulness.

I'd had to pick a bug carcass off one of the ones downstairs before lighting it. It was gross.

Leaf looked around my room and smiled. Posters on the wall, a shelf of my old and not-so-old plush toys. More books than could fit on the bookshelf. A stack of homework that was probably over a month old and could be tossed out. It was a pretty standard mess of a room, save for the copy of *What To Expect When You're Expecting* that I had on my nightstand by my bed. Leaf went for it, sitting down by my pillows as he opened to the first chapter.

"My mom got me that," I said.

"Is it helping?"

"Sometimes, yeah." I sat down next to him. He swung his head my way and looked at me from below his heavy lids. He was a handsome guy, with those ridiculous lashes of his, and when he moved in for a smooch, I was halfway there. His lips on mine felt right—they fit right, they were soft. He never slobbered on me or made me wish I was somewhere else. If anything, he always left me wanting a little more, and a little more, and a little more after that.

Which, he hadn't taken, and I wouldn't push him for. But sometimes I really wished he'd just go for it.

I could go for it.

I mean, it's not always on the guy, right?

My door was closed. We were both properly fed and would be left alone. Why the heck not?

I plucked the book from his hands and twined the fingers of my left hand with the fingers of his right. One kiss became two. Two became three. He leaned into me, groaning quietly. I slid my fingers into his hair, under the ponytail, massaging at his scalp. Closer he came, closer still.

Until…the bump stopped him.

It pulled me from the heady exchange immediately. I reared back, licking my lips, my growing happy tingles whooshing away at the reality that maybe he hadn't gone for it with me because he found my growing bulge icky.

Maybe it weirded him out.

It kinda weirded me out.

"What's wrong, Serendipity?" he asked, drawing out my name, romancing all the syllables and then a few extra I hadn't known were there.

"Nothing. Just—overfull, I guess."

I looked down. There was heat in my face. I must have been blushing because his hand lifted, his pinky finger gliding over my cheek.

"Is that true?"

"It's not even three months away," I blurted. "Like, then I'll start shrinking down again. That'll be cool."

"What are you talking about?"

I couldn't really speak, so instead I motioned at myself. I'd not been all that self-conscious about my body with him to that point, but apparently the stretched-out

Link face over Gutzilla bugged me more than I'd let on. Or maybe it was the class that morning, on top of seeing Jack, on top of Leaf meeting my mom and grandma for the first time compounding into a roiling ball of stress that was whittling away at my sanity.

"Okay, that's your body," Leaf said. "It's very nice. I'm a fan of it."

"...I just know it must be weird for you. I mean, it is weird. And, like, if you looked up anti-sex in the dictionary, you'd probably see my picture there, so... I saw Jack today," I blurted.

"Jack?"

"The baby's father. Devi got gas from him and I went to see him at work. He's going to talk to his parents about it. He has a girlfriend now, which is totally fine. It's just... It was a weird conversation. I was standing there, telling him about our kid, and I felt so fat. My T-shirt didn't really fit, and I feel bulbous and..."

"Aaaaaaah. I get it. Sara, no. I... Come here." He pulled me in close, pressing my face to his neck. He smelled like clean cologne—not one of those overpowering stinks that made my eyes water that the jocks liked to wear. He'd shaved smooth, and I nuzzled at him, liking how his arms settled around me. Liking how soft he was against my soft. This big bear of a boy made me feel safe and I needed it then, for reasons I couldn't and can't really articulate beyond "I was feeling vulnerable."

"First of all, I'm glad you found Jack. That must be a relief. The worry doesn't do you any good and now, one way or the other, you'll have an answer."

I managed a tiny nod and he squeezed me.

"Good. Now for the rest of it—you're gorgeous. I've told you before, I don't care that you're pregnant. It's not why I don't… Do you think that's why we're not sleeping together? We should have talked about this, I think."

I didn't say anything. He stroked my hair and kept right on hugging me.

"I never have," he said quietly. "With anyone. It's not that I don't want to. I do. I think about it a lot. It's just something I wanted to wait to do with someone special. You are special, and maybe—probably, even—it'll be you I want it to be with. But this isn't about you or your body at all. You're great. It's about me and *my* body, and what I want for it. Does that make sense?"

"You're demisexual," I said. "Demi. You need the attachment before the sex stuff comes into play."

"Yes, I think that's a term I've read about and it sounds right. Does that help you understand?"

I was so relieved by the answer, I burst into tears. He shushed me quietly and scooted back onto my bed so he could haul me into his lap. He was as strong as he was tall and wide, and so I sat there, cradled and adored, with my boyfriend whispering in my ear how beautiful he thought I was, how everything was going to be okay, how much he looked forward to seeing me every day and how much he liked my family.

If the talks with my mother and grandmother hadn't been enough to convince me that I didn't need to consider Jack a part of the package deal with my baby, how cherished and cared for I felt in that moment would have.

CHAPTER THIRTY-ONE

Jack took his sweet time getting back to me. It wasn't like he was ghosting me—he sent me a few brief messages to say hold tight, working on it and this is hard thanks for patience, but holding tight and patience were not my strong suits. I was eager to find out what he wanted to do. I assumed the holdup was that he hadn't told his father yet, or that he had and they were losing their minds about it, but neither scenario was particularly reassuring. I did my best not to dwell, though, continuing along my gestational journey one cheeseburger at a time.

Which was a lot of cheeseburgers. I'd remained a big fan throughout the pregnancy, to the point I'd probably never want to say the word *cow* after Cass was born.

While I waited for Baby Daddy to get his crap together, I worked on getting myself into a Lamaze class. I couldn't find an in-person place so late, but I was able to find an online class that'd help. Dr. Cardiff had warned me about them filling up fast. It'd just slipped between the cracks of high school and pregnancy and doctor's visits and new boyfriend.

I was the busiest-not-busy person in the world.

I was okay with the online class, though. The less huffing and puffing I had to do in front of strangers, the better.

"I can do it online," I announced to Devi. "I should start it next week."

Devi peered at me over her phone, smiling. She'd come over after school for a spa day, which was, essentially, her slathering herself with various goos and then chasing me around until I sat still long enough for my own goo-fest. I'd drawn the line at snail cream. She said it was super hot in Korea.

I said I was super okay not being in on the new, exciting snail secretion trend.

"My skin feels like a baby's butt, I'll have you know," she said.

"Did you hear me about the Lamaze class?"

"Yeah, sure, but I hadn't gotten past the snail thing yet. You compliment my skin all the time and I'm telling you, it's the snail. It's ethically harvested snail goo, bee tee dubs. They don't puree snails. That'd be animal cruelty."

I blinked at her.

"Devi."

"Yes?"

"Why are you like this?"

She grinned.

"There's no one left to stop me. Anyway, what they do is they put the snails on a screen and then shine a light on them that makes them happy. The snails happily secrete on the screen, and then they collect the leavings and make skin care with it. So really, you're using the snail version of pixie dust on your face. It's magical."

"So you're saying they get the snail excited, it uhhh… spurts and then you smear it all over your face."

"DON'T MAKE IT WEIRD. IT'S HAPPINESS SE-CRETIONS. IT'S DIFFERENT." She paused. "Oh, and if Jack doesn't call Lamaze dibs, I'll be your coach."

"You would?" I hadn't considered that I'd be there with anyone other than my mom, but the idea of it being Devi—of it being my best friend who'd been my best friend since pudding cup days—made a lot of sense.

"They're going to assume we're together," I said. "When two queers are anywhere together, we must be dating, 'cause that's how it works for the straights, right? What-ever. I'll have the hottest girl in the room, either way."

"You really would," she said. "And you know why I'm hot? Snails. Snails all over my face."

I stared at her.

She grinned back.

Five minutes later, I had snail secretions on my face. True fact: snails do, in fact, make your skin feel like a baby's butt. I was a convert, but for the first application, I winced and whined a lot. Devi called me a baby. Then she took the snail stuff off and put a mud thing on and it hardened until I looked like Pennywise. I was five minutes shy of finishing my clown-bake mask when we heard the clatter from the other room. There was a loud thud, a crash and Mormor shouting, "Attans."

I didn't speak much Swedish, but the swears I knew by heart.

Devi and I rushed out of my room and into the hall. Mom was at work for a few hours yet, so it was just us and my grandmother. Mormor was in her craft room, a place I associated with the West Wing from *Beauty in the Beast* because I'd been forbidden to go in there upon penalty of death. The last petal had fallen off her rose a while ago, leaving her in her perennially salty meat suit, but apparently there were still things to protect in her craft sanctum; the warning she'd issued when we'd moved in almost the same as it'd been when I was five and visiting with Mom.

"Mormor? Are you okay?" I asked, knocking.

"Yes, yes. I'm fine. Just a little spilled paint. Be careful when you open the door."

Open the door? I'm allowed in there?

It was likely a once-in-a-lifetime chance, and so I took the invitation, less because I was worried about my grandmother's well-being—she'd told me she was okay despite the crash—but more because maybe I'd be able to see what magical things she had hidden inside.

The door opened.

My breath did, in fact, catch in my throat.

It was *a nursery.*

There was another small bedroom next to Mom's that I'd assumed would be the baby's space. But Mormor had instead converted her own craft room to accommodate my sprogling. The walls were painted rich navy blue and there were gold-foil stars of varying sizes everywhere. These weren't the sticker decorations you could buy on the internet, either. She'd hand-stenciled about a trillion of them, along the tops of the walls and curving down around the corners of the room. It must have taken her forever to finish them all, but somehow, I'd never caught her in there.

"When? Oh, my God, Mormor. This is beautiful," I said.

Devi nodded. "Wow, this kid's super lucky. Really nice, Mormor."

Mormor sniffed and mopped up a small puddle of spilled gold paint, her smile tight. "Thank you. Little Star needs her space. And it's getting cold out. The yard work is over for the season. I have time during the day when you're at school."

I was emotional. Again. I battled the tears, managing to keep them at bay, but Devi knew. She patted my shoulder and pulled me in for a half hug. I collected myself so I could help Mormor clean up the paint, but when I tried to stoop from the waist... Nope. No go. I couldn't do it. The belly was in the way and I was stuck hovering halfway to the floor. I reached for the door frame, intent to kneel and try to help that way by going on my hands and knees, but Devi shouldered past me.

"No way with that stomach. I got this." Devi grabbed

the paper towels and mopped at the paint. Luckily, Mormor had prepped the room with a plastic drop cloth before work, so the disaster hadn't impacted the Berber carpet.

"You're the best," I said. "Both of you."

Devi flashed me a smile. It made her Pennywise mask crack.

"Except when you do that," I added. "That's terrifying."

"So's your face."

Considering I was as bemasked as Devi, she wasn't wrong.

"Girls." Mormor shook her head and dumped her soiled paper towels in the garbage. She eyed the walls, assessing her work with a thoughtful nod. "How about you wash your faces, I change out of these overalls and we go to Ikea? I think it's time to pick out some baby furniture."

Going to Ikea for not-Swedish people is a harrowing experience. It's big, it's crowded. The overhead lighting is brutal and gets you sweaty fast. They've set up the aisles so you're essentially stuck in a mouse maze and the only way out is to pass their Idaho-sized home goods section full of baskets, art and candle tchotchkes you can impulse buy for a buck.

Going to Ikea with your Swedish grandmother? An altogether different, and somehow more aggravating, experience. Not only did you have all that other stuff to contend with, but you had Mormor's strange Swedish pride, too. At everything. The vast and varied, yet somehow stylistically the same, furnishings became indicators of superior Swedish design, instilled in us by our Viking ancestors. Kitchen cabinets with choose-your-own hardware were a sign of our cleverness. Vikings did, after all, invent the comb, the tent and the magnetic compass, Mormor informed us.

Bet you didn't know Vikings had skills beyond just raiding and pillaging.

They were big on spatial efficiency and modular home living, too.

Devi and I slogged along behind her, carrying the obnoxious yellow bags with the blue handles while Mormor chattered on and on through the aisles, pushing her cart and smiling. I wasn't going to rain on her parade—she'd painted me a nursery, after all—but there were times when I considered perhaps diving into a Kvikne wardrobe with two sliding doors and lots of interior storage space in hopes of meeting a goat-man in Narnia.

"Do you even have any Ikea furniture in your house?" Devi whispered to me.

"Nope. She like antiques and Americana," I whispered back.

"So why's she so...you know. About Ikea?"

"Because she's Mormor," was the best I had.

Devi seemed to understand, though. She nodded gravely and continued on. We were deep in the middle of the cement building, so we had no cell service. We took to hitting each other with our empty yellow bags for fun. Every once in a while, Mormor would look back over her shoulder at us, her expression suggesting she did *not* want to turn this car around, and Devi and I would smarten up for forty seconds before going right back to being brats.

We giggled a lot in spite of our shared misery.

At least our skin looked good.

It took us seventy-three days and nights to get to the baby section, but once there, my reservations about being trapped in Ikea faded. There were ten nursery vignettes scattered around, with cribs and dressers and plushies and soft blankets. I picked up a blanket, and then remembered the navy-blue-and-gold blanket Mormor had been knitting over the past few months. She'd known she was going to decorate the nursery. She'd been planning all along.

"Thank you again, Mormor," I said.

"I like that one," was her reply, ignoring me to point at a white crib with two pullout storage drawers underneath. I approached and ran my hand over the rails, my eyes skimming the ticket that told me all the ways this was an adjustable bed, to grow with my kid as they went from baby to toddler and beyond.

"The white drawers or the natural finish wood would look nice with the blue and gold," Devi offered. "I think I like the white."

I nodded. I couldn't speak. Not then, not when we picked out a bureau and a changing table and an upholstered corner chair so I could nurse. Not when we filled up those tacky yellow bags with baby linens, a mobile and soft stuffed animals.

I had a nursery. A real live nursery for a real live baby that was coming far sooner than she was not coming, and *oh, my God, everything feels so real.*

CHAPTER THIRTY-TWO

The next three weeks were spent with an Allen wrench assembling furniture. I wasn't stuck doing it, more surveying the process and bearing witness to oodles of my mom's go-to swear words and delivering her gallons of much-needed coffee. Mormor had checked out, saying she'd bought the furniture and painted the nursery, so Mom got the pleasure of putting it all together.

Come to find out, big pregnant bellies didn't do well with a lot of things that required mobility, including building a crib with eighty thousand modular pieces. It was official. I had popped.

Cass was a volleyball-sized impediment to productivity. I could no longer pity Erika from my Saturday group without looking down at my own midsection and RIP-ing my feet. The backaches were real; so was the need to pee. Dr. Cardiff hadn't been kidding. The flutterbye baby in my middle, kicking to her heart's content, meant I was in the bathroom a ton, and that number was only going to climb. "So strap in," Dr. Cardiff said at my check-in.

That appointment, she also introduced me to two other OB/GYNs in her practice. I wasn't sure why until she dropped the anvil on my head of, "In case I can't be there to deliver Cassiopeia for whatever reason."

I must have gone pale at the possibility of having an-other doctor looking at my baby-distended wahoo, be-cause Dr. Cardiff rushed to reassure me. "I plan to be there, Sara. It's in case of emergency. I make a wide ma-jority of my patient's births. But *if* it happens that I can't make it, small if, but *if*, I thought you'd like to know my backups?"

I didn't particularly want to meet either doctor, consid-ering they represented my delivery plans swirling down a giant baby-sized crapper, but I sat through short intro-ductions and hollow reassurances that Dr. Cone and Dr. Laghari were *so* happy to be on my birthing team. Point-ing out that they were both men and I really didn't want a man doctor gazing at my spew parts would have been worthwhile to mention, but I was so desperate to get out of there, I stayed quiet, nodding a lot and miraculously not crying. Well, for a while, anyway.

I kept it together until the car, and then I exploded.

The snot and tears flew, Mom offering me piles of drive-through-window napkins to sop up the flood before we both drowned. She stroked my hair, her fingers getting tangled in my black curls, her words quiet and loving. It was exactly what I needed when I was feeling vulnerable. My mommy comforting me. I was really lucky to have her, and that she was so supportive, and had been throughout my pregnancy.

In fact, I was so grateful to her, I...cried all the harder. Look, there's been a lot of crying, I know, but you have to understand your hormones are frantic and weird and unreliable. My brain was a writhing sack of cats far more often than not. I was lucky I could get up in the morning and put on pants without breaking down that everything was awful forever.

"Thanks," I warbled, cramming a wad of McDonald's napkins up my nose.

"You're welcome, peaches. It sounds like she's going to be there, at least. So that's good." Mom stroked her fingers down my cheek and tucked them under my chin. "I'm sorry you're so upset. Is there something I can do that doesn't involve murder? Mommy doesn't want to go to jail yet. Mommy has living left to do, and a grandkid on the way."

"No, probably not. It's just that I don't want a strange dude looking at me when I...you know." The confession made me embarrassed. Dr. Cardiff had been looking up the rude end of me a lot, and yet I still had hesitation when it came to dude doctors, apparently? "It's ridiculous."

"Nah, it's not. I still prefer doctors who have my junk and understand my junk to the alternative, but I'm going to tell you a secret, and you won't believe me, but I swear it's true."

"Yeah?"

"You aren't going to care. Like, you think you will. Remember when you were freaked about the poop thing?"

"But I am still freaked about the poop thing," I said.

"Well, okay then. I thought we were past that. Oops. But I promise you, you are going to be so busy with getting that kid out of you, you won't care who sees what. Seriously. No birth is clean or polite. None. And your body is contorting in weird ways and it's freakish and weird and it hurts and your focus will one hundred percent be on getting through it as efficiently as possible. There were six masked strangers in the room when I had you. Your grandmother held one hand, your dad held the other hand and this army of medical people in a really ugly teal stood there, staring at my parts, and *I didn't care.* Even a bit. And then you came out, and you were slimy and wriggly and gross and I loved you immediately." Mom paused. "It's consuming, Sara. Totally consuming. The things you think you'll care about, you don't care about. It's secondary to the baby. All you're going to know is that you need help and there are people there who are helping you. That will supersede everything, I promise."

"Look at you, with the fifty-cent word," I said.

"I know, right? It's like your mom isn't nearly as ignorant as she looks!"

We shared a smile, and then we shared a Blizzard from Dairy Queen. It was a pretty awesome ending to a pretty lukewarm afternoon.

What was not awesome was that Thanksgiving came and went, and Jack was still giving me the quasi–blow off. He kept in touch, letting me know he was still around, but they were one sentence texts of apologies and excuses about how hard it was and that his family was going to get upset and he was afraid to talk to them. It was confirmation he hadn't ripped off the Band-Aid yet. I was sympathetic to a point—not everyone's families were as supportive as mine—but I was losing patience, too.

I had the much harder job in the vast scheme of brewing the kid.

Nut up, Jack.

The second week of December, when I was sitting in the living room, holding Leaf's hand, staring at Mormor's color-coordinated Christmas tree because she only decorated with Sweden's colors, I said as much. It wasn't out of the blue or anything. Rudolph didn't start playing and I had a crisis of paternity, but he'd sent me another text that said, gonna tell parents after X-mas. Have a good 1.

My fingers were moving before I could think better of it.

Don't bother. Clearly too hard for you.

Yes, it was witchy, but I was thirty weeks into the pregnancy and he'd been told over a month ago. I was in a Saturday morning teen support group and had started Lamaze with Devi. I'd read two books about pregnancy. I knew things about mucus plugs—don't ever Google image search that. And the meconium—*especially* don't Google image search that. I was working my fat pregnant butt off to make sure that my kid came into the world with a half-functioning mom.

And he couldn't tell his father?

Whatever.

I'd been patient enough.

"Are you okay?" Leaf asked.

I grumbled something that wasn't really words, more just a mishmash of frustrated animal sounds.

"You look like you want to eat the phone," he said.

"I kind of do. Jack just told me he wasn't going to tell his family until after Christmas. I guess he doesn't want to ruin the holidays." The bitterness was there, lacing every word. Leaf snorted and rubbed the back of my neck, hissing when he felt how tense my muscles were. His fingers kneaded at them in vain, attempting to get me to uncoil.

Good luck, buddy.

"He's being dumb." He motioned for me to lean forward, and I did the best I could, resting my boobs on top of my belly. His hands moved from my neck to my shoulders and spine. "You've been patient. If he can't appreciate that, he's not worth your time."

"I know, right? I'd hoped he wouldn't be an asshat about it, but I guess that was too much to ask."

"His loss," Leaf said.

Damn right, it was his loss.

Except it wasn't *actually* a loss. Two minutes later, Jack texted me back.

I'm sorry. Gonna tell them now. Bbs.

Okay, so maybe my baby daddy wasn't an asshat. Maybe he just needed a toe up the butt now and then to get him going in the right direction. I could do that. I could be *that toe.*

"Or not. He's telling them now. I guess pointing out he was being a donkey was a quick way to get results. I should have been meaner, sooner."

Leaf kissed the back of my shoulder. "I like you mean. At other people. Mean at me, probably not so much."

"I don't have any reason to be mean to you, though. You should screw up more."

He stopped massaging my shoulders.

"Like that?"

"...never mind. Keep being awesome. I'll save my mean for other people."

He laughed and pulled me back into a hug. My back was to his front, his arms looped around my body, his hands resting on my belly. I went still, so my kid started kicking like crazy. Leaf followed the movement with his hands across my belly button area.

Most pregnant people will tell you in-utero children are offended by relaxation. The moment their fleshy incubator stopped moving, the kid got their tap shoes on. It made trying to fall asleep a fun and exciting game. Dr. Cardiff explained that the babies were lulled by their mom's movements. My walking around equated to "Rock-a-bye Baby." I stopped? Well, Mom just failed the team.

This roundhouse kick to the ribs will show you, Mom!

"She's active."

"She does this lately. Kid doesn't like it when I chill out."

"Are you chill now? More than you were, at least?"

I eyed my phone—the conduit between me and the proving-to-be-annoying father of my kid.

I eyed the Christmas tree, the stockings hung by the chimney with care and the reflection of me and Leaf cuddling on the couch in the black of the TV screen.

"Yeah," I said, nestling in closer to Leaf's warm body. "Yeah, I'm okay."

CHAPTER THIRTY-THREE

Jack's parents took the news poorly.

That is the understatement of the century.

I had a lot more sympathy for him when he called me that night, at eleven, two hours after I'd gone to bed, but I figured it had to be serious if he was willing to use actual conversation instead of text to communicate. I rolled over and picked up the phone, clearing my throat so I didn't sound like I'd gargled with a porcupine.

"Hey," I said.

"Hey. Hi," he said back. "Sorry to wake you. Did I?"

He sniffled.

He'd been crying.

I wasn't going to make a big deal out of it. I knew I didn't appreciate it when people fussed when I was a wet sack of tears, which was frequently, so I went at it simple.

"I sleep all the time. Kid makes me tired. It's fine. You okay?"

"No, not really. My parents are pissed. They want to meet you and your parents. Dad's... He wants a paternity test. He was an asshole about it. I knew he would be. That's why I waited so long. I know how this is going to sound, but it was as much for you as it was for me. My mom will keep him in check to a point, but he's going to be uncool."

I groaned and flopped back into my pillows, my eyes adjusting to the darkness in my room. Back at the apartment, I had those plastic glowy star stickers on my ceiling. I missed them in that moment. They would have given me something to focus on that wasn't Jack's father potentially dickbagging at me and our unborn kid. "Okaaaaay. Well, he can deal with my mother and grandmother. Good luck to him. I'm not sure what goes into a DNA test, but..."

"I looked before I called. We can do spit tests when the kid is born—it's a girl, right?"

"That's the assigned gender. I wanna keep doors open in case they choose another gender, later, though. But that's a talk for another day."

Jack paused.

"Yeah, okay, that's fine. I'm just going to tell my parents it's a girl. I don't think they'll get it, otherwise."

Jack's parents sounded like charmers.

"Anyway, you can get a blood test done now but that's probably going to cost us money and the baby's coming soon. February, right?"

"Yeah."

"Okay. If you're cool with one of those spit tests, my dad is. We can get them off Amazon. He just doesn't want to have to pay support if it's not mine. Which, I—I believe you, Sara, okay? My dad's just tough. He's not always a bad guy. He's just... I dunno." Jack sighed and sounded sad. "Anyway, he wants to get together. It's probably going to suck. A lot. I won't lie."

"Yeah, but I'd rather get it over with. I'll talk to Mom and Mormor and we'll set something up. Text you tomorrow?"

"Sounds good." He paused. "And I'm sorry for the delay, Sara. I was just really scared."

"I am, too, sometimes," I said. "But it'll be okay. I've got plans in place. My school's going to let me finish the last term of senior year at home so I don't have to leave Cass too early."

"That's cool," he said. Then he paused. "I guess you're not going to that Ivy League school you told me about, huh?"

"Not now, but maybe one day. I didn't apply to any for now, though."

It was that time of year when all of my classmates were getting their application essays together for early decision admission. Weller had even set aside a few days in AP English to give us guidelines for writing what she called the perfect college essay. It was formulaic, but it sounded legit, and I wished I had more reason to care about it, but

I was too busy trying to fit a baby belly in between my chair and desktop to give her much attention.

Your priorities shift when you're pregnant.

To Weller's credit, she'd noticed my discomfort, and miraculously, the next class we had two long tables in the back of the room with pull-out chairs. They seated two kids per table, and Leaf had taken to sprinting to class early to claim one for us. Thankfully, the other kids caught on pretty quickly it was for the preggo who didn't quite fit into standard seating and never fought him.

Because Weller had done that, my other classes did it, too. She was a trendsetter. A mean one who called us stupid when we screwed up, but a trendsetter all the same, and I appreciated her consideration.

"However I can help, I will. My mom said she'd help, too. We'll figure it out," Jack said.

"Yeah, we will. Let me talk to my family and we'll get a plan going?"

"Totally. Thanks for being cool. And I'm sorry again."

"Don't worry about it."

I hung up and rolled over. My brain was on fire, doing that thing where I worried not about what Jack had said, but what he *hadn't* said. About why his father wanted the DNA test. Did he think I was a slut? Was it because my last name was Rodriguez? Did it even matter what he thought because he was just the baby's grandfather? Or maybe he was just being responsible for his son, making sure Jack didn't get taken in?

I worried about the gender discussion, too. Was Mr. Ianelli anti-queer? And if so, how would he feel if he found out I was questioning my sexuality and leaning toward IDing as bisexual? Or that my best friend was gray ace? Or that Morgan was a trans girl? Would he teach my kid a lot of toxic things that would, ultimately, hurt people I loved a lot?

I felt like crap. I was halfway tempted to call Devi or Leaf and wake them up with my whining, but the next day was a school day, so instead, I crawled from my bed and went downstairs to sample our leftovers, and by sample, I mean microwave and devour all of them. Mormor had made fried chicken and mashed potatoes with gravy. They were delicious.

Both times that I ate them for dinner that night.

I was sitting in the living room, my only light the warm glow of the Christmas tree, when Mom padded downstairs in her robe and slippers. She caught me feasting and smirked, throwing herself onto the couch beside me and sticking her finger straight into my mashed potatoes.

"Uhhh, why are you so nasty?"

"Because potatoes are delicious," Mom said.

She wasn't wrong. That didn't mean I wanted her pawing my food, though. When she licked off her first stolen potato sample and made motions to take a second, I stabbed the back of her hand with my fork.

Mom flinched.

"Dang, girl. You are bitey."

"Leave my food alone," I said.

"Okay, okay. Did you leave anything in the fridge?"

"...no."

Mom smirked and headed off for the kitchen, returning

a little while later with a jar of pickles, a pudding cup and a quarter pound of lean roast beef with a saltshaker. It was pretty gross, and I frowned as she sprawled out next to me.

"I'm the pregnant one, I thought," I said. "That's food abuse."

"Delicious food abuse. I'm PMSing. Salt, beef and chocolate, baby."

I smirked and went back at my dinner. Mom salted her beef and chewed thoughtfully. "So what's got you up? Everything okay?"

"Jack told his parents. They were dicks about it," I said. "Erm, sorry. They were unpleasant about it. They want to meet."

"Good swear catch." Mom proceeded to wrap a pickle in salted roast beef and eat it. I scowled at her. She ignored me. "We'll get together. If they're dicks, they can deal with me and your grandmother."

"That's what I told him."

"Good. Did you know Vikings rubbed actual salt in wounds? Like, we did that. We may have invented that. We were those people. Jack's dad is going down."

"…you and Mormor say the weirdest crap sometimes, you know that?" I shook my head.

"Yeah, but you love us. And you don't have a murder factory so I take that as a sign that I'm a superior parent."

"As opposed to all of my classmates who do, in fact, have a murder factory?"

"Yes. Exactly." Mom finished her pickle atrocities and moved on to her pudding cup. Realizing she didn't have a spoon, she used her finger to eat it. Out of pity, I cleaned

off my fork and handed it to her. She saluted me and dug
in. "Friday," she said.

"Invite them over then?"

"Mmm-hmm. Bring me the disbelievers. We shall feast
upon their trepidation!"

I stared at Mom. I blinked.

Without a word, I picked up my phone to text Jack
the plan.

Leaf, Devi, Morgan and Erin all offered to come be my
backup for the meeting. I went with Leaf for no other reason than he was a big dude and maybe, just maybe, that'd
slow Jack's dad's roll. Leaf showed up a half hour before
the Ianellis and immediately popped into the kitchen to
sous-chef for Mormor. It was interesting to see my usually unflinching grandmother nervously fluttering about
in her blue dress. She didn't say she was worked up, but
she couldn't sit still. Every time she sat down, she immediately thought of something else she should be doing and
sprung up again.

Mom, who'd just finished vacuuming, whispered to me,
"Stay out of her way. She's turbo right now."

In a way, I was glad for it; if Jack's dad was as bad as
Jack suggested, we'd need her sass. I didn't like the idea
of Mormor being stressed, but...well. A stressed Mormor
was a pointy Mormor.

Pointy was good sometimes.

Mom finished picking up the living room, straighten-
ing the tree skirt under the Christmas tree and putting out
drink coasters. Leaf delivered the tray of meat, cheese and

crackers that he'd assembled to the coffee table. I set the table. We were all quiet, lost to our thoughts. Leaf, dismissed by Mormor, came to help me fold napkins and put out silverware. He'd worn nice khakis with his off-white button-down shirt and black shoes. We were all dressed up—Mom in her pink blouse and black slacks from work, me in a floral-print dress that tucked in under my boobs and flared out and over the bump to call as little attention to it as possible. It was a futile endeavor. My kid was large and in charge, but hey, I'd managed some tights and a pair of shoes that weren't sneakers, so at least I looked cute.

I'd gotten to the point that shaving my legs was off the table. I couldn't bend to get to my calves. It was tights or revealing that the great North American yeti was real and living in New England.

The Ianellis pulled in five minutes early. Mom went to the door and held it open for them, smiling. Mrs. Ianelli came in first. She was small and delicate, with pale brown hair she'd cut into a chin-length bob, green eyes and a Christmas sweater to go along with her jeans. She held a cheesecake in her hands, and she smiled at Mom.

"Caroline," she said.

"Astrid. Please, come on in."

Mrs. Ianelli walked inside, scoped out the Christmas tree and then spotted me not-at-all hiding behind it by the fireplace. Her eyes swept right over to me, first perusing my face and then going down, down, down to the evidence of my and Jack's misdeeds.

"Hi," I said in greeting.

"Hello, Sara. Nice to meet you. I'm Caroline."

Mormor came out of the kitchen toweling off her hands. "Yes, hello. Welcome. I'm Ursula Larssen. Come in, come in." She took the cheesecake from Mrs. Ianelli and the two of them disappeared into the kitchen, making proper introductions. Jack walked in next, in jeans, work boots and a long-sleeved T-shirt. His hands disappeared into his pockets as he looked around.

"Hey," he said. "Nice house. I probably should have dressed up more, I guess?"

"Don't worry about it." I pulled Leaf forward, my hand resting on his back. "Jack, this is Leaf."

The boys shook hands, sizing one another up. Leaf immediately dropped the big white dazzle smile. Jack's wasn't as warm, but I was pretty sure it had nothing to do with Leaf and everything to do with his old man, who'd just shaken Mom's hand by the door and come inside.

"That's my dad. Peter," Jack said.

"Mr. Ianelli, I think is more appropriate given the circumstances," his dad corrected.

Mom and I shared a look. She shut the door and pursed her lips.

"Can I get either of you a drink?" Mom asked. "Soda, beer, water, the harder stuff. The liquor cabinet is in the kitchen."

"I'm set," Jack said.

"I'll take a beer," Mr. Ianelli said. He glanced my mother's way, scowling slightly, his mustache twitching before walking my way. I wasn't afraid of him, but I wasn't eager to make small talk with him, either. Not after Jack's warnings on the phone, and definitely not in the face of his grumpy stare.

"Sara," he said.

"Hi." I tilted my head at Leaf. "This is my boyfriend, Leaf."

Mr. Ianelli just…sorta blew past Leaf's existence. Like he glanced at him and then immediately looked back at me. "Jack said you're a good student."

"Oh, he did?" I looked at Jack. "I, uhh. Yeah. I think I'm ranked second in the class right now? Might be third. I've missed a little school thanks to doctor's appointments but I haven't fallen too far behind."

Mr. Ianelli grunted at me. "That's too bad."

"Is it?" Mom asked, waltzing back in from the kitchen with a couple of beers in hand. She handed one to Mr. Ianelli and took a swig of her own. "I'd say being third in the class is not a *too bad* thing at all."

Mom had that smile she got when she was feral. It didn't come out often, usually when we were at a store and the clerks were rude, or when a waiter was really bad at a restaurant. It looked surface friendly, but it hinted at long angry fangs that would delight in rending flesh from bone.

Mr. Ianelli didn't seem to notice. "Just meant that she'd have to delay going to school is all."

"Sure, but the grades will still be there when transcripts go out. We're lucky—my mother is retired and has already said she'd be willing to watch the baby so Sara can go to class. We just want to make sure we don't push her too hard and force her early. She's a smart girl. She deserves the opportunity to be at her best."

Mormor hadn't said that to me, but I wasn't surprised to hear it. She'd been my babysitter when Mom was working full time and a single parent. My kid would grow up stuffed full of delicious food and *Young and the Restless* and too many garden stores. I could handle that.

"Caroline would help with that, too." Mr. Ianelli paused. He looked from me over to Leaf, his brows lifting. "If the kid is Jack's."

Jack groaned. "Jesus Christ, Dad."

"What? I'm telling it like it is. She has a boyfriend right here. We don't know."

"I know."

Mormor's voice was quiet from the kitchen doorway. Deathly quiet. If Mr. Ianelli didn't realize that he was in imminent danger, he was a fool. Jack's mom clued in pretty fast. She brushed by Mormor to come out to the living room. "Peter, please."

"I'm being practical, Caroline. I'm not saying it's not his, either."

"You're being rude is what you're being," she said.

My esteem for Caroline rose significantly.

Mr. Ianelli sighed and raked his hand over his hair. He swigged from his beer and shook his head. "I'm trying to protect our son."

"Maybe don't embarrass me to death. That's protecting me, too," Jack said. "I'm...really sorry, Sara. Like, so sorry. I just..."

"I'm going to make something very clear now, and then we can have dinner and hopefully talk like civilized people." Mormor moved to stand beside my mother. Her hands were clasped in front of her stomach, her chin was notched up. The left eyebrow was raised in challenge, the tone of voice so cold, it could have frosted hell itself. "My granddaughter is an honest girl. A good girl. If she says the baby is your son's, it is your son's. We will do your testing, mostly so matters of support can be efficiently handled. And there will be support. It takes two to dance a tango. They both tangoed. You can have any opinion you want outside of my home about that fact, but within these walls, you will not insult my granddaughter by suggesting she's a liar. To do so insults me. I will not stand for it."

Mr. Ianelli turned colors. First, it was a red stain in his cheeks. I thought maybe it was embarrassment, but as the color spread, turning to purple up by his temples, I realized it was anger. Hot rage. I took a step back.

Leaf stepped in front of me.

Jack and Caroline stepped toward one another.

"Look, lady, I didn't come here to listen to some bullsh—" He pointed his finger at Mormor and advanced.

Mormor…

Well? She threw a shoe. Lightning fast. It was a motion I'd seen many times before and it was always impressive. Her hand darted down, her leg bent, the shoe went flying, whizzing by Mr. Ianelli's ear and smashing off the Americana swan on top of the TV cabinet.

"STOP," she barked.

Mr. Ianelli stopped, looking stunned.

His hand dropped.

"You threw your goddamned shoe at me!"

"You are advancing in a threatening way. I'll throw the other one if you come any closer."

Jack's father spun. "That's assault. Caroline, this crazy woman just assaulted me, for Christ's sake!"

"No, I did not," Mormor said, her voice even. "I threw a warning shot. If I'd wanted to hit you, I'd have hit you. Trust me, my aim is very good."

We didn't even make it to dinner. Mr. Ianelli dropped his beer on the table and stormed out of the house, cussing and muttering all the while. His mortified wife grabbed her coat and chased after him, throwing apologies as she followed him to the car and promptly started screaming at him in our driveway. Jack looked after them, ashen, swallowing so hard his Adam's apple bounced.

"I gotta go," he said. "I'm really— I want to be in her life, okay? Please don't write me off because of my dad. I want to be a good dad. I know I can be."

"We're not holding you responsible for him, kiddo. Don't sweat it," my mother said, reaching out to squeeze his shoulder. "We're cool. Right, Sara?"

"Yeah! Yeah, it'll be okay. I'll text you, Jack. If you need help—"

"Nah. No. It's not like that. He's not… He'll yell but that's it. I'll be okay." Jack muttered a Merry Christmas at us before escaping the house. The four of us remained in the living room watching the Ianelli SUV leave the driveway. No one said a word until Mormor tutted, crossed the room and slipped on her shoe. She put it back on her foot and stomped her way to the kitchen.

"It's a Christmas miracle, everyone," Mom said, motioning for us to follow. "Free cheesecake."

CHAPTER THIRTY-FOUR

Ham dinner was pretty great. We were short three people, but that just translated to me getting more leftovers when the feed urge struck again. I worried Mormor would be upset that she'd put in so much work only to have our guests storm off, but she took it in stride.

"My cooking is reserved for those who earn my labor. Mr. Ianelli didn't earn it," was the prim reply.

Then she slapped another helping of potatoes on Leaf's plate.

Mormor liked to feed Leaf in much the same

way Leaf liked to feed me. They shared that pride about cooking. She started inviting him to Sunday family dinner with us after that, which worked out well because Leaf's dad worked three weekends out of four each month. Leaf took to bringing dessert, often some kind of layered pastry. Once he even commandeered her kitchen so he could make milk dumplings on the stovetop. They were cinnamon flavored and delicious and I told him I wanted to be buried in a vat of them when I died.

He kissed my forehead and told me I wasn't going to die.

It was sweet, if not overly optimistic.

For Jack's part, he kept in touch with me despite the man my mom had taken to calling Nimrod Father. The night of the disastrous first meetup, I was putting away our dinner dishes and he texted me to apologize on behalf of himself and his mother. Both of them were eager to hear updates about the baby. They'd do so independently of Nimrod Father if need be—he said that his father didn't have to be involved if I didn't want him to be.

I promised I'd let him know how things were progressing, and that we'd figure out what needed to be done closer to delivery time.

I sent him pictures of Cass's assembled nursery. He responded with, That's so cool.

It really was.

A couple weeks later, Christmas fell upon us with all its nauseating good cheer. My two major gifts were baby-related; Mom got me a stroller, Mormor got me a high chair.

"You didn't have to do that, Mormor," I said, eyeballing the antique wooden seat with the removable tray and stenciled duckies. "You got me the crib already."

"But I did have to. This will be in my kitchen. It has to match my decor." She glanced at my mother. "I didn't trust her not to get something hideous."

"Your confidence overwhelms, Mother," Mom said, her hands running over her new robe-and-slipper set, her lips quirked in a wry smile. "It fills me with such love."

"Oh, stop. I love you but you have bad taste, Astrid. In men and furnishings. We know this," Mormor insisted.

Well, okay then. We weren't getting involved in that discussion because we liked our limbs attached to our body.

Leaf's sister came up with his niece from Florida during holiday break so I didn't get to see him as much as I'd hoped. I was, however, invited to come over New Year's Eve to meet Miri and Elana. Miri had what I'd come to recognize as the Leon sense of humor, with the crinkly lines by her eyes and the bold big-bellied laugh. She wore a scarf over her hair, and when I asked about it, she explained it was to show she was a married woman, in her family's tradition. Elana was a riot of big dark eyes and black curls, her toddler fingers getting into *everything*. My future flashed before my eyes as she ran from room to room, playing with not the toy her grandfather had given her, but the empty box it had come in.

She wore it on her head and ran into walls.

"Is this how kids really are?" I asked, watching Elana pick herself up off the floor, don the box again and go right back to bouncing herself off of stuff.

"Oh, yes!" Leaf smiled. "Good luck!"

"Jerk."

"I'll help. I have experience."

To demonstrate, the next time Elana ran past, he swooped her up and kissed her on the belly, birthing a thousand baby giggles that made me think maybe the kid thing wouldn't be such a train wreck after all. Not with people like Leaf and Devi and my mom and grandma around.

I was *super* lucky.

The second Friday in January saw subzero temperatures with a wind chill factor around DEAR GOD, WHY DO WE NOT LIVE IN FLORIDA? Even I, queen of the third trimester hot flashes that left me feeling like overcooked broccoli, was bundled up in triple layers. It was a typical enough school day, with a test, a paper due and a quiz, until lunch when Leaf rushed into the cafeteria with a gigantic grin on his face. He slid into the seat beside me and brushed his lips against my ear, fast like a bunny so no one would catch him being egregiously affectionate.

"Dad got the mail," he said, pulling out Tupperware from his bag.

"And?"

"Not only did I get accepted to Johnson & Wales, I got offered an academic scholarship that covers two-thirds of my tuition. I'm going to be a chef!"

I was so proud of him I squealed, hugging him and not giving a single crap when the lunch monitor, Mrs. Sullivan, came over to tell me to sit down, to stop being so handsy, that I was breaking school rules by touching my boyfriend *so aggressively.* I muttered an apology and stared at her, my hands resting on my stomach. I blinked slowly, waiting for her to give me detention.

Okay, I wasn't really waiting for detention. I was pretty sure she wouldn't give it to me. Putting the pregnant kid in detention was a bad look and she knew it.

I got off with a verbal warning.

As soon as she walked away, Erin reached across the table to squeeze Leaf's wrist, offering her own big grin. She wore a pair of fingerless gloves under her hoodie sweatshirt with cat ears because Stonington didn't believe in properly heating the south wing of the school. One degree colder and they'd have to rename it Siberia. "Awesome, dude. Super proud of you."

Leaf winked at her.

"I got two rejections in the mail!" Morgan offered. "But I also got an acceptance. UMass it is, looks like."

"You okay with that?" Leaf asked.

Morgan shrugged. "It's not Northeastern, but I can still get a decent computer engineering degree. I'll deal." She cracked open a bag and produced a zillion high-protein, low-sugar snacks.

"I'm still waiting to hear back from Emerson," Erin said. "But I've got a couple acceptances for backup schools. My mom's freaking out that I want an art degree. She keeps telling me to do something useful with my life, but I'd rather be broke doing what I love than suffering for the next fifty years doing stuff I hate."

"You tell 'em, baby. That's why Mama's gonna make

the big bucks in programming." Morgan grinned. "In
theory, anyway. But I got you."

"I know you do."

They shared a look that could have melted butter.

"Oh, hey. No-go on hangouts tonight," Morgan said,
abruptly changing the subject. "Tomorrow instead, maybe?
If you two can give up the sacred date night?"

I tucked into my food, moaning quietly to let Leaf know
I appreciated the sarma. It was my favorite of the dishes
he brought, and knowing that, Mr. Leon had taken to
making it once a week. Sweetness ran in the Leon family.

"Sure. I'll let Devi know," I said.

"Cool."

The rest of lunch was spent with Leaf, Erin and Morgan
all comparing college notes and me watching with muted
horror as my child moved around in my gut, causing weird
angles to appear where there ought not to be weird angles. The college talk didn't bother me at the time, but
when I got home to an empty house, with Mom at work
and Mormor nowhere to be found, it started to eat at me,
particularly as I knew Devi was going to chime in about
her acceptance results, too. I was the only one not going
to school and I worried, honestly, that I'd be left behind. I
knew I'd go back to school one day, when I had a clearer
picture of how life would be as a mom, but what if the
friends who were so dear to me moved on without me?
College was a big change. It was exciting. It was new.

…I'd be at home with my kid. Not changing. Not
being exciting.

It weighed on me.

It weighed on me right up until Leaf showed up on my doorstep unannounced, holding a mixed bouquet of flowers.

He didn't have his own car and his father would still be sleeping for work, so I wasn't sure how he'd gotten there. I opened the door and looked past him. Morgan's car idled in the driveway, an old cotton-candy-blue Volkswagen that had seen better days. Erin and Morgan were in the front seat, waving at me, both bundled up in winter coats and gloves. Leaf donned a woolen peacoat with a red-knitted scarf doubled around his neck.

I tipped my head back for a kiss. He complied, pressing the bundle of ribbon-wrapped stems into my hand.

"Come out with us," he said in greeting.

"I have to text my mom and ask." I paused to sniff the flowers, smiling at the sweet smell. "And put these in water. Come in. I thought Morgan and Erin had plans tonight?"

"They lied." He grinned.

"Oh."

Leaf followed me inside, kicking the slush off his boots. We hadn't had much accumulation of the white stuff yet, but there'd been a few flurries over the week that meant our shoes were always wet and the world was painted gray. Gray skies. Gray crusty buildups of snow along the sides of the road. Gray water.

Deep winter in New England could be pretty depressing.

I found a vase in the kitchen cabinet and set the flowers by the sink before grabbing my phone.

"Where are we going?" I asked. "Mom's going to want to know."

"To see your mom."

"…oh."

That made no sense.

He plucked the phone from my fingers.

"Trust me. Get your coat. I'll help you with your shoes," he said.

Month eight of pregnancy meant I was doing a whole lot of cramming my tootsies into slip-on shoes unless someone was there to help. Leaf was happy to be that guy, and I balanced a hand on his shoulder as he slid Keds on me one at a time, him a big tall Romani Prince Charming to my very pregnant, kind of sweaty Hispanic Cinderella.

"Gracias," I said.

"De nada."

A coat, some gloves and my pocketbook and I was climbing into Morgan's car. Erin had vacated the front seat for me, standing by the open door like a chauffeur. When I protested, insisting I could fit in the back seat (and let's be real, I couldn't, but she should be allowed to sit shotgun in her girlfriend's car) she told me not to be silly and helped buckle my seat belt for me. It almost didn't fit, but we managed it with a little prayer and a lot of grunting.

Erin and Leaf climbed in the back. Morgan pulled the car onto the main strip, some girl-band punk rock playing on her stereo.

"I like your hair," I said to her.

She'd styled it in a Mohawk. She wasn't allowed to in school, some crap dress-code rule, but once she'd gotten out and gone home, she'd applied gallons of product. It was back to her natural Irish Orange, as she called it, but the highest spikes were so tall, they brushed the roof of the car.

"Touch it," she said, leaning her head my way.

I did.

The spikes were practically rock.

"Awesome," I said.

Listening to my friends chatter on about a zillion different things, all the while refusing to answer any of my questions about where we were going, helped with the bummed-out thoughts about college. Distraction was often the best medicine. Sure, I'd sweat it again at some point, but not right then. Right then, I was in my happy place. Arriving at an Italian restaurant and being led to a small function room where Mom, Mormor and Devi awaited me—along with Jack and Mrs. Ianelli—was *also* my happy place.

I figured out two steps in they'd thrown me a baby shower.

It was awesome.

Above the doorway, a banner with my name and Cass's name was decorated with gold-foil stars. The favors, the confetti, the napkins—everything was navy blue, not a whiff of pink anywhere to be found. There was a long table with place settings for dinner, a second table for gifts and a third, smaller table topped by a beautiful cake decorated with a pacifier on top.

"I… How? How did…" I motioned at the room, then at Jack and his mom.

Mom came over to kiss my cheek, her arm sliding over my shoulders and anchoring me in case I was a flight risk.

"You go to sleep at like six o'clock. I stole your phone and texted Jack and the gang to set it up. Everyone deserves the hellscape that is a baby shower. And because I

love you, we're not playing pin the tail on the infant. Infant rentals are expensive, come to find out, and stealing
them from the grocery store is a felony. It's kind of unfair."

"Oh. I—oh. Okay. Thank you!"

I smiled at Jack, who looked nervous. He kept shifting his weight from one foot to the other, glancing at his
mom, glancing back at me.

"Hey," he said.

"Hey!"

"Hope you don't mind that we came. But since it's for
my kid, too, I thought—you know."

His mom grabbed his hand, her eyes going big in her
pale face.

"Hi, Sara," she said. "You look beautiful. You're glowing."

They looked kind of pathetic. It was like that scene in
Gladiator when everyone was waiting for me to thumbs-
up or thumbs-down them being there—thumbs-up, they
were welcome. Thumbs-down, they'd be eaten by a pack
of lions. Or Mormor. I'd probably pick the lions myself.

I didn't want them to feel that way around me or my
kid. That wasn't fair—not when they sincerely wanted to
be part of the baby's life, and that was a heck of a lot more
than I had with my deadbeat dad. I did the only thing
I could think to do and left Mom's side to go to them,
pulling them both into a hug that was seriously awkward
with a beach ball–sized fetus between us.

"Yeah! We're family now, right? For Cass? It's cool."

Jack's mom was so relieved she started to cry.

Outside of her blowing an accidental sob booger on my
coat, it was a fantastic day.

CHAPTER THIRTY-FIVE

Tuesday, February eighth was a day that would go down in infamy.

It was the day I did not give birth to my kid. I thought I might but it was a big whopping nada on the reproduction front.

The morning started like any other morning, meaning the alarm went off and I propelled myself from my nest of cast-off blankets and pillows, wishing I had a pulley system and a pair of work mules to haul me to my feet. I waddled my way to the bathroom, my gait more side to side than forward movement. I peed for what would probably be the first time of fifty that day. A noteworthy development was a weird, phlegm-like gob of stuff had passed out of me sometime during the night, not unlike a chunk of jellyfish. I'd seen more like it the day before. I was pretty sure it was my mucus plug, and losing that was totally normal. It meant the kid's head was in the right place in my pelvis and my body no longer felt the need to hold everything inside.

It was gross!

Did I mention bodies are gross? Because they're gross.

My book—and Dr. Cardiff—had told me losing the plug was an indication that my system was doing what it was supposed to do in preparation for birth. It could happen awhile before actual labor, so I wasn't really thinking things were imminent yet. I wasn't due until the sixteenth, after all. Sure, I had nasty backaches that morning, but those had been around for months thanks to the weight gain in my midsection. And sure, I'd had cramping, but Braxton Hicks had been happening off and on for a couple of months. Those were weird practice contractions, where all the muscles in my midsection would tighten up for thirty seconds or so before releasing. My stomach would get super hard for the duration of the contraction, and then it would go back to normal.

The thing was, my Braxton Hicks had never hurt all that bad. They were frequent, sure, but there'd never been pain. I had pain on Tuesday. It probably should have told me something was different, but again, all of the books—all of my talks with my doctor—said Braxton Hicks could hurt and that it was okay and normal. I didn't push the panic button.

What I'm getting at is, the movies make it look like you know you're in labor immediately. The reality is a lot of the symptoms you have are symptoms you've been having throughout the third trimester, and the pre-labor signs look like a slight uptick in your everyday body aches and pains.

Which is how I went to school when I was actually in labor.

Senior year AP English is a slog most days. You're not reading the most engaging material because public schools rarely believe in assigning material written by anyone actually alive. It's Shakespeare and sonnets and Emily Dickinson and stuff that I could appreciate, but not really connect to. Weller had us digging through *Hamlet*. It wasn't my favorite play, but it was better than *Julius Caesar* and *Romeo & Juliet*, and it wasn't as racist as *The Merchant of Venice*, so I'd take it.

Mark O'Hara was busy reading Hamlet's part aloud to us, screwing up the pauses and rhythm of the iambic pentameter because some men liked to watch the world burn.

Weller was visibly twitching.

So was I, but it had nothing to do with Mark O'Hara and everything to do with the increasingly alarming muscle constriction happening in my midsection. It'd been going on from the time I woke up, through the ride to school and into class. Most cramping I could breathe through, as I'd been taught in the online class Devi and I took. But there was one—dear God, there was one where

I saw Jesus. It started in my back and seemed to move around front, to where the baby rested.

I inhaled sharply and squeaked.

Mark O'Hara stopped murdering *Hamlet*. Every set of eyes in the room swung my way.

I didn't care. I was too busy gripping the table in front of me, my fingernails scouring the wood as a solid minute of contraction made breathing almost impossible.

Leaf leaned into me, his concern obvious.

"Are you okay?"

I shook my head in the negative.

"I think that's enough *Hamlet* for today," Weller's voice rang out. She stood from behind her desk, all six feet of her, in her trusty red cardigan and woolen pants. She adjusted her glasses and scanned the room, knuckles balancing on her desktop. "You have a research paper due next week. You can take the next twenty-five minutes in the library gathering your research materials. Wikipedia is not allowed. Now go."

It took everyone a moment to get moving because they were ogling me. Weller barked out an, "Excuse me, did I not speak clearly enough?" and my classmates scrambled to get their things together, practically bolting for the door. I clutched at the table. The cramp passed, but I was terrified another one would come. Leaf's hand was on the small of my back, rubbing in small circles. He knew about the backaches, had witnessed them firsthand. He went straight to what he knew worked best, and I adored him for it.

I breathed deeply and braced as Weller approached. She had the ability to look down her nose at you from every angle. But for once, she seemed aware of it—she didn't want to intimidate me. She crouched before my table. Her gaze swung over to Leaf. I was afraid that she'd banish him to the library with our classmates, but instead she said, "Why don't you call her mother? I should probably send her to the nurse, but this is different, I think."

Weller, queen of the advanced placement demons, was again proving to be the most compassionate of my teachers.

"Thank you," I rasped.

She reached across the table to take my hand. I waited for another cramp. The last one had been awful, like the worst charley horse ever, only in the wrong place. I worried if another came, I'd squeeze Weller's fingers off. I told her as much, but she snorted and told me not to worry about it.

"I had three babies. I'm tougher than I look."

Somehow, that didn't surprise me.

Leaf slipped my phone from my bag and dialed Mom at work. He paced back and forth as he talked to her, explaining what had happened and that Mrs. Weller had told him to call.

"She's on her way," he said a moment later, slipping my phone into his back pocket. "Also, she said it's rude to have your baby on the floor of the high school."

"...she would say that." I managed a smile and slumped into my seat, holding onto Weller with one hand, rubbing my distended midsection with the other. "It could just be Braxton Hicks, too. They like to fake you out, but they've never been like this before."

"It could, but better safe than sorry," Weller said. "Leaf, go get her a damp paper towel from the restroom? Do you have anything you need in your locker, Sara?"

I shook my head. Leaf scampered off to do as he was told, appearing a few minutes later with a sopping wet towel he had to wring out over the garbage before applying to my forehead.

"You're so red." He dabbed at my cheeks with the paper towel. It felt amazing on my skin, and I had the urge to douse my whole body in cold water. I needed a nice, cool pool to walk into.

In February.

Apparently.

"Oh. I'm okay." I paused, slurping in a breath. "I'll be okay."

If I kept telling myself that, I'd eventually believe it.

I'll be okay.

I'll be okay.

I'll be ok—

Another contraction hit.

"The only thing ruder than having the baby on the floor of your high school is having it in my car," Mom announced. "If your water breaks on my upholstery, I'm going to be hella mad."

"Hella?" I asked, trying to get comfortable in my seat and failing. I felt swollen, like a balloon that ought to be floated over the Macy's Thanksgiving Day Parade. Worse, I felt like I was in imminent danger of bursting. "You're not from the bay, Ma."

"No, but I watched a lot of *South Park* when I was pregnant with you. Maybe that's why you're like this. Let's blame *South Park*."

She was trying to distract me by cracking jokes. It worked only to a point. Leaf had stayed at school because he had to—Mom didn't have the ability to dismiss him from class, nor was it time to. Even if it was for-realsies labor, it'd be hours yet unless I was one of those freak-show moms who managed a three-hours-and-done delivery.

Honestly? I would have liked to have been that freak-show mom.

My reality was much, much longer and drawn out. Three hours would have been divine.

Mom pulled into the driveway. She must have called Mormor in advance to warn her that something was amiss, because she was standing sentry by the door when we arrived. The moment Mom opened the car door she swooped in, tutting and circling like a silver mother hawk.

"Are we going to the hospital? I packed her a bag. We should call Devorah so her coach is there."

"Nope," Mom said, sounding emphatic so Mormor didn't bulldoze her. "Dr. Cardiff said five minutes between contractions, and then we go. We're not there yet. There've been a total of…three, Sara?"

"Four," I said, the memory of the last one in the car enough to make me wince.

"How close together are they?"

"Ten minutes apart. About," I said.

"Hmm. I see." Mormor paused. "We're sure she shouldn't go to the hospital yet?"

My mother helped me up the stairs of the front porch.

"We're sure, Mom."

"I'll take your word for it." Mormor hustled along behind us. "Do you want anything to eat or drink, Sara?"

"Nope." I wanted a shower. A cold one. I said as much, and Mom took me upstairs to help me undress. I didn't feel nearly as weird or as self-conscious as I normally would being naked in front of her, and it made me think back to what she said about not caring about which doctor was helping me, only that a doctor was helping me. It seemed a little more believable, particularly as I called for my mom to come back into the bathroom when another contraction hit, this one hard enough that my eyes watered and I clawed at the side of the bathroom stall.

Mom held me up, climbing into the shower with me and drenching her work clothes in the process. She toweled me off. She helped me get dressed in comfortable pajama pants and a soft top.

She walked me around the house, slowly, as we waited to see what was happening.

She got me cold water to drink.

She took me to the bathroom to pee, standing outside the door the whole time to ask if I was okay. More of the jellyfish stuff had come out, and I told her so, and she announced what we were all suspecting.

The baby was coming. Not yet, but she was coming.

Cass-watch was officially on.

CHAPTER THIRTY-SIX

It is a truth universally accepted by New Eng-landers that whenever is the least convenient time for New England to dump a bunch of snow on your head, it will do so. We'd had a season of nothing up to that point, only dustings and cold weather, but God had a sense of humor and de-cided what my pregnancy needed at the zero hour was a gosh-darned blizzard.

Eff snow.

Eff snow forever.

Eight inches in three hours happened right off the bat, with more accumulation expected over the course of the night. It messed up a lot of things, namely Devi and Leaf coming to see me at Mormor's. I was okay, my grandmother and mother were there to see to my needs, but I would have liked my boyfriend and my bestie. I would have liked Leaf's soft words and Devi's reassurances, like she'd learned in our online classes.

I got... Mormor squawking in panicked Swedish before going out to ride her snowblower around the driveway every hour.

"She's like the Wicked Witch out there," Mom said. "Just substitute the broom for a snowblower and turn her green and you've got an eerie likeness."

"She's making sure we can get out of the driveway," I said. I was tired. I was in pain. My contractions were about six minutes apart. I didn't have a lot of good humor to throw Mom's way. "God, my back is killing me."

"I'm sorry, baby girl. I know it sucks. But the good news is, the hormones will kick in soon and all of this will seem like a distant dream afterward." Mom came over to sit on the ottoman, pulling my socked feet into her lap and rubbing my soles. "That's true, you know. Labor is unpleasant, but our brains do chemical whammies on us so we're willing to go through it again in the name of the species not dying out."

"I'm never going to forget this," I promised.

"You say that now, but who knows."

Mom winked.

She'd changed out of her wet work clothes into a pair of black leggings and a big sweater, a pair of snow boots on her feet for the inevitable and unenviable trek to the hospital. It was only twenty minutes to get there, but considering the road conditions and the scarcity of sand trucks out in Mormor's neighborhood, it'd take at least double that, which is why Mom said we'd head over when my contractions were five and a half minutes apart.

So, *soon*.

We'd be leaving *soon*.

I looked out the window from my position on the couch. The snow had gathered in the corners of the windowpanes. It was flurrying so hard, I couldn't see Mormor despite her winter coat being an eye-stabbing bright pink with reflective striping along the seams.

"What if we can't get there?" I asked in a whisper.

"Four-wheel drive, poppet. We'll get there. You texted Jack?"

"Yeah. I texted everybody."

"Good."

Mom had been the one to call Dr. Cardiff, who reassured Mom she lived close to the hospital and for me not to fret—she'd be available. I clung to that knowledge; I was getting scared. More scared than I'd ever been in my life, thanks to the pain and uncertainty. It all seemed so overwhelming suddenly, like all of those classes, all of those meetings with counselors seemed to have been for nothing. I cried about it, and my mom held me tight, telling me in her softest, sweetest voice that she loved me and wouldn't let anything happen to me.

It helped. But what helped the most was Leaf.

The contractions were at a steady five and a half minutes at 11:00 p.m. I texted Leaf to tell him we were packing up the car, that I'd be sure to message him when I got to the hospital to let him know I was safe. He'd kept in touch with me all day, relaying messages from Erin and Morgan that they were pulling for me, too. His frustration that he couldn't be there was evident, but the snow had come on strong, and no one in their right mind would jump on the roads in that storm. Mr. Leon had been sympathetic but firm that Leaf was staying home until it was safer to travel.

It wasn't ideal.

So instead, right before I was supposed to leave the house, he FaceTimed me on his phone. I heard the telltale tones and picked up, hoping I didn't look like a sweaty ham, but totally aware that I looked like a sweaty ham. Labor uglied you up right quick.

"Hey, you," he said, his voice low. "Dad's off tonight. Don't want him to hear me on the phone so late. I think he'd understand, but… Parents, you know?"

"Hey, you. We're heading out," I said. "Mom's getting my coat."

"I know." He smiled and moved his phone super close to his face, so all I could see was his eyes. "I just thought I should tell you something before you go."

"Yeah?"

"I love you. You are amazing. You will be amazing. Your daughter will be amazing. And I am so excited to meet her tomorrow."

He'd never said it outright before. Not the *L* word. And I never in a zillion years would have thought he'd say it to me as I was about to go launch a kid out of my wahoo, and yet somehow, it was the perfect time. It was exactly when I needed to hear it. We'd been dating for months, we'd beaten around the bush by saying how much we liked each other, how good spending time together was. We'd said, "I love spending time with you."

Never "I love you."

Knowing Leaf, knowing how seriously he took sex and commitment, I knew he meant it. He wouldn't have thrown it out willy-nilly at the six-month mark just to placate me so I didn't freak out about having the kid I'd known was coming for almost a year. He'd saved it for the exact right moment—when I could swaddle my frantic rabbit heart in it and find peace when no peace wanted to be found.

"I love you, too," I blurted before the tears started. "So much. I love you, Leaf."

"Go, be excellent for me." He kissed the camera. "I love you."

An hour and twenty minutes in a car with Mom clenching on the steering wheel like she wanted to strangle it, with Mormor griping about how she drove in snow, with me in the back seat breathing through increasingly painful contractions.

This was not the Larssens at their best.

"Watch out for the stop sign," Mormor said.

"Ma."

Mom had that warning voice—the one that suggested she'd bake someone into a pie if she had to.

"Brake now so you have time to slide," Mormor said.

"Ma!"

"Can the two of you knock it off?" I growled from the back seat, both of my hands clasped on my stomach. "I don't need this right now."

"You are upsetting Serendipity. Hush, Astrid."

I stared at the back of Mormor's head, hoping it would spontaneously combust or maybe catch fire, just for a little while. I loved her, but she was obtuse sometimes.

Okay, like half the time.

"We're almost there, kiddo," Mom assured me. She'd said it fifty times over the course of the quasi-epic journey. I officially had trust issues. Every time I looked out the window, I just saw snow, some more snow and a little more snow after that. I couldn't tell where we were—only the dulcet tones of the GPS with its crisp British accent kept us on course.

"She sounds smug," Mormor said after the directions told us to take a left. "Why do British people sound smug?"

"Why do Swedish people sound like that Muppet?" Mom asked.

"Excuse me! I will have you know—"

"STOP. TALKING!" Rarely did I raise my voice to the women in my family. Even less rare did they listen. In that minute? They stopped talking. They went stone silent, and the last five minutes of the car ride became so much more bearable, it wasn't even funny.

Mom pulled Mormor's SUV up to the double doors of the hospital. Mormor grabbed my bag and helped me hobble inside. I sat down while Mormor went to talk to the front desk. I was so focused on waiting for my next contraction I didn't see Devi across the waiting room.

I *heard* her, though.

"SARA. YES. YOU'RE HERE. OKAY."

I looked up. There she was, resplendent in forty-five lay-ers of winter clothes and silver snow boots that looked more like moon boots than anything. Her father stood behind her in his black woolen coat and a ridiculous-looking hat with a fuzzy ball on top. Beside him was a police officer with a mustache holding a cup of coffee in his gloved hand.

"Dad called in a favor to get me here," Devi said, jerk-ing her thumb over her shoulder. "You don't know ex-citing until you're in a cruiser in a foot of snow going too fast to get to the hospital. That was better than a roller coaster. I think I'm going to puke."

"Don't puke on me, please. I am so…so glad you're here," I said, taking the fierce hug she offered and bury-ing my face in her neck. She smelled like Devi always smelled—like flowers and soap and all things good. It was another comfort I hadn't known I needed until I had it. "So, so glad."

"Same, wifey. Same. I wouldn't miss it for the world."

"You nearly did," I said.

"Well, yeah. Okay, sure, but that's on the blizzard not on me. How are you feeling?"

"Ehhhhh," I said, warily watching the clock. I was due for another contraction. I dreaded it because the pain was amping up. I eyeballed the woman at the counter who was taking her sweet time addressing Mormor.

At least I knew Mormor wouldn't allow the situation to continue long. Her fingers were already tapping on the countertop.

"My doctor supposedly is making it in, so that's good. I ju—" I didn't get to keep the thought. The next pain hit and it was a doozy, making me moan out loud and lean forward in my chair, my fingers clasping my pajama'd knees. Devi sprang into action, just like we'd seen on the video, using the cadence of her voice to help me focus, to help me breathe through it. She put her hand on my forehead, not because she was checking me for fever, but because she was ice cold from being outside and she knew it'd feel good.

"You got this, Sara. You got this," she crooned.

I nodded and waited for the cramping to stop. Devi watched the clock. It seemed interminable, but by the time I flopped back into my chair, my heart in my throat, she smiled at me. "Fifty seconds. You're getting close, girl." She paused. "And I won't even hold it against you."

"Hold what against me?" I managed, watching a nurse coming my way with a wheelchair and Mormor at her side.

"I can't puke on you, but you can break your water all over my shoes? How's that fair?"

I looked down.

I'd wet my pants.

And hers.

"Oh, crap," I whispered.

"Yeah." Devi gripped my hand and gave it a squeeze. "Yeaaaaah."

CHAPTER THIRTY-SEVEN

Wednesday the tenth of February, before my eighteenth birthday, I became a mom.

There are things I could tell you about the thirty-six hours it took to have my kid that'd possibly scar you for life. I could talk about walking around the hospital literally for miles hooked up to an IV pole, my mom, my best friend and my grandmother taking turns chatting my ear off to keep me entertained while I awaited the next round of pain. I could talk about hours of nausea and the relief of cup after cup of ice chips. I could talk about alternating between riding out contractions on my hands and knees because my back hurt that badly, to lying on my side in a hospital bed, a fetal monitor hooked up to me so they could watch Cass's heartbeat and, eventually, issue my epidural so I hurt as little as possible.

I could talk about nurses checking on my dilation and saying encouraging things that were lost to the discomfort and whirlwind of giving birth. I could talk about exhaustion— not just mine, but my family's and Devi's, too, because Tuesday became Wednesday and night became day.

But I won't go too far into any of that. Suffice to say, Mom was right. You care about a lot less than you think you will when you're in the moment, launching life from your loins. There was no dignity and I didn't care. I just wanted to get through it for me and my kid.

What I will tell you is that at 3:03 p.m. on a Wednesday afternoon, my feet in stirrups, Dr. Cardiff standing before me in a puffy mushroom-top hat and with a bunch of nurses at her side, I pushed out my Little Star. She slid from my body with a bellow that matched my own. For that matter, that matched her grandmother's and great-grandmother's, too. They victory screeched like a team of conquering Valkyries when the next generation made her way into the world. They celebrated her arrival. They celebrated my bravery and the bravery of all people who share the ordeal of giving birth.

This was the Larssens at their best. Not the arguments or the ridiculous jokes or the shoe flinging or anything else. *This.*

Dr. Cardiff was stalwart through it all. She was the one

to catch Cassiopeia, whooping aloud at a fine, healthy, robust seven-and-a-half-pound, hairy-as-heck infant. My kid was fuzzy all over. A Hispanic yeti kid, just like her Hispanic yeti mommy. We could Nair it up together in the weirdest bonding experience ever.

I'd teach her how to bleach her mustache when she was older if she wanted. It'd be grand.

Cassiopeia was slimy and red and fierce when she met the world. She was placed on my belly immediately upon vacating my body, to keep her body temperature up. They cleaned her up right there on top of me, placing a cap on her head and a heated blanket over her chubby body as they fussed over her and me—yes, her blanket was pink, it had finally caught up with me, and I didn't care one bit. They clamped her cord in two places and cut between it, taking a sample of blood to test her blood type. O negative, like mine, which was a weird bit of pride but I wasn't exactly operating at full potential. They suctioned her tiny nose free of goop. I stared down into her murky eyes and started sobbing my brains out that she was real. That I'd made the journey and it was officially the next phase of my life. Mom joined me in the weepies. Devi, too. Only my grandmother remained stoic, but when they helped me move the baby into position so I could breastfeed her for the first time, I swear I saw her eyes get glassy.

"Her head's all pointy," I said, watching the little mouth working on my nipple. She'd latched immediately, which was good. I'd read about other moms having a hard time with it but that wasn't one of my trials. "Not that I'm complaining. Just more making an observation."

To be perfectly honest, that kid could have had face tentacles and a spiked tail and I'd have deemed her the most precious thing who'd ever precioused. She was mine, I'd grown her and everyone who didn't like her weirdly shaped head or excessive monkey fur could bite me. She was perfect. I would fight them.

...when I could feel my legs again.

"That happens," Dr. Cardiff said, ridding herself of her fluid-stained coverings with the help of my delivery nurses. "Your birth canal squishes her head. It'll even out over the first few weeks. The body hair will fall out, too. That grows inside the womb."

"Weird. Womb fur," Mom said.

"...thanks, Mom."

"You're welcome. She's gorgeous, kiddo. Absolutely gorgeous."

"She has her father's nose," Mormor said. "But the rest of her is all Larssen."

"Does she?" I peered down at the tiny little face—at the angry tiny face, because apparently Cass had opinions about the indignities of moving out of my womb. There was a heart-shaped face with a pointy chin and big eyes under dark arches of eyebrows. There was a tiny bump at the end of her nose that wasn't mine, but definitely Jack's, though his was at an angle thanks to being broken.

If Nimrod Father wanted to insist on the DNA test, I'd do it, but he'd have to be pretty ignorant not to recognize his son's schnoz.

Dr. Cardiff congratulated us again and made a swift, albeit warm, exit. She looked tired, but to her credit, she'd been there for a long, long time and deserved sleep. I was wheeled out of the delivery room and into a regular recovery room. The nurses continued to fuss awhile, checking vitals on me and on the baby, and eventually taking an ink footprint of the baby. They kept one for the hospital, but the other one could go home with me.

Baby's first refrigerator art.

Cass finished nursing on what little milk I had to offer. One of the nurses, a nice woman named Vikki, assured me my milk would be far more plentiful over the next few days, but that the baby didn't need so much at first because her stomach was so tiny. That was reassuring, and I stroked my hand over Cass's back, marveling in the softness of her skin.

"You did great," Devi said with a soft, tired sigh. Somehow, despite hanging out with me all night and most of the day, the witch still looked gorgeous. It wasn't fair. "I'm gonna go get Jack, if that's cool? And I'll call Leaf to let him know. And my parents. They're gonna want to come get me soon. Mom's freaking out that I haven't slept in thirty hours."

"Thanks. Thank you," I said. "You were the best coach. I love you so much."

Devi leaned down to press a kiss to my head. "And I love you! I wonder if Lamaze coach is an excused absence for the day?"

"Probably not, but maybe your dad can call in another favor."

"Truth." She waggled her fingers at me. She kissed Cass's forehead, and hugged my mom and Mormor, and then she ducked out of the room. I smiled and held my kid close. When Vikki the nurse picked up Cass to put some antibacterial ointment in her tiny eyes, I flinched. The baby cried, and I had to suppress a completely irrational desire to rend flesh from Vikki's bones for upsetting my child.

…it was cool.

Everything was cool.

Because after Vikki put a bracelet on the baby, then one on me, she returned Cass back to me. Any longer and she might not have had a face. I was feeling protective.

My mother asked to hold her, and I was considerably less homicidal about my family members touching my kid than I was strangers, even nice strangers like Vikki. Mormor took her turn afterward, singing quietly in Swedish to her. I was enjoying the comradery of the whole thing, the feeling that the Larssen women could conquer the world, when there was a soft tap on the door. I looked up. There stood Jack, his mother right behind him, her hands clasped on his shoulders.

"Hey. Hi," he said, swallowing hard. He looked from me to the baby and his fingers twitched. "Oh, wow. Wow."

I appreciated that Jack had never asked or demanded to come into the delivery room with me. He kept in touch with Devi after she texted him, and she advised that my room was full capacity at three people with my mom and grandmother and her. He'd been cool about it and asked her to message him when we were closer to the birth. An hour before Cass made her for-real entrance, Devi had texted him to come to the hospital, that it'd be done soon. I was fully dilated and ready to rock and roll.

He'd been patiently waiting in the hospital waiting room for news ever since.

With his mother and father.

Devi advised not coming in with his father right away so as not to upset me. I appreciated her concern, but I was less worried about me and more worried about Mormor whipping more shoes at him and getting kicked out. Nimrod Father could wait awhile, maybe after Mormor had gone home to get some sleep herself.

"Come see her," Mormor said to Jack, perhaps a little sharper than she should have. To soften it, she smiled at him and walked his way, the baby cradled against her chest. She instructed him to sit in the chair next to my bed, where Devi had been a little while ago, and then, with the utmost care, she showed him exactly how he had to hold our daughter. He supported her little neck, he notched her into the crook of his arm. He stared at her face and he looked…amazed.

"She's beautiful," he said, almost reverently.

"Yeah she is. And hairy," I said. "But don't worry, that'll fall out."

Caroline moved in beside her son and crouched, her head hovering over the baby's. "Oh, Jack. Sara. She's lovely. So lovely," she said.

…yeah.

Yeah, she really was.

My kid was amazeballs.

nounced to all of us after she'd changed out of her work clothes. She shouldered into her insulated vest, daring to take the weather-liar on TV's word that March wouldn't swing from fifty degrees to twenty. "It's a drama about 9/11. I'm going to buy those anti-snoring nose strips in advance so I'm not rude."

"Astrid! It's relevant social commentary. It has to be better than that thing you had me watch with the space people," Mormor protested. "I didn't like the angry green man. I liked the blond gentleman in the tight pants, though. I could watch a whole movie about him."

"Mom, you strumpet. Lucky for you, there are at least three of those. A Hemsworth for every day of the week."

Mormor tsked before stomping outside to the car. Mom waggled her fingers at all of us, pausing to press a kiss to the top of Cass's big bowling ball–shaped head, and then one to the top of my big bowling ball–shaped head.

"Be cool, my babies. Actual babies and teenagers alike. We'll see you later."

I made Cass's tiny hand wave bye-bye and then, as my friends chattered among themselves, as Leaf adjusted his grip on me so I could better lean against his chest while I held my daughter, I realized how good things were. It wasn't the life I'd planned. It wasn't the life anyone would have probably wanted for me, but it was a life, and it was good.

And most importantly?

It was mine.

That's all that mattered.

★ ★ ★ ★ ★